First Printing, 2016
ISBN 978-0-9977660-11

Cjsummerhayes.com
Cover art by C. J. Summerhayes

*For those who are no longer here with me.*
*To my fantastic husband, family and friends.*
*I just made my dreams come true!*
*Thank You!*

# Acknowledgements

This book has been a work in progress for the last eleven years. It has grown from one character and one idea, to a full Team, and all the family that brings with it. I have had the usual frustration and lack of time, but now I am so very happy to share it with everyone. Firstly, I would like to offer my thanks to those who have been on this journey with me.

My Husband, I love and adore you! Thank you so much for putting up with the crazy in my head as my mind wanders. For taking me to 'Hotel Del' and helping me realize that visiting a place is better than a google search! For being my biggest fan!

Nanny Bubbles, thank you for always telling me to follow my dreams. That being an artist wasn't so bad!

Dad, your continuous support over the years has meant more to me than you could ever imagine!

Miss Fran and Aunt Sandy, I love you both and without your support for many years I wouldn't have made it this far! Xox

My MIL (Mother-In-Law), you read my books and gave me confidence. For that I am eternally grateful.

Lori, an amazing friend who introduced me to Kathleen who became just what I needed in editing. I thank you both and look forward to hearing your thoughts!

To my two best friends in the world. Elisabeth and Kris. Since meeting you both you have always been a strong part of my life. Two strong women I love using as the focal point of my characters.

For those who aren't here. My mom, Dennis, Grandpa Read. Your time, yet brief in my life still left its memories that I treasure. Mr. Jim and Mr. Hev', two men I truly learnt so much from just by hours of talking and listening. The two of you were and always will be very special and I cherish all my memories of you both.

# SEAL Team

## 7

## JAMES'S

## STORY

"So, gentlemen." Lieutenant Commander Daniel MacCafferty, team leader and all-round nice guy said, as he began to finish wrapping up the weekly meeting of Team Seven. He tried to sound a little more upbeat than moments before. He had one last thing to add to their briefing, and he knew the subject would not make the men very happy.

Team Seven is the U.S. Navy's Elite Special Warfare team of SEALs (Sea Air and Land). A clandestine entity and only those who were part of the team ever knew anything about what they did or trained for. With no missions sending them 'Wheels up' and 'Active' for over two weeks, it left the men able to enjoy the time back on base in Coronado, California. Their down time consisting of brushing up on their specialized skills of warfare and spending quality time with their families.

Reluctantly the team leader began. "We have a doctor arriving today at 1230 hours. He's coming to us from the USNS Comfort. Commander James Buchanan will be assigned specifically to Team 7. He'll do the new monthly physical exams and when needed, he'll be joining us from the side lines when we go on away missions."
"Won't that be like having a civilian with us?" Max Vincent asked with a puzzled look on his face.
"He won't have to be right next to you out there but at a determined extraction point or safety zone. It's just in case any one of us gets injured, or any 'packages' require medical attention." Daniel referred to 'packages', and each man knew that term was used

when they added extra bodies, normally nameless and usually civilians to their exit route on missions. It was usually these 'packages' they were saving from something terroristic.

A groan of unhappiness spread throughout the room. "I don't like it either. Neither does the chief," Danny waited a beat. "These are new orders coming down from Washington, and our wonderful Base Admiral is adamant we adhere to this, so for now, men, we are to go along with it."

Silent agreement went up around the room, as each member of the team looked at one another. "Now go get some chow, men. We'll convene back at the "O" course at 1300 hours."

XXX    XXX

The USNS Comfort had been keeping presence with some of the Navy fleet in the South Pacific, almost a day's journey by U.S. Navy Air transport, to the San Diego Navy Base on Coronado Island.

The Comfort had been shipped out almost eight months prior and now Commander James Buchanan looked out at the oncoming Californian coast and sighed. American soil, safer than any of the ports the Commander had been to in a long time.

This transfer made James nervous. Working with some of the toughest teams of men in the Navy would be hard, a sure test of endurance and stamina. James had never had to face any front line combat situations in ten years of Naval service. The closest to combat ever, had been the poor injured fighters who had been brought to the Comfort.

"Commander." A petty officer on the flight crew spoke, breaking James's thoughts. "We'll be arriving in a few minutes, Ma'am."
"Thank you, petty officer." She smiled.

Oh yeah, Jamie Buchanan was scared to hell.

XXX　　XXX

Team Seven all sat around in the afternoon sun, slugging water after their third time through the "O" course. Soon they would be in the cool Pacific water doing some water exercises. Their commander and his XO, (executive officer) Lieutenant Cooper "Coop" Lee, had left to meet their new guy, and bring him back to meet the team, before depositing him in the comfort of his new office over at the medical building.

"I bet he's some skinny little dork." Max said, laughing.
"I can't believe they think we need him." Kevin King joined in.
"If he's a Commander do we call him Doc or by rank?" David asked, seeing as this doctor would outrank everyone on the team.

Before anyone could answer, the little base Jeep,

driven by the XO came in to view and all the men stood up to await their team leader and the new guy. As the Jeep got closer they could see their fellow officers frowning and looking royally pissed off. The closer they got they could see why. The sparkling white uniform sitting behind them, was encapsulating something none of them could have expected.

"Oh shit." Steven said. "The new guy wears glasses alright except he's not a skinny dork or obese." He began to shake his head smiling. "No she's a woman instead." David said what all the men's wide eyes could see.

# CHAPTER ONE

Jamie was betting all the SEALs around her were thinking the same thing their two friends were thinking when they had watched her walking away from the aircraft, only a little while ago. Even over the roar of the engine, she could tell their shock and anger. The Lieutenant Commander didn't even greet her; he had opened his cell phone and started yelling about ten feet away. His XO Lt. Cooper had introduced him from a distance.

In the Jeep when Lt. Commander MacCafferty had finally turned to her, his aviator glasses showed her a distorted view of herself, like the crazy mirrors at the circus. It added completely to the fact he had a large melon-sized head, covered in a dark buzz cut, wide shoulders for a giant of a man, and his look terrified her down to her toes, but she had managed to keep a calm façade. "Commander Buchanan. I hope you understand my confusion and anger about your transfer to us," Danny had said straight out. She liked that; she respected that straight-forward no B.S. approach. "Yes Sir. Your team, and all the SEAL teams are entirely male, and male for a reason. It is not for me to understand, but to obey orders Sir; and my orders were to get my ass here. Sir, I'm just as confused and angry as you are."

Jamie could have sworn she'd seen Danny smile, but if it had been there it was gone before she could look twice. "Well, it seems our Admiral Spears kept the fact you were a female a secret, to see how we'd react. Quite frankly I'm not going to let that asshole get his yearly hard-on from me complaining, so it looks like we're stuck together." He towered over her even from the front seat of the Jeep, where he turned to talk to her, and for the briefest of moments she stopped breathing from fear. She wasn't sure if he had noticed, and hoped he hadn't and wasn't sure how to respond to that, besides a "Yes Sir."

Now Team Seven just looked her up and down as she stood there for all to see in her dress whites. She wanted to crawl under a rock. "Sir, permission to check the Commander, to ensure that she is indeed a she," a male asked, and the comment made the men around her, all of whom over-shadowed her in height and width, either smile or laugh or maybe both she was getting a little claustrophobic. It was all she could do to stay put, and not run screaming for cover. "Lt. Schlome. I don't need to remind you that even here, sexual harassment leads to court-martialing, do I?" the Senior Officer asked, without even the slightest eye contact with the Junior Officer. "No Sir." The Lieutenant stood straight at attention, all of the other men followed suit, and it was then that reality completely sunk in, she wasn't on the Comfort anymore. She was now in the center of SEAL country.

Something she wasn't ready to experience so close up and personal.

"Team Seven. There has been no mistake. Our Rear Admiral just didn't inform us of our new team member's gender. Now this is Commander James Buchanan MD."

"Jamie." She quietly interrupted with what felt the largest lump in her throat.

"Jamie then." He seemed to be smiling again, from what she could see in her peripheral vision. As Danny moved around the inside of the circle of men, his deep booming voice seemed to stay in one spot. "Let me introduce the team." He pointed to his men as he stopped beside her; and she made a mental note exactly how tall and strong he was. "Lt. Ryan O'Rielly. Lt. Kevin King. Lt Junior grade Mathew Taylor. Lt. Max Vincent. Lt. Steven Schlome. Officer Jason Richards. Petty Officer David Richards. Ensign Justin Miller. Lt Lee Kelly. And you'll meet the Senior Chief later."

She just smiled, relaxing a little bit, but she still felt small and over-shadowed. "Well." She coughed out nervously. "You all look like you're kinda busy. I don't want to take anymore of your time, so I will leave you to your training, and get to that office and un-pack." She tried to take a step back, but she landed on the edge of a large shiny black boot, and as her eyes travelled from that boot up she became even more nervous and shy. "Coop, take the Commander over and meet us at the exercise point." Danny's voice boomed, and like the sea that had parted for Moses, the men seemed to break from the huddle, and sun hit her again, the warmth from the sun as the human cover left warmed her instantly.

Having been inside her new, almost empty office for

an hour, she was still trying to shake off the image of all those strong men standing around as if she were a piece of something unspeakable they didn't want near them. The looks had been challenging, and almost mocking, as all their eyes had been hidden by shade from either sunglasses or baseball hats.

Man, to say the team leader was royally pissed off was an understatement, but he would have to learn she had never backed down in her life, and she wasn't about to start. She outranked him and that should be enough.

It should.

Her desk stood in the middle of the room, stacked with boxes of files she had yet to go through; the floor was scattered with more of the same. Big boxes of basic medical supplies for the small examination area, off to the side of the room were there, waiting to be opened and stocked inside new medical cabinets. Next to that was the folded examination table, a wheeling seat and tray caddy, with other important medical tools.

A desk sans a phone, a desk chair and the empty file cabinets; even the office computer was still in the box. There was nothing personal about the space, and not for the first time since leaving the Comfort, she wondered if maybe she should have been a little more vocal over her transfer.

A knock on her office door made her sigh, and she

got up as gracefully as possible in the knee length white uniform skirt. Seeing a young ensign in her doorway, impossibly young, Jamie remembered how innocent things had been a long time ago. At twenty-eight she felt so very old sometimes. "Yes?" she asked. "Ma'am, I'm Ensign Largo, I have orders to report to you." The girl held out papers and Jamie moved over to take them realizing in fact that this ensign was her new secretary-cum-assistant. "What medical experience do you have, ensign?"

"I'm a registered nurse, Ma'am."

"How old are you?"

"Twenty-two."

"You look a lot younger." Jamie finished scanning the papers and looked up. "How do you feel about being my assistant and not working on the hospital floor?"

"Very excited, Ma'am, you are the talk of the base."

"I'm sure I am." Jamie sighed.

"Permission to speak openly, Ma'am."

"As a rule, always."

"Why would you agree to this assignment Ma'am?"

"Good question; I'll let you know once I figure it out."

Unlike the actual office, the small waiting room was half ready to see patients. A couple of comfy basic chairs, a desk for Largo with a phone already connected to the wall, and a computer, which looked as new as this wing of the hospital. Largo was nice enough to run and get them both a coffee, no matter how bad it was, from the cafeteria and had suggested they get a small coffee pot for making some in the waiting room.

Both of them were organizing files into the cabinets, when another knock was heard. Being behind it was nice, as Jamie could share her rolling eyes look with her new assistant, which made the quiet girl smile, and that, Jamie knew, was the start of their working friendship. "Come in," Jamie called out, putting the file on top of the cabinet. To her surprise, two of the men from the team came in, one was Steven, she remembered the name, and the other was Mathew, if she had gotten them right.

"What can I do for you both?" She put her hands on her hips and gave them the look of impatience. Okay, so she knew she was not totally welcoming, but the office had a long way to go before she could start using it. "Commander." Both men stood at attention, and it was the dark, brown haired, amazingly good looking, broad shouldered Mathew with a deep yet friendly voice, who spoke first. He actually gave her a small smile, but she felt as if he were trying to sum her up, which unnerved her. The other was just biting his tongue, you could tell; his eyes were filled with questions. She wondered what it could be he wanted to say, or at least ask out loud. It was a good bet it wasn't polite, or even something he could ask without getting a court martialing, now that made her smile inside as she made the internal joke. "Stand easy men." Okay, so she wasn't a total hard ass, she hated the ram rod way you had to stand straight at attention herself, so she was the absolute last person to ever make someone else do that.

"The Lieutenant Commander asked us to bring this over." His hand came forward slightly and robotically, and she saw the whiteness of paper peeking out from a cream folder. "It took both of you?" Jamie said with her eyebrows raised, not letting them know if she were joking or serious. "I suppose it did." Mathew replied. He was busy trying to figure something out; for glasses without thick lenses, why the woman before him would chose such thick and ugly frames.

"So, what is it?" She waited for the Hollywood-looking man to hold the papers further out, and once she reached to take them, both their hands on either ends of the file, she only then looked up to see his smiling eyes looking at her. She hoped she didn't blush as she turned to read them, but emotions switched as she read the first words and she could have burst out laughing. Their commanding officer was going to make sure she either quit or died trying to prove that she had it in her to be on their super special team. She knew Danny wanted to prove his only point which was that she should never have been sent to Team Seven.

"Tell Danny I'll be there in the morning. You're both dismissed." was her only physical and verbal response to them, and then she watched their slight hesitation before leaving. That had not been what they had expected. "Has it started?" Largo asked behind her, as she read over the piece of paper again. Each day that coming week she would be tested on some skill any one of the team had. It was going to be like being in boot camp, or worse, a first year at Annapolis as a plebe. "Started?" Jamie looked back at Largo, still kind of shell-shocked. "The 'get the female doctor out of the way' tests?"

# CHAPTER TWO

Lt Junior Grade Mathew Taylor noticed the pick-up truck parked directly in front of the house next to his that had been empty for two weeks, after the couple who had lived there had moved overseas. He parked his car in his own drive and noticed a female struggling with a large moving-box as he jumped out of his truck and closed the door.

She was beautiful, wearing only a small pair of shorts that barely covered her ass, and a tight tank top that showed off her amazingly feminine but muscular arms, and an abdomen so perfect you wanted to kiss all the way down between the muscles. The feminine package was all topped off with a tan that glowed in the dusk light, and sat in contrast against the champagne light hair.

Her hair was long and blonde, and reminded him of one of the women from the original Charlie's Angels. "Hi there, let me help you with that." He ran over the short strip of grass that separated his drive from the next noticing her shock at his approach. "That's alright, I have it." she said.
"You sure?" He noticed her eyes; they were a warm hazel that reminded him of the coffee he got from the expensive coffee house on his way to work in the morning.

"Yeah, I'm sure. Do you live next door?" He hoped that wide-eyed look was one of hope. Maybe his year was looking up, and some single, drop-dead gorgeous female would move in next door and they'd have some fun and. "Neighbor, right?" Her words knocked him out of his day dreaming bubble, as she pointed towards his truck he had just left. "That's right. Are you moving in?" If there was a God, he hoped so. "No my sister is; c'mon in and meet her." She gestured with the box towards the front door. "I'll let you grab a box if you do." She smiled, and without being asked twice, he ran over to the truck bed and pulled out an equally large and heavy box, following her like a good puppy in seconds.

He hoped the sister was just as hot and completely available.

"Jay." She shouted. "Where are you?" She put her own box down on another box already on the floor, and turned back to him. "You can put that down anywhere. She must be upstairs. By the way, I'm Melanie." She extended her hand as he stood up from putting the box down next to the pile where she had put hers. "I'm Mathew."
"Nice to meet you Mathew." He noticed that although her hands were soft they had a slight roughness to them.

"Jay." She shouted again as she retrieved her hand, and moved away from him towards the kitchen. The house, like all of them on the street, were pretty similar in design, and this one was a very close mirror image to his own. Of course, the big difference was the pool in the back that took up most of the yard space. "You know; my sister is probably hiding out.

It's like anytime she knows there's testosterone around, she runs for cover." The closer she came back the lower her voice went as if she were telling a secret. "Really?" Mathew asked, confused and wondering if there was something wrong when the weird vibe rang out in his head.

"She's my twin sister, and unlike me she's shy, bashful and probably the other five dwarfs too." She let out a little giggle. "Jay." This time the sounds of footsteps could be heard coming down the hard wooden stairs. Mathew was beginning to feel awkward at invading this space, but he was grateful it wasn't a husband coming down, because he would have known immediately why Mathew had offered to help.

He started to feel like he should leave, cute twins or not.

"Were you shouting at me?" A female voice asked, still out of view in the kitchen.
"Yes. I met your neighbor outside, and he's here waiting to meet you, so get in here."
"Mel." Was all the voice said, but with a trace of a sigh thrown in.
"I'm sure he won't bite." She turned to look back at Mathew, and with a serious voice asked. "Will you?" Ending the question with a wink. "I'll be right there." The voice came back.
"Think you could make it before my plane leaves for Cherry Point?" Mel giggled again at her own words, and Mathew frowned. It was as if this woman was

rolling to the beat of her own drum that no one else could hear. "Cherry Point?" He asked.

"Yeah, I'm stationed out there, I'm a Marine." She looked and saw his surprise. "You seem shocked Mathew. Don't I look like a Marine? It's the hair, right?" She flipped a few strands over her left shoulder.

"No. Well, yes. It's just...." Before he could finish explaining, Mel's sister finally emerged from the Kitchen. Their eyes locked, and she stopped short.

Mathew noticed the difference between the sisters instantly. Unlike 'Mel' the other was wearing sweats, and her hair was tucked under a baseball cap that matched her sweatshirt. Both monogrammed with the words 'Navy' and 'Commander'. Mathew stood straight. Jamie let out the breath she realized she was holding, and waived his respect for a ranking officer with a "Please, we are off base." He relaxed and felt stunned. "I didn't know Jay knew any men?" Mel choked out a laugh.

"Shut up Mel," Jamie said ever so softly. "This is Lieutenant Junior Grade Mathew Taylor. He's in Team Seven here at Coronado."

"Oh," is all Mel could manage to say, behind her smile.

# CHAPTER THREE

"Well, this is a shock." Jamie threw a bottle of water at her sister. "Do you really live next door?" Her eyes were suspicious and hidden behind the ugly glasses still. "Yes Ma'am, I do."

"Well isn't this cute." Mel looked from one to the other as they both looked to her.

"You'll have to forgive Mel. She got all the stupid genes in the womb, and, of course, as normal, feels the need to embarrass me."

"Well, excuse me." Mel chuckled, looking at Mathew.

"I won't take it personally Lieutenant if you'd like to leave here, running and screaming. Sometimes I wish I had that option when she's around." Mathew noticed how Jamie was not looking right at him, but more looking at the spot on the wall to the right of his head, as if she was too unsure to make full eye contact. "Well, I do have groceries in my truck," he said, knowing how lame it sounded, even to him, although he did have groceries in his truck, and he sure did feel very uncomfortable. "But if there's anything I can do to help...." He offered as he took two steps back.

"We should be fine thanks." Jamie responded quickly.

"Are you single, Mathew?" Mel asked, picking up her jacket and keys from a box in the corner as both Jamie and Matt looked at her with quizzical looks. "You don't have to answer my sister's rude and obtrusive question; it's none of our business." Jamie blushed.

"It's okay. Yes, I am. I just got out of a pretty serious relationship." He watched as Mel's smile got wider. "Well then, with that, I'll be leaving you both." Mel announced. "But it is good to know that a strong Navy SEAL is my sister's neighbor. Not to mention the fact that he's single and so is she. Mathew, it was really nice to meet you. I hope we meet again." Mel walked past Mathew. "I'll call you Jay, and see how you're doing in a day or two." She shouted as she walked out of the front door.

The room seemed impossibly quiet and large without Mel in there, and Jamie realized how comforting her presence had been, however annoying. She wondered if Mathew would laugh about this with the rest of the team in the morning. She was sure he'd never speak to her again, not that it really mattered. After all, given a few weeks her butt would probably be back on the Comfort and far away from this hunk. But she noticed him studying her, no doubt noting all the major differences between her and her sister. "I'd better let you get back to your boxes," he said. "Thanks, and I'm sorry about Mel."
"That's okay. I'll be seeing you at work then."
"Yeah."

XXX    XXX

"She's your what?" Steven laughed popping a piece of apple in to his mouth. "I think he said neighbor." Lee finished tying his sneaker. The three men were heading out for a lunchtime run around the base, after a morning of sitting in the classroom, studying up on their various language specialties. "Neighbor, you know, the house next to mine with the amazing pool in the back yard."

"Nice pool." Lee smiled to himself, thinking of how nice it would be to be lazing around the pool with a few beers, music in the background, or even the Padres on the radio coming in for a win.

"And our new Doc is a half of a pair huh?" Steve winked at Mathew. "Is she as dorky-looking as Jamie in those thick glasses?"

"She's weird." Mathew stood finishing off his stretches with some shoulder rolls. "Weird how?" Lee asked. "There are certain degrees of weird." As any man in uniform knew, there were degrees of weird, it was something to do with the white uniform.

"Well she has this funky sense of humor that's really odd, like she's some hippy child, and she's the total polar opposite of her sister." Mathew explained. "So, if they're identical, then the Doc should be as hot as you said her sister was," Lee reasoned. "How is that polar opposite?" Lee asked for clarification. "Yeah, how stunning are we talking about here Matt?" Steve asked. The three men stood talking as the others came and went from the locker room, until it was just them. "I would say in your terms, Baywatch hot. Definitely makes me think about joining the Marines." Matt tried to joke at the end.

"Damn, that hot!" Steve sighed as you could see him trying to conjure up a mental picture.

As they began their lap they saw their Lt. Commander

coming towards them. They slowed down, wondering what was up, and if they were maybe going wheels up. "Taylor, Schlome, Kelly." Their ranking officer said as the distance between them was just a few feet. "I hate to ruin your down time, but I need you three to meet King, O'Rielly and Richards over at the 'O'." He was referring to the ominous obstacle course renowned in the military, as the worst physical activity to train on.

"Sir?" Lee asked.

"I'm afraid I decided to have a team run the 'O' with our new doctor."

"The Commander is really going to run the course? I thought for sure after we gave her that list, she'd transfer out of here." Steve fought back a laugh at the image in his head. "The top brass wants reassurance that their halfcocked idea to do this is going to work. I need to know that if she is caught in a clusterfuck, she can keep up."

"They really expect these new ideas to work?" Lee asked.

"Yes Lieutenant." MacCafferty addressed the question. "Though I'm betting that whether our Doc had been a male or female, neither one could do any of the stuff we're about to test her on."

# CHAPTER FOUR

With the normally hot San Diego weather heating everyone and everything above ninety degrees. Jamie found herself already sweating, as she walked over to the "O" course, away from the comfort of her air-conditioned office. Leaving Largo with the new mountain of files needing to be sorted she felt guilty before remembering where she was headed, and that last thought was forgotten.

Knowing of the notoriety of the course, and how many had failed before her, she'd be lucky to get through alive. Having done similar courses before, she wasn't too worried. It had been a few years, and she wasn't about to tell anyone she had.

Dressed in her Navy issue grey sweats and baseball cap, she wished she'd left her glasses back in the office like Largo had suggested when she had come back from the women's restroom to drop off keys. Her assistant had just shaken her head at her, before offering a small piece of advice. Now, with the large round frames, and the large grey headband holding on securely to the arms to stop them sliding off, she knew she looked like a freak and in a way she was fine with that. She didn't need the attention of the men here.

At about twenty yards away from the course she saw the seven men waiting for her to arrive. They looked neither happy to see her, nor to have to waste their lunch-time having to do this. She had figured from the last conversation with the Lt. Commander, that he and the Senior Chief Chris Polanski were very open about not liking her being there. Believing that her failing the course would prove to everyone that having a doctor on away missions was all well and good; as long as they didn't become a dead weight that the others needed to take care of.

Women did not belong in SEAL teams, and the tight circle of men here sure looked like they wanted to prove that fact to her.

"Let's get started then." Was all the LT CMDR said when Jamie was close enough with them to hear. "Commander are you ready?" The XO asked. "Aye, Aye Sir." She said, slightly sarcastically, knowing as the ranking officer above all of the team, that she did not have to show any respect and call him 'sir', or even salute any of them. "Have you seen the course, Commander? Should we explain anything for you?" All the eyes were on her again as they waited the reply to MacCafferty's question. She made herself hold her ground firm. "Sir, I have seen the course and believe an explanation would be wasted. Sir." "You might regret that," the Senior Chief said. Jamie said nothing, but instead held her gaze firm with the two senior officers.

She had been partnered up with Mathew Taylor. All the men paired up just like in the SEAL training programs. Your Bud would be your stability in getting through training after the hell week endurance tests. Undoubtedly Mathew must be one of their strongest and skilled men to be paired up with her, in case she crumpled and he had to carry her back to be humiliated.

In front of them were King and Schlome. Behind, Richards and Kelly, and then the Senior Chief Polanski and O'Rielly brought up the rear. They would get two minutes between starting whistles. As the moment their whistle was about to be blown on them, Jamie felt her heart rate accelerate, and the adrenaline start to pump throughout her body.

MacCafferty blew the whistle for Jamie and Mathew. After a brief sprint, there was the course. First, the four-foot hurdles, and then the log-beam, before the hundred-foot-high net that you climbed up on one side of and repelled down the other from a separate rope. At the bottom of that would be more climbing, crawling and basic obstacles, before the long, ten mile run around the airfield part of the base, back to where MacCafferty was waiting.

XXX    XXX

Lt. Commander MacCafferty watched in amazement as the one person he had completely expected to fail came in to his view with her partner right next to her.

Sure, they had moved from the second position they had started in to the last position. But the mere fact she had been able to keep up that well astounded him. Polanski stood next to him as they watched the teams come closer and closer in the final stretch.

"How's our Doc doing?" Chris accepted the binoculars from Danny and looked through to see what his friend saw. "She kept up with the whole group, looks like she is pacing Mathew with ease."
"Are we meant to be happy or pissed about that?" Chris asked for clarification.
"I'm not sure yet, but I would like to know how she just did that." Danny grumbled as he looked up to see a jet flying low overhead, cutting off any obscenities he had been about to, or did say, from being heard.

XXX    XXX

Jamie could see all the men up ahead with their commanding officers.

She and Mathew were the last two in but she was grateful to just have been able to keep pace with him. After the men behind them had overtaken them, she'd had a moment's sinking feeling, that they were going to be beaten completely. It made it harder when out of the corner of her eye she saw her partner not showing much signs of a struggle, and she was only barely keeping her knees from buckling. Her sweats were drenched, and they felt two hundred pounds heavier. She knew the minute she stopped she was going to puke or pass out.

Slowing her speed with Mathew's, she came to a gradual stop as did he, just a small distance from the others. She bent over to stop her head from spinning, and to fight the urge to yak and completely embarrass herself. She could faintly hear all their voices around her but her heartbeat was thumping in her ears. Closing her eyes, she sank to her backside and lay out flat on the ground, her eyes still tightly shut against the glare from the sun.

Feeling a hand pull her left shoulder up, she opened her eyes to see Mathew pass her a sweaty bottle of water. Slowly sitting straight up by herself, she noticed Kelly on one side of her and Schlome on the other. The other man was shaking off his run, while the three officers were obviously talking about what they had just seen her accomplish.

"Ah, thanks." Jamie said quietly, and refocused her eyes on her knees although even that was a hard task with beads of sweat falling down her forehead and right in to her eyes. "Are you okay?" Mathew asked. "You look a little pale."
"Why wouldn't I be okay? I mean that was nothing, right?" She laughed slightly, and Mathew noticed, not for the first time, that close up, even with the horrendous glasses, Jamie had a perfect looking face; even more so than her sister's. Her skin was flawless and soft looking, and tanned to a perfect slight glow that made her cheekbones seem to pop out. He wondered why she'd hide behind such ugly eyewear, when Lasik treatment, or even just smaller glasses would make such a big difference.

"You did great," he assured Jamie, as her color slowly came back and she re-hydrated herself by taking long slow slugs of water. "If you say for a female I might have to accidentally mix a diuretic in your coffee," she told him.

"No really, I was going to say non-SEAL." He smiled at her joke, and she noticed how even more boyishly Hollywood he looked. "Yeah?" She raised her eyebrows.

"Yeah, I've never met anyone who hasn't done that before, do that on their first try."

For a few moments Jamie sat there regarding his statement, an obvious dig to find out more. It was so obvious, and she decided that she didn't want to tell anything to the men who wanted her gone faster than she had arrived. She just got to her feet with the three men following suit. "Commander." A new, sterner voice came in to the picture. It was MacCafferty and he looked neither happy nor, glad of her accomplishment. It almost made her burst out laughing but she bit her lip. His two fellow officers were still standing away from the group, talking between themselves.

"I've only ever met one female that could do that course, and she had been training on it for a few months." Danny said.

"Sir. Sorry Sir." Jamie snapped to attention, using the sarcasm that flowed out. "Care to let me in on how you just accomplished that?" For a few minutes Jamie just looked at him, thinking about whether she should tell him the answer or not, to the same exact question Matt had hinted at moments before. "That was not my first 'O' course sir. My father was a military man, and I basically learned to walk on them."

"Really?" Everyone was listening to their conversation.

"Yes Sir. Is there anything else I can do to prove myself to you right now, or would it be okay for me to go back to my office for a hit of some pure oxygen, and a muscle relaxant?"

"There's the weapons test in the morning," he informed her.

"Not a problem Sir. Tell me when and where."

"Tomorrow, 0600 hours, shooting range." Jamie knew the men had to be noticing how she wasn't backing down to their boss. She smiled sarcastically, and left without a response, walking away from all of them to her office.

## CHAPTER FIVE

The Senior Chief and Lieutenant MacCafferty sat in the Lt's office, looking at the morning's weapons test that had been carried out by the new 'female' member. Chris had administered the test with Max and Richards to help as a point of reference, seeing as they were the two best inside a team of the highly skilled marksmen.

As both of the men had suspected after yesterday's course run, there was something unusual about Jamie and the fact her weapons knowledge rivaled some of his own men, only confirmed suspicions.

"I don't want to speculate Danny," Chris said, leaning back in the chair opposite Danny's desk. "But without a further look at her personnel file, I'd have to say that the doctor has been trained by someone, and trained very well. She had a comfort with those guns out there this morning that I have never before seen in any non-combat personnel."
"She scored better than Max." Danny held up the print-out of the scores, his voice maybe a touch higher than normal. "He's one of our best, Chris. I've already put in a request for her full file, but it seems it has to be revised over at Navy Intelligence. They said they'd fax it when it's done."
"Maybe Spears didn't fuck us after all."
"Let's see. I wouldn't be too quick to discount anything; we have the other tests before we can really be certain without proof."

"When is she due to start the new physicals on the team?" Danny asked, picking up different papers on his desk, and looking at them while he spoke with his team mate and friend. "Right now she's still trying to get their files completed. Seems a lot of the overseas medical treatment wasn't in order. But she seems confident that by the Monday after your wedding she'll be good to go."

"Good." Danny thought for a moment; then his office phone rang. "Excuse me." He told Chris.

Chris picked up the file he had been holding on his lap. He had to go over some new training drills he had devised. He wasn't the XO, but he took front seat when Danny was taking care of meetings and the boring side of being the team leader. Danny's upcoming time-off would be a great chance for him to give the team some less relaxing activities than what they became accustomed to when waiting to go wheels up.

"Sorry about that." Danny apologized. "Kirsten and Patti are going over to get their dresses for next weekend," he said referring to Chris's wife Patti. "You know you're pretty calm for a guy that's getting married a week from Sunday."

"I think I'm just glad we haven't been sent overseas. I know it would break her heart if we had to postpone again." The last wedding date had been cancelled when they were sent overseas for four months. Danny had been upset, Kirsten heartbroken, but she had been supportive, and here they were exactly a year later coming in to the last few days before they would get married, and Danny was just petrified the team would be activated.

"But last time was not of your doing."

"True, but I guess I'm just glad everything's going okay. I've been dying to marry her for so long."

"The entire team is looking forward to the dinner party, especially not having to wear their dress whites." Chris smiled, mainly because he was glad more than anyone else. "Well Kristen wanted to make the ceremony more special and the dinner more relaxed."

"That'll work. By the way, will you be inviting our new member or should I send the men a memo not to mention it?"

"Actually I was going to get Kristen to ask her, she's been asking a ton of questions about her."

"I hear all the women have."

"Let's get her an invite then." He reached for the desk phone again. "Nothing like females to gossip and ask questions. We may not need that personnel file after all."

XXX  XXX

Mathew pulled into his driveway Friday afternoon, and realized he hadn't seen his new neighbor and team member since doing the 'O' with her two days before. He had heard about what had happened at the test that morning, and the coming week would be interesting with those tests too.

The following weekend was the Lieutenant

Commander's wedding dinner, and he had been around when some of the guys had mentioned Jamie had been invited, as a step to include her in to the close-knit world of Team 7. He had also heard she was going to be going alone like him, and he wondered if maybe she would ride over to the dinner with him.

Jamie's car was in her driveway, so it was a good bet she was home. The evening was warm, and the last vestiges of the sunset were just leaving the horizon, but that orange and purple hue still lingered.

He walked over and rang her doorbell, ready to ask her to go with him. When he had to press the brass button a second time and there was no answer, he took a quick peek in the window next to the door, and could see the back door open. Moving down the steps, and towards the side gate, he could hear the faint sound of splashing water, and figured she didn't hear the bell because she was in the pool.

"Commander." Mathew shouted as he walked around the side of her house towards the back yard. The stretch of grass was fenceless between their two properties until you reached the back section, and all the yards were fenced off. "I'm by the pool, Lieutenant," she replied. "You know we are off base; you can cut the formality and call me Jamie." She heard his footsteps and was getting out of the pool drying herself off with her back to his approaching footsteps.

He stopped dead. There in front of him was a bikini clad commander that "hot damn" had a really great body, even more toned and tanned than her sister's. He wondered why she would hide it, and how she even managed to tan when she wore those baggy sweats. "Mathew. Are you alright?"

Jamie looked at a suddenly motionless Matt.

Taking a moment to snap out of it, he looked at the now visible front of her body that, moments ago, had been hiding, and was now there for all to see. She had the body all women died for, or at least spent thousands trying to create. His gaze traveled up the front of her body slowly taking everything in.

Her hair was damp, and hung low below her shoulders, with a curl running through it. It looked smooth and soft even after being submerged in the pool. It was then he noticed her glasses all the guys had made jokes about, were missing from the picture.

Instead of answering her question, he asked one of his own. "Why do I suddenly get the feeling your glasses are just something you hide behind?" He crossed his arms over his big broad chest. "Do you even need glasses?"
"You know, you are the first person to ask me that. Yes, I do need glasses, but only to read." She smiled back, following his stance and crossing her arms. It seemed to Mathew that this was a new side of Jamie; the shy female was replaced by someone stronger and more confident, and maybe that was because she was

on her own space. "Why do you do that?"

"In the Navy if you're female, you already have a mark against you; that old-boys' club is still there no matter how much it's said things have changed. Take your team Matt, it's a male world." She paused. "Add in being blonde I found certain people didn't listen because I'm just a doctor after all right; but the moment I became invisible, not so feminine in those male eyes, I was taken seriously. So I hide what is my burden."

"So the glasses, the severe bun hair thing, and the sweats and caps, are a sort of disguise?

"Yep."

Jamie watched him process her and turned back to put the steaks on the BBQ. "So now you know my deep dark secret." She put down the now empty plate and marinating brush. "What's your darkest secret?"

"I was a really fat kid in the ninth grade and couldn't get a date till I was eighteen."

"I don't believe that." Jamie felt her knees go weak just talking to this male version of perfection. He, like all the men on the team were strong, but he wore his dark blue t-shirt and cami shorts with an ease and sexuality she was sure he knew he had. "It's true. I have the year books and mental scars to prove it."

Jamie watched as his eyes traveled south of her face and then over to the pool behind her. "I heard you like my pool," she said.

"Who told you that?"

"Kelly was trying to have a friendly chat today after my weapons training."

"I heard you aced the test."

"Funny no one told me that." She turned to face the pool. "You know you can use this whenever you want."

"The pool?"

"Yes the pool."

She walked back to her barbeque and turned the steaks over with the sizzling sending its mouthwatering aroma to Mathew. "Seeing as you're here and I have more than enough. Would you like to join me for dinner? By the way, why did you come over?"

"There was something I was going to ask you."

"And?" She looked back at him, waiting. Mathew thought he was going to lose his nerve, but there was something new and comforting about her. "The dinner party next weekend; I wondered if you'd like to ride over there with me? You know, seeing as we're both going anyway."

Considering the question quickly Jamie didn't want to sound too relieved at not having to go alone to the dinner. "What will your date think about me crashing in?"

"I'm not going with anyone."

"Oh, sorry, did she have plans?"

"I'm not seeing anyone." He moved a few steps closer. "I told Mel that the other night."

"Right, sorry, I was so mortified about her. So, are you staying for steak?" She had to turn away quickly as he got closer.

## CHAPTER SIX

Jamie and Mathew sat comfortably opposite each other on her deck in the back yard. The steak had been devoured, along with the salad she had prepared, and now they were working through a nice fruity red wine. The conversation had been light and friendly, as if they had been friends and neighbors for a while. Mathew thought how he would eat it over and over again, just to stop the inevitable time to go home, from getting closer; anything to keep Jamie talking. Once you got her to talk she was amazing, intelligent, and very witty, completely different from her twin.

"So you're an army brat then?" He put down his almost finished wine.
"Navy brat actually."
"What division was your father in?"
"The SEALs."
"So the 'O' really isn't new to you then?"
"Not really, our father had us in the Navy brat club until we were old enough to rebel. Their weekly idea of exercise on base was a course of some sort." The expression on her face, he noted, was blank, as if the memory wasn't either happy or sad.

"If your dad's an ex-SEAL then why did Mel join the Marines?" Matt wanted to know as much about her as he could, he found himself so attracted to this young woman before him. When he had found out earlier she was only twenty-eight, he was so shocked. Jamie came across as older, like his grandmother would call it, she was like an 'old soul'. "To rebel our father's lifestyle and ideals and to prove that jarheads are just as tough."

"And you joined the Navy? He must be proud." At his comment Jamie just laughed, and held up her wine glass. "My father believes females should be bare foot, and pregnant, and without any rights Mathew. I joined the Navy at twenty to get financial support in getting my medical license. I did my last two years at Annapolis before my first deployment."

"You went to medical school at twenty?"

"I was eighteen actually. I finished off my last two years, thanks to them, and the Navy cleared all my outstanding college loans." Now he was really stunned. Beauty and brains were a lethal mix.

"What about your family?" She flipped the questioning around.

"It's just me and my brother Peter now, our dad passed away a few years back."

"I'm so sorry, that must have been hard." Jamie paused not wanting to see that sad look cloud his face again. "Where did you grow up?"

"A little town in Ohio that you've surely never heard of."

"I wish I had been in one place long enough to make friends and settle."

"Was it hard?"

"Very hard."

Jamie's phone, that was beside her on the table, began to vibrate around, announcing an incoming call.

"Excuse me. This will be Mel, she's getting shipped out tomorrow."

"Sure." Matt watched her as she got up and slipped her hooded sweatshirt over her bikini, walking to the pool where she sat down swinging her feet in the water.

He loved the way her hair had dried into these beautiful natural curls that hung enticingly down her tanned back. There was something highly provocative about her wearing just her bikini and sweater. Her skin looked soft and smooth, and pulled tightly over her perfect thighs. Mathew stood up quickly, banishing the thought from his mind. He decided to preoccupy himself and took their dishes in to the kitchen, where his thoughts would stay under control.

"Okay, you too." Jamie disconnected her call and turned to see Mathew in her kitchen, the only light spilling out from the overhead fluorescents above him into the night sky, as the sun had left them long before the wine had been uncorked to breathe. "Thank you for cleaning up," she told him, leaning on her back-door frame. He turned, closing the dishwasher with his foot. "No problem. Thanks for dinner."

"You're very welcome. By the way, my sister said to tell you 'hello'."

"Hmm, you told her I was here."

"I even told her you and I were riding together to that dinner."

"She believed you? I mean she seems to think you're scared of men."

"Oh, she believed me. She just thinks more to it; and as for me scared of men? I wouldn't say scared, just a little shy is all." Her eyes twinkled, and he knew then for sure that he was lost. "And anyway, you seem like a real nice guy Mathew."

"Well, gee thanks Commander." Jamie loved those big wide smiles he gave, the slight appearance of a manly blush as your attention turned to that strong jaw line, sparkling perfect teeth and the list went on.

And oh how Jamie had noted everything in that list during dinner.

Moments passed in to minutes as they just stood looking at one another. Jamie's eyes glistened like the ocean at dawn, and they pulled him in. The calmness in them rivaled her twin's hazel eyes, that were filled with something else. Mathew just wanted to uncover the mysteries of the oceans floor all night long.

"So, I should let you get some rest so you can enjoy your weekend relaxing," he said, shaking loose his thoughts. "I have to go in to the office tomorrow; I won't be getting too much relaxation." She sighed inwardly hoping he didn't hear because she didn't want the night to end. "On the weekend?" Matt asked, bringing her back. "I have little in that large space, and there's a doctor retiring who said I could have some of his things, and the only time to do it is tomorrow."

"Need some help?"

"Oh, I can't ask you to do that. I appreciate the offer, but I'll just ask whoever is floating around when I get there."

"You never asked and I wouldn't mind at all." His

smile made her knees weak. "If you're sure you won't get in to trouble with your team then?"

His smile faded slightly and he shook his head. "The team isn't going to have a problem with me helping you, Jamie. We've been told to let you in on everything."

"Really?"

"Yes, really." His smile came back. "I guess you could say you impressed the bosses."

"Little old me?" She joked, waving it off, and he was pleased she had mellowed out a little. "So, what time?" Matt asked.

"I was going to leave mid-morning."

"Then come knock on my door when you're leaving, I'll ride over with you. I have only stuff around the house I had to do."

"I'll see you in the morning then, Matt, thank you."

"No, thank you for a great meal and good conversation." He gave one last wide smile before turning to leave towards his own house, and Jamie just stood there and watched.

XXX     XXX

From his bedroom window he could watch her swim laps in her lit pool. Her strokes like a graceful fish. He kept his light off so she wouldn't know he was watching her like a dirty little peeping tom.

Countless laps later he watched her walk up the steps at the far end of the pool, and with her back to him untie her bikini top and throw it down on the bench, replacing it with the zip front sweater she was wearing earlier, except now, he had the image of her naked underneath.

Mathew closed his eyes to steady his heartbeat, and when he re-opened them she was nowhere in sight, and the lights had been turned off.

XXX    XXX

Sleeping was such an uncommon luxury after being at sea for so long.

So when she was awakened by a noisy lawnmower outside her window she stumbled out of bed, ready to yell at the person who had dared to wake her up. She stopped just as her eyes focused, and through the sheer white curtains the noisy bastard came to her attention. The very muscular bare chest was a sudden surge of energy her body wasn't ready for.

In the yard next door was a gleaming chest of hard muscles, his lower body covered by a shabby pair of jeans and sneakers. There were no signs of strain in the arms as he moved the lawnmower, but he sure did look good. His face was hidden under his cap and the fact she was looking down didn't matter, those Hollywood good looks were in her memory.

Jamie walked away and into her bathroom to take a cold shower before she passed out from overheating.

# CHAPTER SEVEN

Having known he had to be home, Jamie had gone and knocked on Matt's door like he had told her to. He appeared wearing only those jeans she had seen him in earlier that morning. He'd ushered her inside, and she'd stood in the doorway, noting how immaculate the living room off to the side, looked. She heard him upstairs, and he reappeared wearing a black t-shirt and a different, less tattered pair of jeans.

She had worried it would be awkward on the drive over to the base, but they talked and laughed as if the dinner they had shared had made them best friends.

Matt was in his element, even as they tried as hard as they could to maneuver the leather couch down one floor and along a corridor, not really made to let the old furniture through. The more time he spent with Jamie, the more attracted to her he was. Even wearing jeans and a sweatshirt with those ugly glasses in place, her hair in a bun, he now knew what she looked like outside of work.

Once they had everything in place, he lay back on the same couch, thinking the office was beginning to look more welcoming, as she carried a few of the boxes from one place to another. They were laughing over a joke about one of the team, as he tried to warm her up to each of them. Not thinking nor watching what she was doing she lost her footing on the rolled-up corner of the rug they had placed down before the couch; and while the box wasn't too heavy and fell on the floor, her body fell to land on his. Their faces so close.

"This is a little uncomfortable," Jamie said nervously. Even with her body screaming, her hands palm-down on his chest, she knew she should move, but part of her didn't want to. "Feels kinda nice if you ask me." Matt smiled, and Jamie became tongue-tied.
"I think we're all done here." Her mouth barely squeaked out,
"I thought we were just beginning." He wanted so much for the space between them to close, to taste those lips before him. "I meant the room." Jamie gently pushed herself off of him, wishing that hadn't sounded so harsh. "Shame." Matt whispered out as he too sat up and took in how nervous she looked. It was an awkward situation he wasn't going to allow to get worse. "Jamie." He began but she spoke at the same moment so he waved her to go ahead but she clammed up as if words were stuck or lost.

"Thank you for all of your help." Jamie said, as neither had said anything to the other until they had arrived downstairs in the parking lot. "My pleasure." Matt told her, with one of his famous smiles. "Somehow I feel like I'm playing with fire, but you have to let me make you dinner to say thank you." "How dangerous can dinner be?" He stopped beside her on her side of the car. "That depends on whether I was the only one affected back there." Each of them watched the other for a reaction; Matt was shocked she had even brought it up. His odds had fallen the other way in his mind.

"Oh, I was affected."

"Matt I...." Jamie began, but he stopped her.

"Dinner sounds great and I promise to behave." Matt winked.

XXX     XXX

Sitting on the back deck of Steve's house the next day, Matt tried hard not to replay the second evening he had spent with Jamie having dinner.

Pasta and beer, how could a man be more satisfied than that?

Okay, so he knew another way he could have been satisfied, but as he'd relaxed in bed that night, he'd known starting something would probably have been a mistake. He'd known her days, he knew little personal things about her outside of the normal things, but he couldn't deny himself the image of holding her and kissing the hell out of her, as her hair cascaded down all loose and soft.

"You've been quiet since you got here." Lee commented to Matt. The three of them had planned on putting together a shed Steve had bought at the local garden center, but the moment beers had been opened that had been forgotten. For Lee it was an escape from his wife who he loved dearly as well as his step daughter and baby girl, but some off-base guy time was a welcome relief.

"Just thinking about stuff."

"What's her name?" Steve kidded, only slightly.

"Her?" Matt looked at him.

"It has to be a female; you got that look when that bitch Anna dumped your ass. She hasn't called, groveling or something, has she?"

"I'd hope you'd be smart enough to turn that down," Lee joined in, it was fair to say no one had really liked Anna as much as he had and he'd been blinded by her controlling nature, which had been more obvious to everyone else but him, until they'd broken up. "I wasn't thinking about Anna."

"Good, it must have something to do with where you were when I called last night about going to grab a few beers." Steve was the player of the team, always looking for the next piece of tail. A trait very few of the women he trolled liked when they found out. "I was having dinner with a friend." He told Steve.

"What's her name?" Lee asked laughing.

"Why does it have to be a her?" Matt asked.

"That means he has some female locked up somewhere." Steve translated with a laugh, and a look shared with Lee the other side from Matt. "I'd like to keep it a secret for a while."

"Why the hell would you do that?" Lee choked.

"God, it's not that nasty lieutenant over in admin whose been flirting with you is it?" Steve pulled a face that made them all laugh.

"No." Matt reached for another beer. "It's just new and I want to see if it will even go anywhere first."

"Matty has a secret girlfriend," Lee said, with a high whiney voice.

"She isn't my girlfriend."

"What, you didn't get any last night? A man who buys dinner should always be taken care of." Steve belched out a manly loud of beer carbonation. "That's you Steve, and I didn't buy, she cooked."

"She cooked and you didn't repay her?"

"It's new."

"Lame excuse." Steve opened his second beer he'd pulled out of the cooler, they used like a coffee table. "You at least kissed her right?" Lee asked. "Nope." Matt said after a pause.

"Sounds like another bad relationship, cut it off now." Steve urged; the man had never been in a long term relationship, and Matt wasn't about to take advice from him.

"But she's a very nice, funny, smart woman."

"If you won't tell us who it is, will you at least tell us if she's good looking?" Lee pushed.

"She's an eleven." The response was immediate.

"Out of what?" Steve waited.

"Ten." Matt grinned.

"Is she on base?" Lee was trying to think of any 'tens' on base and there was a very tiny group. Of course it was hard sometimes, because some women looked terrible in uniform but off base with a little make-up, well, that sows ear was a purse for sure.

"She works on base."

"Navy, Marine or civilian?" Lee continued, as he crossed off the women mentally one by one. From the look on Steve's face you knew he was doing the same thing. "Navy." Matt answered Lee.

"Give up Lee, you should know from experience he

isn't going to give up anything good." Steve figured he knew anyway.

"Are you two doing the test for the commander tomorrow?" Steve was the one to change the conversation. "Which one is it?" Matt asked, knowing which ones he had been asked to help with but not which days without the schedule they had. "It's the pool test." Lee downed the last of his beer.
"I'm on the side-lines for that, I am doing the simulation rescue on Wednesday." Matt said.
"I got stuck with that too." Steve grumbled.
"All I know is, I'm looking forward to it." Lee shocked them both. "I overheard Chris and Danny talking about it, and supposedly it's going to be us against her."
"Why?" Matt had to tread carefully now and not give away anything he might be beginning to feel for her.
"Something along the lines of us being ordered to give her as much hell as possible, while she tries to lead the simulation."
"Seems a little harsh." Matt said, cringing inside; he knew what the guys all thought since her arrival, didn't matter what Danny said, what order they were given. Some men just weren't ready for women to be amongst them.

"I mean, she's only here on orders and to keep our collective asses safe. It's not like she skipped Hell week but wants the same rights and glory as we get." Matt finished and hoped it came out right.
"You know Mary said something along the same lines the other night when I was telling her everything, but

it doesn't change the fact she's on our team now."
"I understand Lee; would you be as mad if it were a guy?"

Both Lee and Steve looked at each other and then at Matt who was waiting for an answer. "Male or female, it doesn't matter," Lee responded.
"I do have a bigger problem with her being a woman," Steve admitted.
"At least you're honest." Matt sat forward preparing for another beer.
"Hey, speaking of the commander...." Steve began.
"Any interesting gossip you've seen from your house, we can use?"
"I happened to see her in the pool the other day when I was in my kitchen, but nothing else."
"Shame."
"Are we actually going to get this shed done?" Matt wanted off the subject. The less the commander was talked about, the less trouble from his two friends he could get in to. "Why, somewhere you have to be?" Steve looked like he was incredulous. "I might have dinner plans."

The shed was never even taken out of the box, and Matt left around four, hearing the ribbing of his 'secret girlfriend' from his two closest friends, as he walked around the front to his truck.

He hadn't seen Jamie since the night before, and nothing had been mentioned about eating together tonight; but it had been the only thing he could think of all day. He took out his cell to dial, and realized he didn't know her number. As he put the truck into reverse, he called information, and there were listings, but both were unlisted and couldn't be given out. He knew he could call the base exchange, but the less people who could connect their spare time together, the better.

"Hey Pete," he said to his brother when he answered the phone.

"I was going to call you later. Thanks for the loan again." His younger brother had been through a tough divorce the year before and along with that, he'd lost his job when the local manufacturing company had sent their jobs overseas. As he was out of work, Matt had suggested he go back to school and get his business degree; he was a wiz at computers and it was better than nothing. He now lived on the little money he had left in the bank that his ex-hadn't been able to grab. But the tuition had been due at the same time as rent, and Matt didn't mind, it was only Pete and his mom these days.

"Don't mention it, you know if you wanted to do it the easy way you'd move out here with me, go to SDU and let me take care of you."

"I know and thanks for the offer. I have one semester left, and I promise I'll pay you back when I start working again."

"No rush, I doubt the Navy is going anywhere for me to lose a job."

"That's true. How are things?"

"I called because, aside from catching up with you and making sure you are okay, I also wanted to ask for a favor of my own."

"Shoot, of course."

"I need a couple of numbers." Matt decided to pull the car to a stop along a residential street, so he would be able to write down any numbers.

"Give me the name."

"James Buchanan; could be under Doctor Buchanan."

"Are you sick?"

"No."

"Is it a San Diego number?"

"Yeah."

"Would you know the address?"

"Next door to me."

"Next door, then why'd you need some guy's number?"

"I wanted to know if dinner...." He didn't get to finish before his brother butted in.

"This isn't your sick way of telling me you're gay is it?"

"Gay?" He chocked out. "James is a woman."

"Called James?"

"Jamie."

"Oh." He let it sit and digest for a moment.

"I found her." Pete told him. "Which number do you want?"

"You have a cell and home, right?"

"Sure do." He knew if anyone could find it, Pete could. His thing as a teen had been finding ways in to things on his computer; some of it had landed him in trouble, some had just been pure fun. He wrote down the numbers as Pete said them to him, and then Pete asked. "Is she someone you like or something, I mean, she didn't give you her numbers."

"She moved here last week and we've hung out a bit."

"What is she like?"

"She's fantastic." And he only admitted that to his brother because that's what you did, shared stuff like that, no matter how far away.

Watching cars drive by he dialed her cell number, figuring if she weren't home she would still answer this number. "Buchanan." He heard her voice in his ear and for a moment he froze. "Hello."

"Hey Jamie; its Matt."

"Hey Matt, I was over at your place looking for you earlier, and I left you a note; did you see it?"

"No, I'm on my way home now; was there something you needed?" Man, she had left him a note; he knew it was too much to pray it told him she wanted him.

"There was."

"And?"

"I needed to borrow a hammer and a Philips-head screw driver."

"Needed?"

"Well, I did the screws with a knife, and as long as I don't lean too hard on my coffee table, it should hold."

"I'll be there in twenty."

"Why were you calling me if you didn't see my note?"

"Oh, I wondered, you know, as I was going to do this anyway, if you hadn't eaten, I was going to get take out."

"Take out what?"

"What do you fancy?"

"Hmmm, that would be telling." Was he hearing her right? Was that a flirtatious comeback?

"What are my choices between here and where you are?" She asked.

"Mexican, American fast food, Thai, French, Italian."

"What do you fancy?"

"That, I certainly can't say." He wanted to see if she had knowingly flirted.

"For dinner Matt." Her voice got so quiet in his ear. "I'm easy."

"I'm sure you are." Okay, he knew she was playing this flirting game now, too. There was absolutely no way she would say that otherwise. "How about Italian, I should get plenty of carbs before tomorrow's swim test."

"That sounds good. Why don't you order a few things from Carlos's, it's on Paradise Valley highway, I'll pick it up and be there soon."

"Okay, I'll see you when you get here."

Hanging up, he threw his cell on the seat beside him, and knew he was smiling like a fool.

# CHAPTER EIGHT

"That pasta was so good." Jamie sat across from Matt, trying hard not to show any emotion as she sipped the second glass of red wine. "Carlos's is a great place; I should take you there some time."
"Like a date?" Jamie enquired. They were sitting out on the back deck again, and while she had taken the food from him at the front door, he had run to his house, getting the hammer and screw driver, which now sat on the other end of the table, waiting to be used.

"Would that be so bad?" He slightly avoided her eyes. She liked those warm grey eyes. They held a lot, fun, excitement and at certain times, since they'd been hanging out alone, heat. "I just don't understand why you'd want to; I mean take me on a date."
"You're kidding right?" He half laughed.
"No I'm not."
"Have you looked in the mirror lately, without the disguise?"
"Every morning and night, at least."
"Then why do you ask?"
"I don't see what you do, I suppose."
"Jamie, you're beautiful."
"Matt." Nervously she started tidying up their dirty plates and napkins.

"Hey." He tried to grab her wrist gently as she went past towards the kitchen door, but she dodged him slightly. Instead he got up, following her into the brightly lit kitchen. "Did I say something wrong?" he

asked, standing behind her. "No, you didn't." She
shook her head and turned to look at him. He had
been tongue-tied when he'd dropped the food off. She
wore a pair of cut off shorts, and just her bikini top
which she had been quick to cover it up with a t-shirt;
but he had the image photocopied to his imagination.
She had a great body, one he would love to explore.
"I find you attractive Jamie, but if that makes you
uncomfortable I'll not tell you again."
"It doesn't make me feel uncomfortable."
"Then what?"
"I have a concern, something I can't get out of my
head."
"Tell me."

She fidgeted with a frayed thread hanging from the
bottom of her shorts. "You've known me less than a
week, we've had dinner three times and...." She
stopped.
"And?"
"And I can't shake the feeling that this is part of your
team's plan to get rid of me. I'm obviously not turned
away by these harsh physical and mental tests, so why
not try something more personal. Take the cutest,
nicest guy on the team, and get him to work his way
in to my emotions and pants, and when he gets the
morning after grossness, it will make me feel too
uncomfortable to be on the team."
"This has nothing to do with the team; none of them
know anything aside from me being your neighbor."
"Really?" He could see her skepticism.
"Really." He paused, letting it sink in. "You think I'm
the cutest on the team?"

It took a few seconds, but she smiled.

"Yes I do." She moved closer to him. "That's all you heard wasn't it."
"Admittedly, yes." He laughed.
"Be warned, cute or not, if I find out you've been playing me, then I'll dish up something very special when you come in for your first physical."
"Noted." He smiled wider. "Now why don't you lead me to that coffee table, tell me why you needed the hammer and then I can let you get some sleep."
"Sure." Jamie watched as on his knees Matt tightened the legs on the low table, and she could admire his backside very well in that position.

XXX     XXX

She had been given her orders along with her schedule.

They were very specific that she wore standard issue away-team gear for her swim, including the boots. As she walked across between the buildings to the pool area from her office, she felt like a midget. The pants were too big around the waist, and held up by a belt Largo had stolen from the 'lost and found', wherever that was inside the medical building. Her boots felt a size too big, even with the thick socks which had appeared with everything else, and the black t-shirt was just soaking up the suns heat. Of course, wearing a bathing suit underneath everything didn't make it any more comfortable.

I'm sure someone could have figured out her size better. But that was part of it, she knew the game, and intended to play it the best she could.

Jamie had her glasses on still and in her hands were a pair of Speedo goggles, which she would have to try hard to put on without anyone taking too much notice. Not that anyone but Matt seemed even to look at her twice.

There was a lot of noise coming from the pool area and turning the corner she got a glimpse of some recruits getting a different kind of pool test in part of the deep end. At least, she hoped there was a shallow end, but as she got closer she saw it was all six foot or deeper. "Commander." She heard Danny's distinct voice, part growl, from the side to her left. Looking in his direction she noted only a few of the team members had joined him. Matt was one, and she would bet he was hiding the normal look he gave her, behind his sunglasses-if he wasn't playing her, and she hoped he wasn't. There was also Coop, Max and Kevin standing there.

"Are you ready?" Is all Danny asked Jamie.
"How many laps?" Man, there was even a roped off lane for her she noted, and her stomach dropped.
"Forty."
"Am I being timed?"
"No, just finish them all."
"I'll try," she mumbled to herself.

Turning her back on them, she put the towel which had also came from the Navy supply company, on the back of a basic plastic lawn chair, a white one like every back yard had, and there were a few dotted around the edge of the pool area. She was quick to change the glasses for goggles and wished she could take her hair out of the bun, and leave it in a ponytail; but she had to forget about that and get started.

Standing on the edge of the pool, she stretched her arms over her head and then rolled her neck. Getting in to the diving position she counted to three, took a deep breath and dived into the fresh salt pool. The moment her body sliced through the surface she knew it certainly wasn't heated for any comfort.

Talk about a sudden change for her body temperature.

Matt stood there, saying nothing, beside Coop; Danny had left after lap twenty, and seeing Jamie had the strength to pull the added weight of the gear across the water didn't seem to make the team leader any angrier or happier. At the other end was Kevin and Max just in case she got a cramp or something and they had to fish her out. One thing about their team leader, he might not want her on the team, but he wasn't going to let the woman drown.

By the time Jamie had counted her thirty-third lap, her arms were killing her. It was easy to say that no matter how much practice she got from her own pool, or a short stint on the swim team in high school, this was the single hardest thing she had ever had to do.

The burn all over her body was so intense she almost felt numb, but she wasn't about to give in and prove anyone right.

Coop was on his cell before Jamie's hands even touched the wall on her last lap. Matt was there looking down as she pulled her head up. He admired her strength and stamina. As in her backyard, she had swum with ease and grace, her turns fluid and professional. He could just make out Coop's words behind him, and he knew none of the team leaders had expected her to finish.

But her face was red, and she was breathing very hard, it even looked like her goggles had taken in some water, and he held his hand out to her as he knelt down. She took it and he knew when she was relying on his strength that she was worn out. He lifted her on to the side of the pool before crouching down beside her. "You did good."
"Thanks." He noted she made no attempt to remove her goggles. Her hair was falling out of that ridiculous tight bun, and was plastered around her face and neck. "If you had any ideas about dinner tonight you can forget it," she whispered out, pretending they weren't speaking as he stood up, but where she remained sitting on the edge. "I'm going to be asleep before my ass even gets out of my car."
"I'll cook; I'll be over later," he said, before leaving her there to catch her breath.

Jamie felt him leave, and sighed inwardly. On legs which felt like jelly she said absolutely nothing to anyone else, but went to get her towel and glasses, changing her eye-wear quickly. Then she sloshed in wet leather combat boots back towards her office, to change into her dry uniform. The sun was still hot and she felt like she was in a walking sauna, as moisture just stuck around her like bees to a honey pot.

"What the hell did they do to you?" Largo asked; the air conditioning inside the medical building had made Jamie start to shiver upon entering the controlled climate, and it felt like miles she had walked. "So I do look as bad as I feel."
"I thought it was a simple swim test?" Her assistant kindly took the rolling desk chair from behind the reception desk, and maneuvered it so Jamie could sit. "It was forty laps."
"Forty? Why the hell so far?"
"I have no idea, maybe they have to swim to whatever ship they sail on."
"Why are you doing this Ma'am?" Largo had fetched a dry towel for her,
"Because I can."
"For now, what if they give you a test which will kill you?"
"No such thing." Jamie pushed herself up so she could go inside the privacy of her office to change. "How is the filing going?"
"I have about three files complete, still waiting on over two hundred away-mission records out of four hundred."
"You should get going; we have all day tomorrow which is test free. We'll make a dent in it if that fax machine ever starts giving us anything.

Once she heard the final click of the the door closing behind Largo, Jamie shut her eyes, shivering down to her bones; she wanted a shower and possibly a box of tissues to cry in. She was beat physically, and it was going to take every ounce to make herself move anytime soon.

XXX    XXX

Having grabbed a few things from his place after a quick shower, he had seen the lights on in the back of her house, and carried over the food he was going to cook. He found her on one of the sun loungers, asleep, a beer precariously held in her left hand. He didn't have the heart to wake her after the long day, and swimming the one-thousand-meter distance given to her. He was a little disappointed; all the way home he had been looking forward to this.

"Where are you going?" Her voice made him turn back, and he placed the items on the patio table.
"I thought you were asleep." He sat on one of the neighboring sun loungers.
"Just resting my eyes."
"How tired are you?"
"Not as tired as I am hungry, I haven't eaten since lunch."
"Then why don't you relax and I'll cook."
"No argument from me, I don't know how I'll get my arm to lift a fork, but I'll eat somehow."
"I'll feed you."
"Really?" One of her eyes finally popped open.

"Yeah, really."

"Do you always work this hard to impress every female you like?"

"Only the special ones."

"Special?"

"Just like you." He gently touched the back of her hand as he got up to go start cooking.

She wasn't sure what he was making; he was in and out of the kitchen, the grill had been turned on, and at one point he had even switched her beer for a cold one. He didn't say anything, and she wondered if he thought she had fallen asleep. "Are you still hungry?" The smell of something good filled her nasal cavity. She felt the cushion move slightly as she felt on her bare thigh the roughness of his shorts, as he sat facing her instead of beside her, like he had earlier.

"Famished."

"Try this." He was holding out a fork with what looked like a small shrimp on it. She sat forward, and as delicately and lady-like as possible she took the piece off. The flavors which hit each taste bud were so mouthwatering. "Oh my God." Her hand went up to her mouth.

"You don't like it?"

"Are you kidding? That has to be the best damn thing I ever ate?"

"There's more."

"And although the thought of you feeding me is tempting, the least I can do is sit erect and be sociable."

Jamie wasn't sure how quickly he moved or how

slow she was being, but before she could get to her feet, Matt had crossed to the table, put down the plate of food and the fork, and then returned, scooping her up inside those strong arms. "I think you're taking this a little too far, Matt."

"Taking you to your bedroom would be going too far."

"I couldn't do anything but be there if you did." The words came out of her mouth so fast she didn't have time to blush, but Matt did. That was something she had noticed since they had started hanging out together. He played a good game, but he was still that shy guy underneath those cami pants.

Eating the grilled shrimp with pineapple mango salsa was good, the baked potato was light and fluffy, but it was the third beer to wash it down which was making everything kinda swirling. They joked and laughed, and she sure was feeling a lot more relaxed around him.

"So tell me about the Comfort."

"It looks like an oil tanker painted white with red crosses painted on the sides."

"You know what I meant."

"Oh, that we don't have weapons, and to fire at us would constitute a war crime."

"How long were you serving on there?"

"Five years."

"And was there anyone on there who was you know, special?"

"Everyone was special." He watched her eyes sparkle.

"I just want to know if I have any competition."

"No, no one like that on there."

"How come?"

"I wasn't looking for anything like that."

"Are you looking now?"

"I wasn't when I arrived, I just wanted to survive; but I think it's fair to say, someone has snuck up on me, and made me see I could live with that."

"Could you really?"

"I'm game."

"No more reservations?"

"Only one. Working on the same team; I don't expect Danny to put up with this, I might get transferred, I could be back on the Comfort before we know it."

"I want to give this a go." He waved his finger between them.

"This?" She copied his movements with a gleam to her eye.

"See what could transpire."

"Be careful what you wish for, Lieutenant Junior Grade."

"Meaning?" Was she about to share whatever secrets about herself, and the family she never spoke of?

"I've heard the stories from my assistant; one day you guys are dating, the next they're married and popping out kids."

"That's the least worst thing I could ever think about." She watched him, not sure he had chosen the right words, but he smiled at the end, when he knew it was right. "With me?"

"Yeah with you."

"Marriage and kids with me, am I hearing this right?"

Jamie had to ask.

"Yeah, all of it with you."

"Are you a sucker for punishment or what?" She was only partly kidding, the rest, the stuff she didn't want to tell him, held maybe ninety-five percent of that.

"You let me figure that out for myself." He got up and took her plate.

"Thanks for dinner." Her legs were able to get her to the kitchen with the bottles for the recycling.

"Anytime, how about again tomorrow night?"

"I would love to, but I have the feeling I'm going to be spending a late night in the office."

"I'll bring something in."

"I couldn't ask you to do that." She started to protest.

"You didn't, I offered." He held her chin gently in his fingers.

Jamie held her breath as she knew Matt's entire being was upon her, his fingers gently holding her close to him, and his face slowly coming closer. Instinctively she licked her lips slightly, and as she took a breath his lips touched hers, and her hands gently held on to his shoulders.

Matt's head felt like it would explode. The synapses in his brain were firing at the speed of light. He let go of her chin and wrapped his arms around her, he knew it was a brief, hunger-filled kiss filled with promises and heat, and he was willing to work slowly at this, make sure it was something she wanted too.

He already knew he wanted a lot more moments like

this with her.

## CHAPTER NINE

Jamie's sleep had been so deep that when the alarm woke her at six she only wanted to hit the damn machine and crawl back under the covers. Aside from sleep, she wanted to get back to that place in her dream where Matt was doing a lot more than the simple but sweet kiss he'd given her the night before.

Her office was beginning to come together. With a few trips to various stock rooms she had everything she needed in the small examination area to actually see patients. The room felt comfortable with the leather arm chair and matching couch. They were set in the middle of the room, with her desk and the two chairs, welcoming people to come in and talk to her.

She just wished the filing cabinet was coming together as well.

Around two she had been called down to the Admiral's office. The man was middle-aged and wreaked of that butt-head attitude behind the stiff authority he tried to show. She was guessing he was getting some real strong pleasure out of Danny being so freaking pissed, because he couldn't stop telling her how amazingly she was doing; how of all the candidates in the medical field for this trial and position, she was making him personally proud, and had reported so to the secretary of the Navy.

Feeling a shower to clean off the schmuck she had arrived back at the office to see Largo with a mountain of papers and a hole-punch. Some more of the files had arrived, and together they dealt with them until around five-thirty, when Jamie dismissed Largo for the night. The fax machine, as if on cue, started spewing more paper ten minutes after she left. Jamie just sighed as she took what came in to the office, and set them on the floor in piles of which patient they belonged to.

"You weren't kidding." Matt's eyes opened wide when he appeared in the darkened doorway. The only light was from the lamp on her desk, and she snuck a look at her clock; it was almost nine. "And I have so much more to do." With her legs in front of her she leant back on her hands. "Tell me inside that bag in your hand is something to eat."
"I'm starting to think you only want me for the food."
"Among other things." She patted the floor beside her. "Have a seat, join us mere paper pushers."

"How is it going?" He placed the bag down on his other side and leant over to kiss her cheek softly; it was a simple maneuver, but it felt so personal and newly right. "Oh Matt." She leant her head on his shoulder as he tucked her in to his hold like a mother bird using a wing to protect its young. "Forget being given the 'we don't want you on the team' treatment, this paper work will kill me first."
"I have faith in you, you'll get it done."
"Thank you."
"And seeing as I'm being a distraction, then I'll put in a few hours and help you."
"You brought food; that is a good distraction."

Matt watched as Jamie began eating what he had made at home and brought in. It might be wussy to admit it but he liked to cook, and cook for someone else. All day during classes and training he had been thinking about her, what she might be up to, and what to make them for dinner. He had decided upon a simple salad with fresh raspberry balsamic vinaigrette and grilled chicken.

Around midnight they had the piles sorted and the fax machine had stopped. He was lying on his side while Jamie was on her back looking up at him as they laughed over stories from the Comfort, and when Matt had been at Annapolis. They found they knew some of the same people, which was a long stretch when you factor in how many people were in the Navy.

"My sister called me earlier."
"How is she?"
"Crazy as always."
"Glad you said that, she has a real odd sense of humor."
"Yes she does, she's dealt with some stuff over the years, her loud openness is due to that I think."
"Like, what kind of stuff?" Maybe she would slip and reveal something about herself. "Family stuff."
"Like?"
"Our mom died when we were young, Mel was closer to her, and I guess she never really got over it."
"How about you? Is that why you became a doctor?"
"No, I just wanted an honest reason to see lots of men

naked." Her answer made him laugh so hard. "I know you want to know about my past Matt. One day you will. It's just hard for me to open up, and for now let's keep it simple."
"Simple it is."

XXX    XXX

When Matt left to get back to base the next morning, the first thing he noticed as he carried his backpack and coffee out to his truck, was that Jamie's car wasn't in the neighboring driveway.

They had arrived home to their separate houses around midnight the night before, and in some ways he'd hoped she would invite him in. But she had instead just offered to make dinner the following night, that's if Danny's test didn't have her killed first.

Walking in to the locker room on base where a few of the team were getting ready, he said "Hi" to each of them before going over to his own locker and opening it. He had his shirt off and his sneakers slipped off, when he heard movement to his side and saw Kevin stood there. "So I heard an interesting thing this morning." Kevin crossed his arms over his chest, while leaning his back on the locker two down from Matt's. His voice was low, and fear prickled the skin on Matt's entire body. "Which was?" He avoided eye contact. "I was over at the medical building, getting things for this morning's test, and I heard from one of the guys on security detail over there that the commander had a late-night visitor last night?"

"And?"

"A guy, my friend swears it's a guy on Team Seven, but couldn't think of his name."

"Shame."

"Until I gave him a few, and guess what?"

"What?"

"He said it was you."

"He was mistaken." Matt lied totally avoiding eye contact.

"Come on Matt, I saw you with her at the pool the other day, the two of you tried to make it look so normal but, you two were talking."

"I just asked how she was."

"Matt, Matt, Matt. I don't care if you're screwing the commander, but come on, give me some juicy secrets to be in on."

"We're neighbors."

"I know that too."

"We've had dinner a few times like last night."

"In her office?"

"Yeah, in her office." Matt sat down. "Do me a favor Kevin, don't tell anyone on the team."

"I wasn't going to, Steve's only just got off his punishment for dinging Danny's car, I can only imagine what Danny would do to you if he knew."

Even with Kevin's ability to keep the biggest and most outrageous team secrets longer than anyone had ever known, Matt was still freaked about being caught, when he walked in to the class room where they were going to get the mission briefing. The room was an unusual few degrees darker, and he took his seat in the middle. It was set out with leather desk-chair-style seats in a college lecture room fashion, and it was comfortable being in there for hours doing boring stuff.

Not everyone on the team was there; the exercise was going to use only six of them. The Senior Chief was playing the injured party who was going to need rescuing, and then there was Max, Kevin, Steve, Lee and himself. Danny was starting the run-down early seeing as they were short a person, the important person, Jamie.

XXX  XXX

"Should I expect different orders by the end of the day?" Largo kidded when Jamie walked out of her office wearing the latest get up. The same style cami-pants, boots and t-shirt, but she had to wear the shirt that matched the camouflage pants. They'd even sent over the floppy hat the same color as the clothes. In addition, she had to wear what they called a flak-jacket and even with all the pockets and compartments empty, it weighed a ton. Seeing as she was the medic-slash-doctor, she also had to carry the pack holding the supplies for seeing to the injured.

"Now, now Largo, there is no way this test will beat me either."
"Even Wonder Woman needs a little help, and rumor has it this is the test they expect to break you with."
"The rumor huh?" Matt had warned the same things

in not so many words, and she understood. No matter how much he may or may not like her, his loyalty was to his team. If their higher-ranking officer gave him an order to do everything but what she needed to get through this, then he would have to side with Danny. It didn't offend her because Matt, having such strength, was a good quality. "Don't go listening to rumors Largo."

"Yes Ma'am." Her assistant laughed, as she clomped out of the office waiting room and down the hall.

Cheating and getting a ride over to where she had been ordered to get to appear, she passed a few of the team in the hall to the class-room. They gave her smiles with well-hidden smirks behind them, and she returned with just as big a smirk.

Knocking on the closed door, she was beckoned in by Danny's strong voice. She wanted to say something sarcastic, but instead bit her tongue. "Commander, please come and take a seat." She was waved to a spare seat in the front row, and heard the few snickers as she thumped past everyone. The clothes certainly did nothing but hide her figure, which was a plus but also made her look frumpier.

Sitting there listening to Danny obviously tell a different version of what was going to happen, her mind began figuring out ways to outsmart whatever the team had already been told. They were going to be dropped by helo where Chris was waiting; he was not in the room. She was to assess the situation and give the appropriate treatment. He would then be carried back on a stretcher the twenty miles across desert-like terrain, to coordinates which were inside a leather pouch she would be given once they landed.

It sounded easy, but Jamie knew for sure they were planning something else.

# CHAPTER TEN

It started with the thirty-minute flight over San Diego, North East towards the hilly landscape, and the Marine Base Camp Pendleton that sat just outside the city limits. The area that went on for miles and was all dirt, rocks and sporadic sprinklings of California native brush, she sat on the floor with her back leaning against the rear wall of the helicopter, while each of the men seemed to be dangling legs over the edge of the opened doors. She had shared a quick look with Matt through their sunglasses while boarding, but she was letting him do what he needed to do.

Thinking she could see Chris in the distance, she heard Max point it out to the others, and sure enough, she could vaguely make out a person lying in the dry sandy dirt. She made sure she had all her things, and once the helo lowered down enough for them to jump off, she was there along with the others. She had done that kind of insertion many times before when on the Comfort, and they'd had to go in to enemy territory to collect one of their own.

Reaching Chris, the men just seemed to stand in a sort of circle around their friend, with their backs to him. It all seemed very odd, and she laughed to herself when she saw what they had done to make her know his pretend injuries. Someone had written in thick black marker on pieces of paper, and pinned it to where the injury would be; a broken leg, arm, possible neck injury, partial burns and a head laceration. All of those were pretty easy to pretend fix with splints and bandages, and in a few minutes she was done, except she threw her own one in there and it had made Chris open his eyes with concern and looked at her.

She just smiled.

Having had to carry the fold-up stretcher too, she held the IV bag she had inserted into Chris's arm: his shock at her action was clear and said, "Schlome, King, help me get the chief on the stretcher." Without responses they both moved and did what she asked, but were back in their positions straight after. "I'm ready to go, let's move him," she said, and not one man budged, but they did all turn in to face her. Normally those big strong mean-looking men glaring down at her would have made her tremble, but she had been waiting for the first sign of defiance and here it was.

"I get it, here is where you were ordered not to follow my directions." Jamie just nodded her head and looked each of them in the face. "Okay, well I can understand all this posturing is because none of you want me here, but I don't particularly feel like standing around all day being ignored, so, I tell you what, guys, I'll give you a good damn reason to get your asses moving." She noted the slight twitch in jaw muscles, and opening up her bag she took two clear liquid filled vials from her kit, and a syringe. "What are you doing Ma'am?" Kevin asked. As the corpsman he had also just noticed the IV bag which hadn't been in their equations. "Why don't you tell your team what this holds?" She threw one bottle to Kevin, with which she had already half-filled the syringe. "Epinephrine," he answered.

"And this one?" Having the syringe now filled she threw the other one and tapped the needle for air bubbles before grabbing the IV bag and squirting it into the valve. "Beta-blocker."

"Care to give the team a science lesson about what happens when you give that much of each medicine to a person mixed together?"

Even Chris's eyes had opened wide, and she chuckled internally.

"It depends, I read a paper which says to some it is harmless but to others it could cause serious side effects."

"Name one." Max told Kevin.

"Chris could stroke out." Kevin's cool was gone, sweat was beading down his face and Jamie could see. "And I set the bag for fast hydration." She held up the bag quickly. "Then it could kill him faster, depending on the exact dosage." Kevin finished.

"This isn't how this was supposed to go down." Max was the first to break that order from Danny.

"Then I suggest you help me carry that heavy son-of-a-bitch to our rendezvous point or he's gonna die." Closing her bag, she took the leather pouch with the information for the pickup sight and threw it to Steve, who caught it with a quick hand to his chest.

It worked.

Three each side at the six grip sections, they paced each other as they jogged with a strain in their arms in the direction they were supposed to be headed. Jamie had delegated that job to Steve in the front opposite Matt, while she stayed in the middle holding the IV bag.

They stopped once, took swigs of water and each switched sides to stop tiredness weakening their hold on Chris. Jamie wasn't sure when, but she knew the moment the Senior Chief figured out what was going on, and she knew the man winked at her.

An hour and a half later they reached the helo, moored on the ground with its engines off. Danny stood there smoking a cigar waiting for them. As per the way she was getting used to, Jamie took in his scowl.

"You better help him." Max yelled at her, throwing his body up close to her, once Chris was on the stretcher inside the helo. They all watched the exchange. "He'll be fine." Jamie said, throwing her weight back, and shocking Max, who took a step back. "You all think your special but guess what, I didn't need a medical degree to figure out this was a pretty important fucking test today. Someone should control their tongue better, because the entire fucking base knew about it." Jamie pulled off the flak jacket, stupid floppy hat and shirt which was drenched, and held her hands up. "I didn't ask to be your fucking thorn. I was more than happy to remain on the

Comfort. But guess what, someone else had the notion to send me to you. So why don't you start throwing your weight at them, and not me, or next time, when this isn't a bloody drill, then I may just forget everything, quiver and shake like a girl and kill you."

Turning back to Chris, she ripped off the tape holding the IV needle to his skin which she had pierced slightly, when pretending to insert it. She took the bag in the other hand and moving back to face the men, hurled it at Max who caught the bag it on his wide chest. "If you think for a second that I would do something as stupid as that just to get you to move your asses, then you need a shrink on the team not a doctor. My only mission to be tested on was to have Chris on that stretcher and us here. I did my end of the test, so what if I made you assholes think something which was a lie."

Reaching in to her cargo pocket on her thigh, she took out her cell. "Now if you'll excuse me, I'll get my own damn ride back to base with people who will actually fucking treat me as a human, and not like a useless piece of shit."

Okay, so she knew storming off was a very female thing to do, but she was making her own point, and from the silence behind her, she knew she'd shut each and every one of them up.

She put fifty yards between them and called a friend, told them briefly what had happened, and after hanging up, a few minutes later heard the squawk of the radio in the silent helo behind her.

"Commander." She heard a shout and recognized Chris's voice. She stayed where she was, looking west, as the crunch of the ground below his boots got louder. "We have orders to stay with you ma'am until your ride gets here." She saw he had a wide grin on his face. "You're bringing in Marines to get you?"
"Trying to make a point, you'll see."
"I think you were smart, what you did out there this morning Commander."
"Yeah, and what does your team leader think, after all it's him I need to win over."
"Oh trust me, you have. You did the first week you were here. He's just one of those men who sticks to something just so he doesn't look like he has egg on his face." The soft rumble of helicopter blades emerged from the distance. "But I still have one more test; he's going to put me through it."
"You've aced everything so far Jamie." The use of her first name sounded nice in a way. "Somehow I think you'll do the same tomorrow."
"But I'll never be one of you guys, and I don't want to be Chris; at the end of the day I'm not GI Joe."
"We know, the biggest thing for Danny was that you wouldn't slow us down or danger us and you haven't."

The helicopter landed between Jamie and the other helo. The back door lowered, and out came a flight-suit wearing guy with aviator glasses and a smile a mile wide. "Commander." He stood at attention and saluted her, and she saluted back before patting his arm. "How is everything, Brandon?"

"Change of pace, but I'm getting used to it."

"Good, want to meet the team I've been thrown in to?"

"You mean the ones who you want to ditch so you can ride in a better class of helicopter?"

"Something like that." She laughed, and walked closer to the team with him.

Jamie introduced Brandon to the men who were still quiet. She could tell from the look Matt gave her that he was trying to figure out who this new man was, and why she would be able to call him in. The man had to have dropped everything to get there from Miramar that quickly, or was he from Pendleton not thirty miles from where they stood?

"How do you know the Commander?" Danny asked.

"We worked together a while back." Brandon watched Jamie stiffen, and knew the woman who was still a mystery and an enigma of a human had just had the same mental flashes as he did when thinking about it. "James was on the Comfort not far from the coast of New Orleans the day after Katrina hit, and hated the fact that they couldn't do anything, out in the water waiting for casualties that never came. Story is she went over her commanding officer and found out which Marine response teams were helping out already. I was in a team just arriving to get people air-lifted out. Our orders came down that we had to pick up a doc and get our asses back in the air."

"Must have been a tough assignment." Lee said.

"I won't lie; we were in the air flying with four pilots on rotation to keep going, aside from refueling." Brandon caught the woman he admired collecting her things.

"James here never took a break even when...." He stopped.
"Even when what?" Matt asked.
"It was late the first day; we got a call from the local dispatchers, who were fielding constant calls. There was a disabled man on a roof, as his house was filled with water up to the ceilings, the neighborhood houses were all ranchers. His wife had been trapped getting him out. Anyway, he wasn't calling for himself, but for the house two down from him. He'd been unable to help as a mother lost her footing and was swept away but there was a four-year-old girl up on that roof. We went immediately and as with houses before, we lowered James down to assess the situation, and bring the tiny girl up. But then the girl wouldn't let her go. She harnessed her to her back and went down for the guy. We got him up, and then both of the girls came up, and I could hear over the headset as James began trying to find out who the family was for the little girl." Even at six-two and wide, Brandon still got choked up recalling this, and all the men could see that emotion as if it was just yesterday.

"Both parents and an older brother were lost in the storm, and James was adamant, against orders, to keep that girl safe while we carried on. For seventy-two hours she did her job with this tiny little girl always on her back."

"I think that's enough now Brandon." Jamie didn't
want it to continue.
"No, go on." Chris pushed.
"While in flight James had been making calls all over,
one to DC to someone she knew there, and by the end
of the second day she knew who was left for this little
girl, and personally called them. I heard her breaking
the news to an aunt and uncle, and when our seventy-
two were up, we met them at the landing pad. Aisha,
the little girl, went running over to her family. It
seems Aisha's parents had moved them down a year
before, for work, from North Carolina. Anyway,
James got chewed out by her admiral for keeping the
girl aboard our helicopter, but took it all. My team
and I all put in commendations for James, and she got
her new rank as Commander."
"I'll meet you on board." Jamie told him, and he
watched her walk away far enough to not hear, and
saw the other men watching her too. She held strong,
shoulders tight and they knew she was never one to
cross.

"I don't get your SEAL ways, I've ferried a bunch of
you guys in the past, and if I were you I'd be honored
to serve with the commander. I'd have her on my six
in a heartbeat."
"We do things differently around here." Danny said.
"Sure, but make your choice now. Welcome her
completely and give her a ride back, or you let me
take her back to Coronado. I know for a fact it won't
be me answering questions about a member of your

team, whether you like the idea or not, being dropped off by a Marine from Miramar." Brandon let it sink in.

"Tell Jamie she's welcome back here." Danny said.
"I think you should tell her yourself?"
"Fine." The team watched as their leader left them and went to where Jamie was sitting inside the other helicopter. "I didn't know you were allowed to use copters for your own personal trips." Max wasn't so bought by the morning's activities and revelations.
"Being a teacher I get a little leeway."
"And you just dropped everything for her?"
"Anytime she calls." Brandon replied firmly. "I didn't know she was in San Diego but I knew she would call one day." Taking a look back he saw Jamie looking reluctant to come back, walking beside Danny. "Just one piece of advice," he said, taking his shades off and wiping his hand across his forehead. "Be careful, she has a wicked sense of revenge."

Matt watched with eagle eyes while hiding his look through his sunglasses, as Danny kept on walking and Jamie stopped to speak briefly to the Marine. Something niggled him, he wasn't sure if it was a stab of jealousy over some man who could have enjoyed Jamie, he may know things she wouldn't tell him. He was just glad that her smile wasn't as strong to him, and there was no hug but a handshake and then a salute.

Getting aboard the helicopter with the team was a real pain in her ass, because she didn't want to have to make small talk with anyone; she was tired and felt they all needed more time to stew.

Once that helo hit the tarmac at Coronado she didn't say anything, didn't stop, just got off with all the items she had to carry, and walked away in her own direction towards her office.

# CHAPTER ELEVEN

Spending the rest of the afternoon in her office she had left the base noting that Matt's truck was in the lot over near the SEAL building as she drove past. She had a few errands to run before going home and had cut out a little earlier than days before.

Once home she changed into her bikini and a pair of shorts before getting the food ready, and then swimming a few laps. She was just going out to sit on her front step with a beer, when she saw Matt pulling in to his driveway. She knew he hadn't been home, and as they hadn't spoken since the night before, she wasn't sure after that mornings blow up if he would still talk to her.

"Hey." Matt noticed Jamie sitting on her front step when he went to grab the bag from the bed of his truck. "I was hoping to catch you," she said, as he began walking towards her carrying his bag on his shoulders "A man likes to hear that, good for the ego."
"I wasn't sure if you still wanted to come over for dinner."
"Give me ten to grab a shower and I'll happily come back over."
"Okay." Jamie got up smiling a tiny smile.
"You alright?" He stopped his moves to leave, and came closer, seeing the sadness in her face; had she been that worried he wasn't coming over? "I'm a little embarrassed about earlier today, I'm sorry."
"Sorry for what? Teaching all of us a lesson?"

"I went a little far calling Brandon."

"Not really; so is he part of the past you won't tell me about?"

"Brandon and I never...."

"That's all I needed to hear." He gave her a smile and this time left her to go clean up, because he wanted to get back as soon as possible.

Jamie was just placing marinated pork chops on a broiling pan when she heard the kitchen's screen door open and close behind her. "I thought I'd cook inside tonight."

"Smells good, is there anything I can do to help?"

"Get yourself something to drink first." Jamie saw the reflection of the inside light on the window and then the noise of the door closing before the hiss of the cap from the beer being opened. "That envelope on the counter is for you." She said turning quickly and making sure he knew what she was talking about, before putting the chops in the broiler and checking the rice pilaf.

Opening it, Matt was speechless seeing what was inside; two tickets to see a Padres game; they were for the following night and at a quick glance the seats were awesome. "And what did I do to deserve these?"

"Actually I was given them by the Admiral for kicking ass today, exact quote."

"And you don't want to use them yourself?"

"I figured you might enjoy them more."

"You have to come too."

"I thought you'd take one of the team."

"And I want to, you." He put the envelope down and

came closer to her. "As of this afternoon we've all been ordered to swallow our problems and treat you as one of Team Seven." He paused. "A real member."

"Everyone?"

"Danny was very specific."

"Interesting."

"So I don't see a problem with us being out or seen by anyone."

"Are you sure?"

"Very sure."

He stole a kiss and then went to sit at the kitchen island to watch her finish dinner.

XXX     XXX

Sitting in the open air of the stadium during the game Jamie reflected on how different the day had been. The pool test had been more of a training exercise as Danny had some of the men show her ways to float and then ran through using breathing equipment which would be an unlikely thing she'd need but just in case. Danny had seemed pleased with her want to learn even if it was completely new to her.

Matt sat there in his tan pants and polo shirt an arm around Jamie as the breeze picked up chilling her in the pretty summer dress she had been wearing. The tension from the last week was gone as the team opened up and let her in. He wasn't about to go around yelling he liked her because there was still a team and rank issue but the dread she might get reassigned was gone for now.

He explained the small points in the game finding out she knew little about the sport and where they sat not far behind the home team's dugout he had an advantage point for doing that.

In his truck on the way out without the roar of the crowd and the noise from the loud speakers he asked. "Your dad not a ball fan?"

"No, he likes football; at least he did years ago."

"And now?"

"I don't know."

"When he comes out to see you I'd like to meet him; it's always cool meeting an older guy from the teams, find out what's changed."

"I doubt you'll meet him."

"Not keeping me around?" He'd half kidded.

"I'll keep you around, at least until another guy sweeps me off my feet." She smiled and he melted not wanting to pursue the topic of her family again; that wall behind her eyes always came up and he knew he wanted her with or without knowing the stupid little things like her family. If they were anything like Mel, he could see her embarrassment.

"Want to come in for coffee?" She asked as the truck stopped in the driveway. "Sure." He'd kept his promise and taken her to Carlos's for dinner before the game. He felt comfortable in her house as if it were his own and he sat waiting in the living room while she started the percolator, their conversation continuing while she made the coffee.

"So I think tomorrow night I should go and look for something to wear for Saturday." Jamie carried in the two mugs.

"Can I come and help?"

"No." Jamie sat close beside him and laughed. "I have a girlfriend I'm going with; we went to school together decades ago when I lived here."

"Well I don't want to get in between girl time but you'll have to make it up to me."

"I guess I can make that happen." She smiled cheekily.

"You know I try not to care, to not think about things but Jamie you are one hot female and I just can't believe there has been years since your last relationship." He waited seeing her stewing over how to answer. "I'm going to respond to part of that question first and say thank you for your kind words about my attractiveness but I've never thought of myself as hot."

"Well you are."

"Okay, and to answer the other part, I have this fear of being hurt, being lied to, used and it all comes from my last relationship, it wasn't healthy."

"How long were you with him?"

"I'd known him for years, thought I loved him and he never noticed me and then something changed. We were together for over a year but by then I realized it was infatuation and he was trying not to lose something he realized he wanted."

"I'm sorry." He squeezed her hand he was touching that rested on her knee. "I'm no quivering virgin

Matt, I've had lovers and a couple of relationships but there's always the past that comes back somehow to screw it up." Jamie leant forward breaking her eye contact with him. "I think I realized the first night we had dinner together that I was attracted to you Matt, not in an infatuation way but in a damn I want that man in me way. I know you want to know absolutely everything about me and in time I'm sure you'll get to see the darker side of my life but I really just don't want to not get to know you because that's getting in the way."

"I'm okay with that Jamie, I am."

"Are you sure?"

"When you say stuff like you want me in you all the other stuff doesn't seem to matter anymore." He chuckled

Jamie felt his hand on her back and she turned her head to see his eyes and they meant it, she was fool enough to make herself see it if it weren't there.

"Come on." She pushed herself up off the couch. Matt had been about to say something when he watched her lift the sundress up and off leaving her in a pair of little white panties and a strapless white bra. The material fell from her fingers as she turned the corner where the stairs were and he was up and off the couch. He caught her mid-way up the stairs and gently put an arm around her waist lifting her toes clear of the last few steps and while he carried her he kissed her neck feeling her hair tickle his jaw.

It was almost instinctive he knew which her bedroom

in the three rooms upstairs was. That and he could see two had boxes in them and a smaller room was the main bathroom. At her doorway he lowered her and her hand had already taken the hand around her waist. He followed her to the bed where she stopped and said nothing but raised up on her tip toes and kissed him. Sure they'd kissed a few times but this had an urgency, a need he hadn't expected. Her hands were now inside his shirt touching his skin and he lifted his shirt in one fluid motion letting it copy the fall her dress had made; only disconnecting their lips for the briefest of moments before he lowered her back, touching as much of her soft smooth skin as possible.

Jamie scooched back a little further on her bed watching as Matt let his shorts fall down his legs. Just looking at him turned her on and now with the few outer clothes off she felt volcanic as the heat rose through her entire being. He was gentle but sure as he came to lie above her, his elbows at her shoulders while his fingers played with the long strands of her hair.

He could kiss like a pro, he tasted so good that she was lost in the sensation and didn't realize he had sat them both up and his fingers had deftly unhooked her bra and let it fall off. Her first moment of partial clarity was when he took one of her nipples in his mouth suckling while the other was manipulated to a peak with his fingers. She sighed and squeezed her legs around his thigh between her legs.

Matt wanted to take this as slow as possible but the

sighing noises she made turned him inside out with the need to be where she had spoken she wanted him. While he gently lowered her panties he as manly as possible shimmied out of his shorts and he took her lips for another kiss as his fingers played in the junction between her legs. She was hot and ready and he tested the waters inserting one, then two fingers inside her as he used his thumb to add a little pressure to her love button. When her own fingers found his hardness he almost died. All thoughts of being a caring and patient lover went out the window and instead he lowered her again and lined himself up at her entrance. "Oh Matt." Jamie's entire body almost convulsed as he entered her.

He didn't want to look at a clock because he knew there was no way he'd kept it going for an hour but when he caught a glimpse of the large red numbers on the bedside table he knew he had done better for time than he thought and his doubts left him. They had made an absolute mess of the sheets and he liked her lack of inhibitions in bed. She knew what she wanted and how to get it and he'd been a more than willing participant.

Jamie could still see the stars from her release behind her eyelids and could truthfully admit to herself that she had never been loved like that in her entire life. It was almost as if Matt fitted her perfectly, both body and style melded in to one fusible being and moments which she wanted to repeat already.

Lying in his arms she turned on to her side and

looked up at him while her hand snaked down the length of his hard abdomen. "How soon can you go again?" She whispered in his ear before trailing little butterfly kisses along his jaw line. "With your fingers doing that." His back arched. "In a few minutes." "Really?" She leant up on an elbow and looked down at him.

"You don't get it, just looking at you I've been a walking hard on for days and now all I wanna do is." Jamie kissed him swallowing whatever word he was going to say.

# CHAPTER TWELVE

Humidity had risen during the night, and it made Friday hotter than sin on the base. The Team were due to go out and do some ocean exercises, and it looked like the commander was off the hook for the day. In a way some of the men needed the time to truly get their head around the idea they had a female member, who was there, could pull her weight and then some, and also keep them alive if they were injured.

Matt had known he was grinning the moment he entered the locker room, and both Steve and Lee noticed it. "I think Taylor finally nailed the secret girlfriend," Steve said, changing out of his cargo pants and into the peanut butter colored shorts. Matt just grinned more as he removed his sunglasses, and moved closer to his locker. "When are we going to meet this woman?" Lee asked.
"I'm not sure." Matt internally laughed; if only his two closest friends knew.
"Are you bringing her to the dinner party tomorrow night?" Steve pushed, as he tucked his black t-shirt into his shorts. "I'm not sure."
"I heard you were riding over with the commander." Lee who was sitting down was tying his laces on his boots. "I am."
"That's so not fair Matt." Steve groaned. "I must have called ten girls and none of them can go, and you get to go with two?"
"Maybe they don't like being referred to as girls?" Lee shrugged with a laugh.

"Two?" He'd been lost in his own thoughts of the night before. He'd gotten very little sleep and had not left that bedroom until just before dawn, when Jamie had insisted they should get ready to go in to work. "Oh no, you didn't." Steve hissed out but with the widest smile on his face.

"Didn't what?" Matt was glad he was changing shirts, and his face was covered, because he wasn't sure if they asked straight out, if he could lie. Not that either of them had talked about it, but it was like a mutual agreement that keeping things off radar was a very good idea for the time being.

"You and the commander?" Steve continued.
"The timing fits." Lee had thought about it a moment, and Matt's behavior had changed around the same time Jamie had arrived. "I don't want everyone knowing." Matt whispered, as he looked around.
"I can see why." Lee had taken a moment to picture Jamie, and could only picture the dorky way she looked. "You don't get it guys." Matt changed into his own uniform shorts as he spoke. "The glasses are like a disguise, as well as her fierce hair pulled back. Get her off base, in her bikini with her hair down, and contacts in." He shook his head hoping just that small description didn't get him hard again. "I knew it." Steve had tried to picture the commander off base and knew she had to be partially Baywatch hot, seeing as Matt had described the twin sister. "Just keep it quite okay, we're going together to the party tomorrow, but pretending only because we're neighbors."
"So you did get laid last night." Steve waited for the

answer, while Lee was just taking it all in. "Yeah, I did."

"Hooyah." Steve shouted so loud, every man in there looked up.

## XXX    XXX

"I think we have almost got them all." Jamie walked out of her office to where Largo was at her desk, printing up new charts and forms and the usual office junk. "Could you get a message to the Foster, and make sure the doc onboard knows we still don't have the info on Richards's treatment."

"Yes Ma'am." Largo stopped typing and took in her boss. All morning she had seemed different. "Are you happier that all the tests are over, and the Team seem to be embracing you?"

"Why?" Jamie frowned.

"You just seem so happy today."

"I think there are a lot of factors." Jamie bit the inside of her cheek. "Whenever you want, you can go get some lunch. Just do me a favor and let me know in case that phone rings, and I'll get it."

"Yes Ma'am."

Jamie was sitting in her office, making herself familiar with a rundown of every Team member's medical history by skimming through each file. She found it prudent to know, so she was prepared; some old injury could cause problems in the field, or she may want to keep an eye on something. She was actually part-way through Matt's file, when the intercom on her phone beeped, and Largo's voice came on. "Ma'am, one of the Team is here, wants to know if you have a moment as he's feeling under the weather."

"Send him on in Largo."

"Yes Ma'am, and I'll go get some lunch; can I get you anything?"

"No, I think I'll wander down to the cafeteria later."

"Yes Ma'am."

In the few seconds she waited for her office door to open she wondered who it was, who would come by. When the door opened and closed she knew, and she felt her cheeks redden from the heat she felt seeing him, knowing what he looked like naked, and how he felt buried inside her.

"Lieutenant Taylor." She said just for the benefit of Largo as the door closed behind him. "What brings you over here?"

"I have this pain." The moment he said that she was out of her chair and motioning him to follow her to the examination table. "Where?" She took her stethoscope from the counter as he placed a hand in the middle of his chest. "You had childhood asthma, any symptoms since then?"

"No." Matt frowned as he sat on the table. "How did you know that?"

"I'm your doctor, it's part of my job," she said softly. "Take your shirt off." She held the round metal end inside her palm. Warming it. She hated how the coldness of the metal made patients flinch.

All that bronze skin, even if she had touched it, tasted

it, slept a little on it, still made her blood pressure rise. She placed the end of her stethoscope on the upper left side of his back and said. "Take a deep breath in, hold it, and then let it out." He did as he was asked. "Okay, and again." Then she moved the stethoscope forward, and this time she was listening from his chest. "Your heart and lungs sound fine, are you suffering from anything else?"

"Yeah an ache."

"Where?" She noticed a twinkle in his eye as his focus shifted to the front of his shorts. "And what does this ache feel like, I need graphic detail or I might misdiagnose you." She decided to play along. "It needs the touch of a certain woman, a woman who manipulated it so well last night."

"And this morning." Jamie added on the end.

"Yeah, and this morning." He agreed when he let an image of Jamie doing things with her tongue to him. Things few other females he had known had perfected in their art as she had.

"Hold on a moment." Jamie walked over to her door and made sure it was locked. Matt watched her as she came back towards him, taking those glasses off, and putting them down on top of the filing cabinet. "We have to keep this as quiet as possible; I don't want the office down below getting any ideas."

"Then you better bite your lip," he kidded, as he slid off the table; the noises she made, the slight moans and sighs, had turned him on, over and out. "Or you can bite it for me," she teased as he took her in his arms. He turned her so the lower part of her back was against the table and while he did as she asked, and gently nipped her bottom lip, he picked her up so she was sitting on the edge of the desk. He pushed her skirt up to almost around her hips so he could get between her thighs. One of his hands cupped the back of her head, while the other began opening the buttons on her uniform shirt. She had his shorts undone and falling to pool at his feet, while he bared first one, and then the other breast to his eyes and hands. He stopped his movements momentarily as her fingers again found him, freeing him and he pulled her panties off as he lifted her butt up.

He entered her deep and quick.

Jamie was so focused on Matt and their connecting; even when he walked them, still joined to the couch and lay her down on her back. It was like the office, base and world had melted away in the background. They had moved over to her desk, her butt sitting on the edge again, when her intercom sounded, and Largo couldn't have had worse timing, she was close, knew he was too, by that twitch in his jaw. "Ma'am I'm back, is there anything you need help with your patient?"
"He's having a breathing treatment Largo, everything's fine." God, she hoped her voice sounded less pleasured. "Yes Ma'am."

"She's gonna know," Jamie feared, as his hips kept moving, she whispered in his ear. "Bite me." He whispered back and when she frowned at him he said between breaths. "Bite me so you don't scream out like at home." Jamie wasn't sure, she didn't want to hurt him but as she reached the peak, she couldn't make a sound, and instead gently nipped the soft flesh at the base of the neck.

Holding her as he too came down to earth, he could have laughed out loud at being almost caught, and how good it was. The look on her face was the icing on the cake, knowing what he felt was coursing through her veins as well.

"I'm going to miss you at dinner tonight." He said pulling his shorts that he had retrieved from where they had fallen while he took in her fixing her bra and shirt. "You've had dinner with me the last seven nights Matt."
"A man gets used to certain comforts in life easily."
"I'll make it up to you."
"I know you will."
"You are very sure."
"Hmm, because I am going to leave my front door unlocked, so whatever time your shopping adventure ends, you can come over and do to me whatever you might want."
"Anything?"
"My door will be open."
"Could be pretty late."
"I'll still be naked in bed."
"Then I'll see you later Lieutenant."
"Thanks again for seeing me without an appointment," he said as he opened the door.
"My door's always open." Jamie had to laugh.

"Ma'am." Largo was at the door before there was a

chance to have it closed.

"Yes Largo."

"I just wanted to see if you needed me to clean up after the breathing treatment."

"I'll get it, Largo."

"Oh, I forgot to tell you. We got a call from the supply company; those masks and oxygen tanks you needed for things like breathing treatments won't be in until Monday." Jamie groaned internally, busted beyond belief. She could feel the sting of embarrassment stain her cheeks. "That's good to know Largo, thanks."

"Don't worry Ma'am, I won't tell anybody."

"Thank you Largo."

XXX    XXX

At the end of the day Matt stripped his wetsuit gear down to his waist, as they waited for the pick-up truck to meet them at the shore point. The entire team was there; each one of them had been a part of the training exercise. Even Danny, Coop and Chris had gotten wet and from the looks on their faces they had enjoyed being out in the ocean.

"Nice bite mark." Steve pointed out to him.

"What?" Matt tried but for the life of him couldn't see where Steve was pointing at the junction of his neck and shoulder. "You didn't have that earlier."

"I probably got caught by something out on the exercise."

"Looks like it was pretty big." Steve looked closer and smiled. "Where did you go while we ran the base during lunch?"

"Why?"

"Because I've had a few bites of my own which looked like that." He stood back. "That's a female bite."

"Is it?" He may have admitted some stuff that morning, but he wasn't about to admit to an on-base escapade. "You better cover that up before someone sees it."

"No one but you would know it's a woman who bit me."

"Ryan." Steve waved over one of the other men. This one had put on a t-shirt over his chest while wearing the wet suit like the others, after having suffered some serious sunburn the week before.

"Yeah?" Ryan asked.

"Tell me what that mark on Matt's shoulder looks like to you." Matt stood very self-consciously still, as the other guy looked close. "Which female did you let take a bite out of you?"

"See." Steve said before Matt could answer. "He has a new girlfriend." He explained to Ryan. "Anyone we know?"

"She works on base." Matt said with a cough.

"Well, as long as she's not another Anna; she was a real bitch."

"Hooyah to that." Matt agreed.

"So are you bringing her tomorrow night so we can meet her?"

"I have to see what her schedule's like." Steve gave Matt a head shake and walked away.

Arriving home, he had forgone the shower on base, and more questions if anyone else had seen, or if Steve had again pointed it out. He went upstairs to his bathroom, turning the water on in the shower and then pulling his shirt off so he could see what the damage was. He smiled when he saw the partial hicky, the teeth marks. It hadn't felt like Jamie had done anything strong, but that sure was a whopper of a mark.

He spent the evening doing small stuff, but constantly listening when a car drove up the street. He caught the Padres playing the Mets away in New York, so it was a short game, as he'd turned on in the fifth inning. Heating up a microwave meal had been unappetizing, and the beer didn't taste so sweet. Around nine he gave up and went to bed, hoping if he fell asleep, then Jamie would get there sooner.

XXX    XXX

Shopping equaled torture.

At least that's how Jamie had always seen it.

It had been wonderful to see and catch up with Katie. She was one of those well dressed, highly manicured mothers of three, who also worked a six-figure salary job. While her friend walked around the mall wearing the latest from Donna Karen, or whoever was the latest big designer, Jamie had been feeling even frumpier in her white, sticking out like a sore thumb in a civilian crowd, uniform.

Pulling in to her driveway it was a pleasure to be home, her home for the past week at least. She saw all the lights off in Matt's house; and although the urge to go inside her own house and shower, before crawling below her own sheets, was calling to her, she knew at a very deep level her body was craving something only he had been able to bring alive inside of her.

Running in quickly to leave her purse and to have a shower, one of those quick in-and-out kind, she threw on a pair of her pajama bottoms which were cropped to mid shin and a t-shirt, forgoing anything underneath. She slipped her flip flops on her feet before taking only her keys to lock up behind her. Then feeling slightly giddy from the adrenaline the action was giving her she got to his front door and turned the knob carefully, finding it unlocked like he promised it would be. Then slipping off the sandals and tip toeing up the stairs, she could hear his even breathing and followed it through the dimly lit hall to the end, where the mirror image of her own layout was his bedroom.

"Your hands are cold." His sleepy laughter made her laugh as she let her hands roam all over his bare chest. "I'm sorry." She kissed the skin near her; it was his shoulder. "Hey, no biting me again, that mark already got me in to a little trouble today."
"You told me to do it." She liked his arm engulfing her.
"I know, and I wouldn't take it back." His own

fingers began roaming too. "I'm hoping you were wearing something when you ran between our houses."

"I was." She'd slipped them off when walking down his hall.

"How was your evening?"

"Don't get me started." Jamie groaned before her breath caught when his fingers found a nipple in the semi darkness. "That bad?"

"Let's put it this way, I like wearing a uniform because I don't have to shop for anything other than underwear."

"I thought women liked shopping."

"I think Mel got all the patience for that."

"But you have civvies, where did they come from?"

"They're hand me downs from Mel." Jamie laughed. "See, she got a fat ass, and I got the tits, in the womb."

"And man am I grateful."

"I can tell." Knowing where his face was now, her orientation was complete. She leant in and kissed him.

"I still have to go back out tomorrow and get something to wear still."

"Go naked."

"I'm already petrified about the team seeing me differently, out of my comfortable bubble."

"Don't be."

"Katie pulled out some fantastic dresses to wear, except I shot them all down as they were sexy and fitted. She hated everything I chose because they were frumpy and old lady style."

"Get something sexy and revealing just for me."

"Just for you; but I thought we agreed to ensure people didn't know about us."

"Well Steve and Lee know."

"So does Largo," Jamie admitted and Matt had actually been braced for something harsh.

"Because of me coming to your office?"

"I made a huge mistake telling a lie I couldn't back up."

"What did she say?"

"That we didn't have the breathing treatment equipment yet."

"Ouch." He held her closer liking the feel of her naked length and how perfect she was inside his arms. How perfect she could be sheathed around him.

"How was your evening?" Jamie asked him enjoying the banter.

"Boring, I actually came to bed in hopes of falling asleep until you got here."

"Did it work?"

"It took a little while to fall asleep but being woken up by a naked female was my dream."

"Any certain naked female in your dream?"

"Yeah, you."

"Well that earns you something very special."

"How special?"

"Let me show you." Her hand went much lower than where it had been on his abdomen where he lay on his back with her head resting on his chest.

# CHAPTER THIRTEEN

Hair was done. Down with volume, and a few meaningful curls to the long blonde lengths. Nails were dry, she was showered, lightly perfumed and just a minor amount of make-up that felt unusual but made her features stand out. Looking in the mirror in her bathroom, Jamie felt like she was looking at her sister, not a reflection.

Not having an appropriate dress to wear to a formal wedding dinner, outside of the dress uniform she had worn to the only other wedding she had ever been invited to, she was forced to spend the morning after an unsuccessful night, scouring the mall for something to wear again.

Thankfully Katie had the patience of a saint. Basically, it was just your usual little black dress, a sheath of black silk fabric that scooped down with a flow of fabric at the neckline, with a back that exposed most of her back, stopping just above her rear. It ended a little above her usual skirt, but with her long legs, it looked even shorter.

Katie, her helpful shopper, had picked out a matching purse and shoes. Pointy and stylish, the stilettos were going to kill her feet, but Jamie had been promised it would add to the effect of the dress.

Jamie took another look in the floor-length mirror. With everything altogether, and her hair flowing around her shoulders she felt uneasy and more nervous than usual. Having to dress like this, with her new team about to see her in this new light, made it worse. The comments about her appearance had not been lost on her since she had arrived.

She was worried a few of the men might think differently about this woman before them. This wasn't the woman they had allowed to join their Team.

She felt like a movie star inside though; like one of those people who do those extreme makeover shows. They go in all frumpy and ugly, and come out a totally new person. Oh yeah, deep down she loved this dress; she just hoped she didn't break her neck in these shoes.

The doorbell rang, and she had kept the door open and the screen latched, just in case Matt arrived. "Come on in. I'll be down in a minute."
"Take your time, I'm early." Taking a deep breath, she stood just behind the top of the stairs.
"Promise you won't laugh," she shouted back.
"I promise." He chuckled, and she knew he would be genuine in his response. She descended the stairs and caught her breath as she saw him standing at the bottom, waiting for her. He was all dressed up in his black and white formal tuxedo. His face freshly shaved and his hair still wet from his shower.

Mathew looked up the flight of stairs at the sound of her heels on the hardwood floor. There, emerging before him, was a female who took his breath away;

she looked angelic and sexy all in one very seductive package. He couldn't seem to get his mouth to do any more than just gape open, as she took the stairs down to him. Even if he could get it to work, there were no words he could string together, to convey what his body was feeling, especially his lower body parts. He kept his eyes on her; clear eye to eye contact, nothing for her to hide behind. No f-ugly glasses and sweats, just a knockout of a woman. A vamped-up version of the woman he had spent the last week with, and the last two nights in bed with satisfyingly.

Jamie kept her eyes locked on his, and after taking the last step, she broke it off, looking at the floor and touching the sides of her dress, almost as if she were trying to make it longer. "Well at least you had the courtesy not to laugh." Her voice quiet and reaching for the keys on her hall table, and purposely keeping her body away from his, moving towards the door. "Shouldn't we be going?"
"Hold on." He grabbed for her arm, pulling it with as much gentility as he could. "I'm sorry, I was trying to find an appropriate compliment to give a commanding officer without getting my ass thrown in the brig."

Jamie pulled her arm free a little more forcefully than needed because the moment Mathew had realized she would bolt, he had the same reflex. "Please let's just get this night over with before I make a run for it," she told him.
"Why would you run?"
"Isn't it obvious?"

"My God Jamie it isn't; why don't you explain it to me?"

"I look ridiculous." He shook his head.

"Ridiculous my ass. I'm sorry but you are so incredibly hot I don't think I want to take you out in public, except to make my ego bigger that such a woman would be seen dead with me. I don't want any of the other guys to see you; I want to keep this Jamie for myself, for when we're alone together, and naked." He paused. "I don't want to let anyone else know how hot you are, because I fear suddenly that I may not be enough for you."

"Matt." It was Jamie's turn to shake her head. "You are the hot one, but thank you." She knew he was serious his expression was so genuine, no gag reflexes hidden deep down. Having nothing witty or funny to comeback, with and feeling even more nervous, Jamie just kissed his cheek in thanks, and grabbed her clutch, before walking out towards his truck.

XXX    XXX

Hotel Del Coronado was the oldest, most beautiful hotel on the beach on Coronado Island in San Diego. Its architecture was impressive, all lit up at night, with the sun setting behind it, as Matt pulled into the covered valet stand. She took it all in. This was a strong piece of history for the small island, connected by a large bridge to down town San Diego. At one end of the island was this expensive beach and tourist community and the other was their base. It was like night and day, comparing the Coronado section to the North Island base end.

Every day she drove the bridge to the island like nearly anyone who wasn't living on base did. You had to drive past the multimillion dollar houses in all shades and colors but when Matt had driven towards the hotel she had seen the stretch of grass running down the center of the main drag, the trees showed as much opulence as the houses and stores. It was a shock even more so when he had pointed out the 'Del' a few traffic lights back from it. It made sense now why she had heard that a lot of important people used the 'Del's' facilities, especially from the base.

Waiting for Matt on the red carpet laid out at the valet stand, she felt impressed as he took her arm in his and they started for the steps leading to the building. The crash of waves could be heard from one side, and the soft sounds of classical music from before them at the doorway. A slight hum of chatter and the occasional shutting of car doors behind them was whisked away by the smell of ocean, floral notes and something sweet like honey or chocolate. Whatever the scent was they added to their hotel; it was just perfect and soft.

The staggered stairs led them to a lobby that was as rich in its wooden décor and antique elevator, as it was in the expensive looking clientele standing around the check in desk, coming out of the stores, or just looking at the carved wooden second floor that was visible from the square opening directly above the lobby.

Jamie watched as couples walked down the stairs that wrapped around the right of the elevator, old fashioned with the heavy brass doors which a man who looked as old as the hotel still opened for guests. The floor beneath her shoes was so soft and carpeted with what must have been a cloud, she was still taking in her surroundings when he stopped her before a set of open doors to the right of where they had entered.

"Ready?" he asked, letting her go reluctantly. He could explain holding her to get up those stairs in those heels, but not all-night long. He had seen her looking around, and knew she was impressed. Shame it was at least three hundred bucks a night for a storage closet sized room at the Del, or he would have gladly booked a room for the two of them that night. He would take her to his favorite hotel over in La Jolla sometime; that would be more for half the price at the spa.

Nearly all the guests had arrived. Danny had spoken to all of them personally as they came in. They were waiting for Lee and his wife Mary, and Mathew and Jamie that he had been surprised to hear, were coming together until Chris had explained that they were neighbors.

He noticed while he and Kirsten were making their way to the dining room that the level of chatter had suddenly dropped, like those around them they turned towards the lobby entrance, to the 'Crown Room' where they were having the party. Chris was a breath away and he leaned closer speaking to Danny so that only he heard. "Looks like our new member just arrived."

"And what an entrance she made." Danny almost silently responded.

There before them was the personification of everything men dreamed about in a woman. Gone was the dorky, nervous doctor that shied away from the Team but stood firm when her back was against the wall. Here she was shining and beautiful, a mix of angel and sexy goddess. Every female had noticed her, and took note even more so than the men.

XXX    XXX

Jamie could feel everyone's eyes focused directly on her and if her nerves weren't already at maximum level they certainly would have been up there, from this. She wanted to just turn and leave, pretend it was all a big mistake; find something to hide behind even, or maybe somewhere dark. She could feel the warmth of Mathew's hand on the bare skin of her back. "I need to get out of here, get some air for a minute." She said. "I'll be in the bathroom." Without looking back Jamie made a quick exit back out to the lobby.

He, like everyone else watched her walk away, and it was only a brief second before the conversations started up again. Steven was already weaving his way through everyone towards him with a cocky grin on his face. "Was that really the Doc?"

"Sure was." Mathew took a quick look back to the exit.

"You were right; she sure does scrub up well. Where'd she run off too?"

"The bathroom, or maybe to the car, hopefully the former."

"Jamie sure raised some eyebrows just then." Steve took another glass of champagne from a waiter's tray as it went past.

"She like your date?" O'Rielly sidled up from behind. "I figured we were both coming here it was stupid to bring two cars."

"Right." Steve laughed, knowing the truth, swigging back the drink in one long swallow. "She's gone from butt ugly to gorgeous in one day. I heard Mary ask Lee which part of his description of Jamie did he forget to tell her about."

"Wow. That was...." Kevin said hiking a thumb and joining his friends.

"Jamie? Yep." Mathew answered. "She's been nervous all the way here."

"I'd like to know where she got that dress." Steve turned as the couple-to-be came over.

"Danny, Kirsten. This place looks amazing." Mathew shook hands with his boss and gave his fiancé a quick kiss on the cheek. It was an unspoken rule that Danny did not want his rank used outside the base; actually, none of them really even used the rank system when referring to each other. "Thanks Matt," the man said. "Where'd Jamie run off to? I was coming over to say hello." Kirsten said.

"I believe she's gone to the bathroom to compose herself Ma'am."

"You know; I could do with a quick freshen up. Will you men please excuse me?"

XXX     XXX

The more she stared at herself, the more she felt ridiculous. Who was she trying to impress, and what was she trying to prove anyway? This dress was all Mel, the hair, even the make-up and nails. Forget about these shoes, they'd been on her feet less than forty-five minutes, and her toes already felt like they'd been given a local anesthetic.

Hearing the door open again Jamie didn't move, hoping it wasn't someone from the party she had just run out of. The hotel was a very busy place, so she hoped she was right, but the odds were slim. "Jamie?" She heard a female ask, busted! "Yes," she replied coming face to face with a beautiful brunette who she had seen standing next to Danny minutes before. "You must be Kirsten." Jamie held out her hand which the bride-to-be accepted. "Thank you for inviting me tonight. It's nice to feel included."

"I'm glad you could make it; I've been dying to meet you ever since Danny came home in a royally pissed-off mood." Jamie was given a huge wide smile.

"That sounds right, and by the looks of it out there, I have a whole set of other issues to deal with now." Jamie leant her hip on the counter top. "Forget about all of them, they'll calm down the minute they remember you're there to help bring their significant others home in one piece."

"Maybe."

"I know that knowledge will make me sleep better when you all go wheels up next." Kirsten gave her a large smile.

"Okay." Jamie smiled as best she could

"But you have to be aware of what the men must have said when they were asked what you looked like. I know what Danny said was, well. Anyway and then in walks you tonight, with this amazing dress and a body half of the ladies would sell their souls for." She paused as she looked in the mirror fluffing a slight curl. "Trust me, I have heard each of them complain about some flaw, I do it myself all the time."

"Stop, you are beautiful." Jamie told her.

"And so are you, embrace it and let the men see you are a strong woman in every facet of your life. It makes them really insecure when you do that," she ended with a laugh.

"Let's go out there, I'll take you around and introduce the ladies to you, and then they'll all know how sweet and nice you are." Kirsten continued.

"How do you know I'm nice and sweet?"

"Because, darling," she said in her Texan accent. Jamie had known she had a twang of something in her voice. "You would have stayed in there hanging all over Matt, giving off the biggest and bitchiest attitude, if you weren't so sweet."

## CHAPTER FOURTEEN

The small section of the larger Crown Dining room had been decorated in all creams and pastels, which contrasted well with the dark rich wood that made up the entire area, from window up through the entire rounded wooden ceiling. The room was rounded at the end, and the windows let in the dark night, blending well with the framed panels in the ceiling. The soft candlelight and the beautiful music playing, and the look was straight out of a fairy tale.

The tables the guests were sitting at were all round. With six guests at each table. Jamie was sitting with Steven on her left and Mathew on her right. Opposite were Lee and his wife Mary and between Lee and Steven was O'Rielly, the quiet and simmering looking SEAL. His quietness alone made the hairs on the back of Jamie's neck stand on end.

Her initial impression of Mary had been one of complete contempt. The woman seemed unwelcoming and icy, a complete bitch. But as time went on she had opened up and showed what a loving compassionate woman she really was. Mary and her husband Lee seemed really in love, looking into each other's eyes and kissing when they thought no one was looking.

"So, Jamie; Lee tells me you have a twin sister in the Marines," Mary said, leaning away from Lee, who had turned to talk to the young ensign crouched between the chairs. Their conversation seemed animated, and Jamie had wondered what it was all about. "Yes I do."

"Identical?" She seemed genuinely interested.

"Pretty much; I mean she got the looks, I got the brains."

"Oh honey, the two of you as teens must have been hell on your father."

"I guess." Jamie sipped the ice water she had chosen after the second glass of champagne had been finished.

"Tell me." Mary leaned just a little closer, and lowered her voice. "Where did you get that dress?"

"I found it at Macy's this morning."

"You didn't need tailoring or anything? Just straight off the rack huh?" Mary laughed. "I wish I could do that. All the clothes I buy need to be shortened at least an inch."

"I was just lucky. I mean it's the first real dressy thing I've ever bought, so I wouldn't know."

Feeling nervous, Jamie asked. "How long have you and Lee been married? You seem very much in love."

"Ah, don't we? About a year, it's my second marriage, and I have a seven-year-old and a four-month-old."

"Wow. That's great."

"What about you? There must be someone special in your life."

"There's no one. I just moved here." Jamie blushed, and she became very aware of Mathews hand on the back of her seat, his thumb gently stroking her back in a soothing motion.

"Where did they pull you from to assign you here?" Mary continued.

"I was out on the medical ship 'the USS Comfort'. I've been serving on board there for about five years."

"No one special on there?"

"No." Jamie finished her water, and had placed it down for a moment, before a waiter filled it up once more. She needed something to change the subject from her. "I hear you and Lee had an interesting start." She remembered hearing something. "Actually yes, but it's a long story."

"I've got all night." Jamie smiled sweetly.

"Well, I was the secretary for the Admiral who ran the base before the new one was assigned. Lee and I met over at the Base Exchange, where we were both trying to buy the same thing that they only had one left of. Then he and my ex-husband almost got in to it too, over something he caught happening." Mary looked down at the cutlery before her and started fiddling with the fork. "Lee was working base security, my ex and I were separated, and the admiral had put me up in housing on base. Lee responded to a complaint and anyway what he did caused some problems for me. So, we didn't exactly have a very friendly relationship to begin with. I thought he was an arrogant pig and he thought I was a Bitch. He helped me through some tough stuff even though he didn't have to, and what became a friendship soon turned into something more romantic." She laughed, taking a sip of her wine.

"That's a happy ending." Jamie gave her a smile

wondering about the part in the middle that was glossed over. Jamie had a nosey way about her, but mainly because she wanted to help and fix things.

"So where are you from?" Jamie asked her. "I noticed you have a slight accent."
"Georgia originally."
"That's where my father and step-mother live."
"Really, your last name is Buchanan, right?" Mary frowned a little in thought.
"That's right." Jamie flinched, and Mathew's hand stopped its rhythm, and momentarily laid flat in the same spot. "Actually, my Dad plays golf with a Buchanan at our country club."
"Oh."
"Your father isn't Richard Buchanan is he?" Mary could see Jamie's uneasy body language.
"Yes he is."
"Now I'll be damned. Our fathers have been friends for years and he never once told me his friend's daughters were in the military."
"That wouldn't surprise me."
"So your Dad's know each other?" Lee asked re-joining the conversation halfway through, his other conversation having finished. "It seems they do, Honey."
"Will you all excuse me please?" Jamie stood up to leave. The men stood too as a courtesy and Mathew asked. "Are you okay?"
"I just need a little fresh air. I'll be right back."

"What was that?" Steve asked, having been listening with deep interest to the two women talk.

"Mathew, has Jamie ever mentioned who her dad is?"

"Like everyone else, I don't know her that well."

"I'm sorry; I saw you two and thought...." Mary fixed her place settings nervously. "Don't apologize." Matt told her.

"What is it Honey?" Lee asked.

"I think I may have upset her by mentioning her father."

"You know her dad?" Steve joined in, still eyeing up one of the waitresses.

"I think I do." Mary looked at the men at the table. "My dad is friends with him, I've actually met the man on a few occasions over the years." She waited a second, and each man seemed to lean further in. "Her father is the senator of Georgia."

XXX     XXX

With the waves crashing continuously out past the shrubbery and sand, the restaurant and bar behind her almost empty and void of any of the paying guests. No one was walking out on the sand and no sounds of water splashing from the nearby pool. The palm trees swayed with a very faint rustle against the waves, but it felt like no one else was staying at the lavish old hotel.

Jamie never heard anyone walk towards her. The party was on the other side of the hotel and she had snuck through their beautiful courtyard to get to the beach side of the property. She stood out on the empty restaurant patio with a propane patio heater beside her, and the hiss must have covered the sound of footsteps. A flute of champagne was suddenly next to her in a strong, familiar hand. Turning, there was Mathew, a blank look on his face looking at her, searching her eyes for the problem.

"Thank you." She took the drink from him. "I wasn't going to drink. These shoes are hard enough to walk in without this in the mix." But she downed it anyway.

"You went missing," he said

"They do the speeches yet?"

"Just wrapped up; you missed Steve trying to not spit his dessert out when all the romantic stuff was mentioned."

"I bet that was a sight."

"Will you be able to dance in those heels?"

"I might." She smiled at the sparkle in his eyes.

"Good. Let's get some more champagne and dance. Then maybe while I'm trying not to stand on your toes, you'll tell me what's up."

"I'm just not used to having people ask me so many questions about my life."

"It's about whatever the problem is between you and your father? It's that, right, that got you upset in there?"

"My father? Let's just say it's a mute subject."

"I'm a good listener."

"I know you are."

"Did I ever tell you much about my uncle who I'm named after?" Matt asked her as he led her over to a bench. "No." She shook her head, she did know Matt had mentioned the man only once, and only when explaining why he had joined the Navy. "He came to live with us when I was about eight. He was my dad's oldest brother, and instead of going to live with my grandfather, he came to us. My parents had a small farmhouse that had been in my mom's family forever.

I didn't know why at the time, but he had been dishonorably discharged from the Navy. He used to drink and get mean, and he would fight with my dad all the time, but my dad wasn't as strong as him, so he never left unless he wanted to leave. He would smoke inside the house even though my mom asked him not to, and he would steal money my mom set aside, for his booze. There was one night that the argument got so bad he actually punched my dad, and my mom called the cops; but he left before they arrived." "What happened to your uncle?" Jamie asked she had put a hand on Matt's knee during the time he had been talking.

"My dad died when I was sixteen, but my uncle didn't show up for the funeral, no cards or condolences. When Pete and I left for college, mom sold the farm and moved to Cleveland and became an assistant at a nursing home. My granddad died, and she tried to find Uncle Matt, to give him his share of the inheritance. It took about a year, and she found him through a VA contact I had made being in the Navy. Seems Uncle Matt, sometime after leaving our place, shacked up with a woman from Chicago. He pissed off the wrong person there, and ended up in Cook County jail doing twenty-five to life for murdering some guy."

"How does your uncle become a murderer?" Jamie was shocked.

"The woman he shacked up with was mixed up with some bad stuff and he died protecting her, or so the story goes." He touched Jamie's cheek.

"I tried to contact him, wanted to see him, but he didn't want to see any of us. He died from liver sclerosis about five years ago."

"I'm sorry. That still must have hurt you."

"It was hard. To have my mom talk about him you would think the guy was an angel, these days my mom thinks everyone is an angel."

"You don't talk about her at all." Jamie watched his face wondering if she got the same look as he did.

"You don't talk about your dad." Matt countered. "I do better on my own." Jamie's statement was blunt as if putting a wall up between them. All comments and questions did not seem welcome. "It's easy not to get nervous or scared by yourself is that it?" He wondered if maybe she was meaning alone as in without him. "Partly."

"Does your father know you're here?"

"Matt; I can't not here." He saw the tears begin to build in her eyes.

"Okay, maybe later?" He leaned in closer. "After I thoroughly enjoy you." He was about to lean in and kiss those lips.

"Jamie, that's where you are." A female voice came from the building. It was Mary. Mathew took a deep breath and stood up, and it was then that Jamie noticed how close he had been. They had been so close the past couple of days and the last thing either of them should do is make their relationship so obvious. "I've been looking everywhere for you." The pretty little redhead said. "We females are going up stairs for the hen night, and you just have to be there for everyone to talk to. Mathew you don't mind do you?"

"We were just talking." He explained whilst lying, he would have taken her, and kissed her there and then, had they not been disturbed. "Jamie come and find me when you want to leave okay."

"Thanks Mathew'. She paused. "For everything."

The two women watched as Mathew made his way back in to the hotel. "He's such a great guy." Mary said. "He and Lee were in BUD/S together and they're like real brothers."

"That's nice."

"He would be a great catch for anyone who might be interested."

"Shame there's no chance of that here then." Jamie tried to play off.

"Whatever you say." Mary laughed, knowing from what she had seen tonight, the two of them were perfect for each other.

## CHAPTER FIFTEEN

Two hours, well, one hour and forty-seven minutes later, Jamie was still being subjected to the banter from the women half of the SEAL team's gossip. All the wives and girlfriends really were a very nice bunch, very friendly and willing to share their lives with her. She felt, for the first time, very comfortable and included. It seemed their doubts about her had vanished.

She especially found herself getting along really well with Patti, an older lady, who was married to the Senior Chief, and the most visible president of this lady's club. She had told Jamie about her two teenage boys, and where the family had been able to vacation last Thanksgiving, and about how wonderful Mathew was. Jamie didn't miss the hidden meaning in that information.

She knew Matt had told both Steve and Lee. Had Lee told Mary who had slipped it into the gossip mill the women all seemed connected by?

The men of the team had been gossiped about nearly the one hour and, oh, fifty-two minutes; from who is the best in the bedroom, to who walked around the house naked when on leave. Someone had mentioned a man mowing the lawn naked, that Jamie had missed the beginning of, and wasn't about to ask who it had been. The visual in her head had been of Mathew from the week before, when she had watched him from her bedroom, and how good he had looked. She had to stop herself there before she made her cheeks flush.

"So, did anyone actually find out what went wrong?" Jason's girlfriend Emma asked. Jamie looked over towards that part of the small sitting room they were in. "I heard he isn't very well endowed, also a little lacking in the sack, you know," Sarah, Kevin's wife said.

"Well, I think that is complete crap." Mary interrupted. "Have you seen him in his Speedo's at the pool?"

"I have." Wanda fanned herself as she raised her eyebrows, to exaggerate her words. "That man has plenty to work with."

"Maybe he's just inexperienced. You know, I hear one of the guys has yet to lose his virginity." Mary grinned.

"And maybe that's him." Sarah didn't want her gossip to be shot down.

"Who are you guys talking about?" Jamie made the mistake in asking.

"Mathew," Karen, Max's girlfriend replied, and it took all of Jamie's effort to hold her champagne in her mouth.

Patti came back from the bathroom, having obviously heard the conversation, and said. "Now ladies let's not scare Jamie off Mathew, before he gets the courage to make a move." Jamie almost did spit out her champagne at the comment. "That's not going to happen," Jamie said, trying to compose herself, and hide every truth bubbling up inside her. "Why ever not Jamie?" Mary asked winking.

"Because the only reason we arrived together tonight was...."

"You live next door to each other," everyone said in unison, and then burst into laughter.

XXX     XXX

Mathew loved seeing how Jamie had been so overly embraced by the women of the Team. The men were waiting for their female companions to arrive, and the ones who weren't, were still in the bar, drowning their single status. He watched with them as all the women came down from the suite they had all been hanging out in for the past few hours. He could tell from the way she was, that she'd had fun, but he could see that a lot of that had to do with a steady supply of champagne. She glowed from it; still steady on her feet, there was now a slight bounce in there.

"You look happy." Mathew commented when she walked over, leaving the other women behind her. "I am." She gave him a somewhat crooked smile. "They are all very cool."

"Alcohol always makes everything look rosy." He smiled wide.

"Sourpuss." Jamie jibed. "But you're probably very right."

"Probably." He laughed. "Are you ready to go?" Mathew offered his arm for her to hold on to, knowing only a few feet away was a set of steps down to the valet parking.

"So, you liked the women of Team Seven huh?" He asked after giving the valet his card to get his truck back. "They were all much nicer than I had imagined." She looked up at him, there wasn't much of a difference in their height with the shoes she was wearing, but she still seemed dainty. "Of course they were. You just expected the worst."

"To begin with I wanted to run screaming or hide in the bathroom, but Patti and Mary are both just too sweet."

"Not as sweet as some." Mathew said, her eyes were sparkling, and they were only a foot apart. He had seen so many variations of Jamie but this happy, obviously slightly drunk version, was probably one of his favorites. "After the looks when we arrived, well, I'm sure you can imagine what I was thinking."

"I was thinking the exact same thing as everyone else, except I have the image of you naked imprinted in my head, so I'm very lucky."

"Huh." Jamie frowned as the truck pulled up and Mathew jumped in to the driver's seat the moment the young valet was out. She made a quick attempt to run, and gave up on the gravel drive. Getting in as Mathew was ready to go, after fixing the mirrors and seat.

"What did you mean out there?" Jamie asked.

"There wasn't a man in there wondering what it would be like to get you in bed, even the married ones, Jamie."

"Shut up." She laughed as she playfully punched his arm

"It took everything I have not to gloat."

"I bet it did."

"I wanted to stand up and shout it out."

"Mathew, I've consumed a lot of alcohol and as a senior ranking officer in the truck I order you to not tell anyone." There was absolutely nothing serious about that in her voice and she actually chuckled a little at herself.

"It was the dress wasn't it?"

"I like the dress." He pulled in to the main road from the drive. "You did a great job picking it out."

"It was one of the ones Katie suggested, I just went back and tried it on again and decided she was semi right."

"You'll have to keep it ready to wear because I am certainly taking you out again wearing it."

"You know if you like it so much you can borrow it whenever you want, just let me know."

"Ha, ha." He looked at her, his eyes lit from the oncoming car lights.

"I'm being totally serious Matt. I think your body would do this dress justice."

"Jamie are you drunk?" He had to laugh with her.

"Oh, Matt, I'm just feeling the buzz."

Yep, she was drunker than a skunk.

# CHAPTER SIXTEEN

Mathew had walked Jamie to her door, but now, as he stood in the dark lull of his house, he wished he could rewind, and re-do the chaste goodnight on her porch steps. He knew little about her personally yet she reeled him in when they were close and made him feel like they had known each other for years. His attraction was stronger for her than his ex, and that had been amazing to begin with.

He had been a little unsure about the end of the night. She was in a different place in her head after all the champagne, and it had been almost natural when they had gone to their separate doors.

He wanted to know everything about her even though he said he didn't have to.

So she had talked about her sister a bit, but only after Mathew had met her, he was sure. But her father being a senator in Georgia? She had stayed far from that, and had been visibly upset when they had found out. Knowing that, he could see how close she was to no one, even her twin. It made him wonder why; his own family, though small, was so close. Sure he spoke to his mom when he could and he and Peter had spoken a couple of times in the past few months but they e-mailed each other all the time. Being alone was showing up a lot in her life, maybe that was a safe way to live, but it made him wonder what had happened in her past to make her feel like that.

The darkness in his house was disturbed by a light shining from outside. It came in through the kitchen and illuminated his body lengthways. If he were a person of less common sense he would think, he was being invaded by aliens.

Then he heard it, the sounds of water and knew instantly that Jamie was in her pool. He walked over to the window above the sink, and from there he could see her, sure enough, doing laps. First he waited for a second to make sure she was ok, she had been drinking; and then he watched her as she gracefully swam hardly disturbing the water. After a few lengths she stopped at the farther end and wiped the water from her eyes, before pulling the wetness from the length of her hair.

She seemed to turn and look directly at him from the safety of her pool. He took off his jacket and loosened the bow tie, before pulling that off too. He turned to place them on the back of a bar stool and she was gone, she was nowhere in the area of the pool. He felt his body groan with the thought of her having gone inside before he could watch her some more, like the pervert he was quickly becoming.

When his phone rang he was momentarily stunned and freaked out. "Taylor," he answered after the third ring. "Mathew, are you still awake?" It was Jamie's soft voice.
"Ah, yeah."
"I was in the pool; you know, trying to do some laps, but I'm just not into it."

"No?"

"I'm still wired from the party, well, the champagne. And if you're, you know, the same, maybe you'd like to come over, maybe swim a little? Just chill out? It's nice out, the humidity has cleared, and well, I would like your company, I miss you being here, and had hoped you'd come in with me, but you didn't seem to want to." Her rambling making him smile.

"You miss me?"

"I know it's weird but I do." She laughed.

"I wasn't sure you wanted me to come in with you, I'm sorry, I would have, had I known."

"It's okay, so will you be over?"

"Give me a few and I'll be there."

"Maybe you'll stay over?"

"I think that's more than a maybe."

XXX    XXX

As she put the phone back on the wall unit, Jamie wondered why she had fallen so quickly for Matt. Attraction or loneliness? The thought made her very nervous. Yes, if she was truthful with herself, she did have a great deal of attraction to Mathew; he was one hell of a lover and made her feel alive all the way deep inside. But they were Navy, career Navy, and there were no exceptions to fraternizations among the ranks. Especially the fact they were now in the same unit and that was even worse.

Standing there, she suddenly felt very self-conscious of what she was wearing, just her plain black bikini that had seen better days, and her other bikini was even skimpier than this one. She knew it didn't matter seeing as he had seen her naked, but she didn't want to be so obviously one of those women who came across as trying too hard. Over the noise of the relentless crickets in the yard she heard Mathew's back door open and close, and she grabbed her jersey short shorts and zip front sweater.

Jamie almost bumped into Mathew as she closed the screen door, turning around, balancing two open bottles of beer and a chip-and-dip bowl in her arms. "Here." She offered a cold, sweaty bottle.
"You sure you need more alcohol?" He smiled. Jamie looked him over and saw that he still had on his tux shirt and pants with the top few buttons of his shirt open, and a nice chunk of his bronze chest showing through.

"Mel would call it the pre-hair of the dog." She sat down at the deck table in the same seat as those nights before, and he sat opposite just like then. "Mel is definitely a pearl of wisdom." He took a mouthful of the cold liquid, and savored it as it flowed down his throat. "I wouldn't say that." Jamie's eyes sparkled.
"I was being sarcastic. She sure has her opinions, about drinking, about you." Jamie didn't miss a beat on that comment. She knew he was looking for her to open up, give him that long story.

"She knows me as well as anyone."
"She's your twin. I thought they were close."
"Twins aren't joined at the hip. We've led different

lives."

"I know they're not. How did you have different lives?" He watched her as the windows of her eyes drew the inevitable curtains across, and he knew she was figuring out how to change the subject. "I just want to know you a little better, Jamie." He paused. "Please."

"What do you want to know?" She asked after a heartbeat.

"Seeing as you're not offering the information how about you choose."

"It's hard opening up. It's not an easy thing for me to open up and talk about myself."

"It can be, but how about you start by asking me something, and then you'll see you won't drop dead from talking about yourself." Jamie sat there wondering what to ask.

"How did you feel when you found out about your uncle?"

"Sad." Mathew put his beer down and rested his elbows on the table, to bring the top of his body closer as he spoke.

"I called, tried writing, but he just returned the letters and declined my calls."

"So you never spoke to him again?"

"No, I got a call from my mom when he passed, and that was that." Mathew never broke eye contact.

"How did you feel?" Jamie asked.

"About him dying?" Jamie nodded her reply. "It sucked, it really sucked. I didn't know this man who I had been named after, and all my memories of him were bad."

"Memories are powerful." She simply said.

"Only if you let them rule you." He returned.

Jamie watched his eyes and his body language, noting the hard part, and the slow recovery of his broken heart. "But it got easier to forget?" Her voice sounded unusually small in her own ears.

"Yes, life goes on, but I started looking at my dad's photos my mom had. I can see why they named me after him, because as babies we were the spitting image of one another." He paused. "Making new memories, especially with an amazing woman who enters your life; that's how you get over the bad memories." He smiled a little brighter. "But now it's my turn to question you."

"Your turn huh?"

"Fairs fair Jamie." He waited her out, knowing the longer he took to ask her something the longer she would sit there sweating below her adorable blue sweat shirt and shorts.

"What is your relationship like with your father?"

"I don't have one." She remained composed.

"Okay. Why don't you have a relationship with him?"

"I haven't spoken to him since I was fourteen."

"He isn't proud of your career? That you are Navy? Does your sister speak to him still?" He knew he should go slower, one question at a time. "I don't know if he cares or knows where I am, and I don't give a damn about the son of a bitch either; and Mel's permanent address is the same as his." And he saw the anger and hurt finally. "What about before your mom died?"

"Mom died when I was eleven. The good senator of Georgia remarried three years later, and I went to boarding school, where I then joined the Navy after two years of medical school in Chicago."

"What about Mel?"

"She was sent to St. Teresa's too, yet she went home for holidays and vacations. Richard's new wife Margaret doted on her, and thinks the world of her, they get along very well from what I hear."

"You were never allowed to go home?"

"I never wanted to go to his home; and then I left boarding school for college at sixteen, and from that day I didn't speak to Mel until we were twenty-one."

"Why?"

"If she was going to have all that she had growing up, she was told to forget about me and never to mention my name in his home. Seeing as how Mel's insecure and needy, you can see how she'd make that work for her."

"Do you have any other siblings?"

"Not anymore."

Mathew decided to let that one pass, feeling that her openness was going to end at any moment, especially as her eye contact had wavered to nonexistent in the last few minutes. "Why would your father do that?"

"Matt, that's something I really don't want to talk about." She stood up, walking to the pool area holding her beer. "I'm going for a swim," she announced, putting the bottle at her feet and taking off her shorts and sweater. "You coming in?"

"In a minute." He answered.

Not looking back, Jamie dove into the pool and swam the width and back under the surface. Coming up and pulling the water from her hair, she came face to face with Mathew as she opened her eyes. He stood at the side, waiting for her. "You changed fast," she said sounding breathless.

"I didn't," he replied looking down. She followed his gaze. He was in the pool with his shirt and tux pants on. "They'll get ruined."

"Do I look like I care?"

# CHAPTER SEVENTEEN

"Hey, you have goose bumps," he said, reaching out and rubbing her upper arms.

"The water's cold," she lied.

"Is that really it? It feels fine to me."

"Mathew." He stopped any more words coming out. "Don't lie."

"About what?" A sneaky smile broke out on her face.

"You know the waters fine."

"Maybe it's something else in the water."

"Like?" He pushed.

"You." She watched as he unbuttoned his shirt painstakingly slow and stripped the sodden cotton off his arms, throwing it behind him in a wet puddle.

"Then why the goose bumps? Do I make you cold?" he asked, as he turned back.

"No."

"Nervous?" He sank down in the water to cover his broad bare shoulders, and looked up at her, waiting for the answer; he had the warmest and most beautiful blue, grey eyes she had ever seen. "Why would you make me nervous?"

"You tell me." He took her hands under the water and gently pulled her down so she was as submerged as he was.

"I think you're just as nervous around me as I am around you," Mathew proclaimed.

"I make you nervous? And you were talking about me drinking too much."

"I didn't drink as much as you."

"Then why?"

"You're a very attractive woman, I think things I probably shouldn't when we are together, and I find it hard to control myself."

"Hard, interesting choice of words Matt; but tonight was just cosmetics, I don't normally look the way you saw me, now Mel does." Her lips started to shiver as his hands moved up her arms.

"Even if I was attracted to Mel, which I am not, I'd have to gag her, so she wouldn't say something stupid, and that wouldn't be any fun for me."

Jamie didn't know what to do except laugh, and she realized that Matt had a way of doing that, making her feel at ease, and open up like no one else could.

"Mel isn't as half bad as you think."

"Is that so?" He raised an eyebrow.

"Okay she is." She felt Mathew lace his fingers with hers.

"Now that we agree on that, how about you come here?"

"Here?" He saw what he thought was a wink in her left eye as she moved closer. "A lot closer would be nice." He tugged on her arms gently again and she slid towards him, a leg either side of his legs. Their faces were very close, and her body came into contact with his bare chest.

"Can I ask just two more questions?" Jamie asked.

"Sure." He could barely breathe from the closeness of her body to his; as always it was doing crazy things to him. "Do you think this is wise? Us getting so deep and acting on our attractions all the time? I mean it wouldn't be so bad if I wasn't a member of Team Seven."

"I wouldn't worry, once I get to know you even better, I might find out you really are like your sister." Jamie's face looked horrified at the idea. "I was joking," he said wrapping his arms behind her back, making sure there was no way to escape. He looked into her deep sparkling blue eyes, and saw everything he had doubted, including her amount of attraction to him.

"What was your second question?" He reminded her.
"Can I get a ride to the wedding tomorrow?"
"Sure."
"I have just one more question Mathew." She looked at his nicely shaped mouth a moment.
"Just one?" He seemed to be looking at her mouth too.
"Are you ever going to kiss me again like those wonderful ones before?"
"I was waiting for you to ask."
"Weren't."
"Was." He leaned in closer, as she did too.

Their lips had just touched slightly, but a shiver ran through Mathew at how soft she really was. It was gentle, almost feather-light as they both seemed to be testing the waters, one toe at a time, unlike when she had been so strong and urgent in their kisses when they had gone up to her bedroom. Jamie sat up a little on his lap, and used her tongue to lick his top lip enticingly. He was shocked she would be so bold. Returning the gesture, and finding his tongue coming into contact with hers, he felt her shift again, as her arms went around his neck and held him there.

Opening up to Jamie he felt her barriers come down a little more and she gave in completely to his mouth and the wonderful things he was doing. She was enjoying this as much as he was and seemed always to do. He felt like a teenager sneaking a kiss in the pool away from the eyes of parents looming close by. If Jamie was closed off to her feelings verbally there was no doubt she opened up when faced head on with kissing him. He never wanted it to end.

Jamie opened her eyes, that she had been keeping shut, to find Mathew there looking at her. She smiled as she pulled back a little, reaching up and untying the knot of her bikini top, letting the string's fall down her shoulders; giving him more of a smile, as he reached behind her, pulling her torso into contact with him, and undoing the other string at the middle of her back. Pulling her in with a kiss that made her forget what she had just done. Taking her dress off for him that first night they'd made love was one thing, but this was out in the open, and so very unlike her, but he seemed to bring it out in her.

"Jamie." His words were incredibly husky as he kissed his way from her mouth down her slim tan neck to her collarbone. "Mmm." She asked in the only language available, her head rolling back as his mouth came into contact with the last bare skin visible above the water, and the top of her right breast. "Jamie." She opened her eyes to his as his wet chin dripped water between them. "Are you sure here in the pool?"

"More sure than anything right now."

"I don't think...." Jamie stopped him with a soul crashing kiss.

"No thinking Matt, just us here now," she said softly into his open mouth.

He felt her hands moving down his torso between them to his waistband, the tips of her fingers under the wet fabric doing the movements and touches he was already familiar with. "Please," she pleaded, her eyes gleaming deeper than the water behind her. "Hold on, I want to do this somewhere a little more comfortable," he said moving his legs from between hers and picking her up. Jamie's legs wrapped around his waist and their chests pressed together, in case any of the neighbors were looking out, even at that late hour.

As he effortlessly walked out of the pool carrying her, his pants dragged from the weight of the water.

"Where do you want?" Mathew asked, looking around.

"Let's go upstairs," she said

"Good thing I know where to go," he joked.

"Can you if I do this?" She asked, taking his lips with hers, while moving her hand lower in his pants, her other hand around his neck, gently playing with his hair. He groaned from the feeling of her fingers touching him intimately, and he stopped once his feet stepped up the one step to the coolness of the wooden deck. "No." His voice was deep. "I can't."

"Then sit down." She whispered in his ear, knowing he wouldn't, and wanting that experience of loving someone outside, in a taboo place. He moved slightly, did something, and still connected, he sat and she found him to have lowered his pants. The only thing between them now was her bikini bottoms, and it was no kind of barrier as his fingers moved the fabric aside and filled her with what felt like two of those elegantly long and strong fingers that were like magic on her skin and inside her.

"Oh Matt." Her head rolled back as his mouth worked her neck again, his movements between her legs making her hotter. Her mind couldn't focus on just one of the sensations. "Stand up a minute," he told her, and she complied, feeling her legs not strong enough to support her for long. He was quick to remove the scrap of black material baring her to his eyes, and he could only feast more on her. She was perfect all over, and he knew she had seen how hard he was from the sight of her. Placing his arms around her waist he moved her back, and as he kissed her on the lips, their tongues dancing, he felt her slide down his entire length, and she paused for a moment as he did, loving this intimate feeling between them. Her muscles were fluttering around him, and she could feel his slight twitch as they remained there connected to the hilt.

On the table a phone started to beep and vibrate loudly, against the silence that was the neighborhood. "Damn it." Mathew said, not wanting this to end so soon.

"It's probably mine." Jamie remained where she was on his lap, impaled by him, but leant over to reach the two phones. "It's more than likely mine. I wouldn't put it past the Admiral to make us go wheels up, only hours before Danny and Kirsten's wedding."

"Would he do that?" She picked them up and passed his to him.

"You did meet the same admiral as me, right?"

"Yeah." Jamie smiled, remembering the butt-head.

"Not mine." Mathew reported, putting his cell back on the table.

"No, it's mine, it's a DC number." She moved off of him reluctantly releasing him from her prison, but he wasn't going to let her go far, and she stood on the deck. "Who do you know in DC that would call at four-fifteen their time?"

"This is Commander James Buchanan," she said into the phone, as she watched Mathew grab a towel from a pile next to the door. "Yes, that is correct sir, but I...." Jamie looked confused and he watched her as she went to her shorts and sweater. He used the towel to wrap around his waist, and then remained standing behind her, listening. "You must be mistaken, that's incorrect. If I could just speak to...." She was obviously stopped. "They're wrong. That is the wrong information."

Mathew watched as Jamie nervously began to pace back and forth on a three-foot spot, her face getting paler and paler. He went to her, and began to use another towel to dry the ends of her hair as she remained on the phone. "Yes sir, no sir." A pause. "I understand that sir, except that's an impossibility. Sir, please, I can't." She was silent for a long moment. "I understand. Yes, Sir."

Jamie's eyes were welling with tears, as she clicked off her phone. "Who was that?" Mathew got a bad feeling in his gut. "That was Admiral Clark at Navy Intelligence. He called to tell me Mel's squad were ambushed just outside Uzbekistan on the Afghanistan boarder. They don't have many details, but he wants me in Washington ASAP."
"Washington? DC?"
"At the Pentagon. He said there's a transport leaving the base in forty minutes, that I have to be on."
"In forty minutes?" Mathew could see her on the brink of a flood of tears.
"That's my orders, yes." Jamie left him standing there as she walked into her house to change and pack an overnight bag.

He followed her in, gently grabbing her arm as she stood on the bottom step of her stairs. "I'll go and get dressed, and meet you in the driveway; I'll drive you over."
"You don't have to do that."
"I'll meet you outside in ten minutes."
"Matt." She stopped him from walking away; he didn't turn to face her. "I'm sorry."
"There's nothing to be sorry for. Go to Washington and bring Mel home."
"But...."
"I'll still be here when you get back." He cupped her cheek, and then kissed her quick, before leaving to

change at his house.

# CHAPTER EIGHTEEN

Feeling totally exhausted and in need of some strong coffee, Jamie took the flight of steps from the transport at Andrew's Air force base just before eleven am Eastern Time, later that day. On the flight over the country she served she hadn't been able to get any sleep, thinking about the fate her sister might have already met. Also what she had begun with Matt, and what had just started when they had been interrupted. How she had found a comfort in San Diego with him, and missed him already.

By the time she had thrown on her uniform and stuffed clean undies and her regulation scrubs in her bag, and packed two spare uniform whites in her garment bag, she had caught a glimpse of Matt standing in his driveway, waiting to take her. He had put on some dry clothes, and looked menacing in the dark night. His fatigue pants and black t-shirt made it hard to see the strong lines of his body in the shadows, but she knew they were there.

"If you need anything you'll call, me right?" He had asked when they were driving over to the airfield.
"I probably won't but...." He stopped her.
"Anything, even if it's to just talk, or let me know you got there. I know you'll probably be pretty busy once you get to DC, but if there's anything the Team or I can do, you better call, okay. We're your family now too."
"Thanks." She paused as he pulled his truck a few feet from the transport at the side of the runway.

"Matt, I think there's something I should tell you."
"It's fine Jamie, when you get back, we'll finish what we started." He hoped he would be over the serious case of blue balls before then too. "I hope so." She tried a faint smile.
"Trust Mel to mess it up; if I didn't know better I'd say this was some major set-up."
"Even Mel's not that cruel." Matt was happy she could make a joke.

"I should get on that plane." She reached for her bag at her feet.
"Just one more thing before you go." Mathew leaned over and cupped the back of her head with one of his hands, drawing her face closer. "Just one?" Jamie's voice was all husky, and at that Mathew wanted to take her away from all the things going on, and never let go. He could feel himself falling deeper and faster.

She leant further in to the kiss, and all her worries at that single moment ceased to cloud her mind. She could imagine he was still inside her, the feelings it had provoked in her, and that they were really back on her deck. Instead, it was soft, slow and extremely sweet. It seemed forever before he finally let his tongue wander into her mouth, gently stroking her own waiting tongue.

It was the engines firing up on the transport that broke them apart. "I better go before they leave without me."
"Remember, Mel will be fine and call me, okay."
"Thanks again Matt, I will call." She closed the door,

opening the back door to get her garment bag.
"Damn, Matt." She leaned in the window of the door
she had been sitting at. "I completely just forgot. Tell
the Commander and Kirsten I said congratulations."
"They'll understand" He reached over the passenger
seat to take her hand. "You better go, Jamie."
"Bye Matt." She felt as she walked to the transport,
how final that bye had been, as if her intuition were
telling her something.

Now as the late morning sun was keeping everything
warm and sticky with the notorious DC humidity, she
stood on the tarmac, looking for her ride to the
Pentagon. Over to the side was a man leaning on the
hood of his sleek black town car, a female standing
with the driver's door open, her arms resting on the
dark metal. Sighing inwardly, she walked over to
them, suddenly feeling like time had turned back five
years.

"Well lookie here." The tall man stood up from the
hood, throwing his cigarette on to the tarmac. His
thick North East Coast accent was familiar, just like
his ever-expanding waist-line. "If it aint James
Buchanan in some very sexy white uniform." The
man, tall and broad, walked over taking her bags from
her. He threw them on the ground and grabbed her up
in one fell swoop. "Hey Dumont." He shouted to the
short stocky woman at the car. "Put me the fuck down
now, Nick. Don't forget I can kick your ass; and just
wait till I get my weapon back." Jamie hit him square
in the shoulder, but it didn't seem to alter his stance,
as he turned to the other female there. "This here is

the most devious of us all." He lowered the
Commander, and picked up her bags from the ground.
"So I've heard." The butch looking female said
deeply.

"I can't tell you how good it is to see you Buchanan,"
the man told her, walking by her side to the car.
"Wish it were under better circumstances, Nick."
Jamie replied.
"Buchanan, this is my new partner, Betsy Dumont"
He introduced them
"Howdy." Dumont tipped two fingers at her.
"Likewise." Jamie returned, turning back to Nick.
"Any news on Mel or her team?"
"Like us little people get told anything!" He laughed,
and his neck seemed to shake. "Does Robert know
anything?"
"He's on assignment, so I haven't heard from him,
but I doubt it."
"Who's been brought in?"
"You, Buchanan."

Jamie's face paled as she looked at him, unsure she
heard him right. "I'm not on the team anymore, Nick,
you do remember, right?"
"I know, I had nothing to do with this. I didn't even
know the mission file still existed until I got the call
about picking you up. I guess your employers over at
Navy Intelligence are cooking up some plan. I'm
guessing they finally got the real James Buchanan's
file"
"Firstly, that's a lot of guessing, even for you, Nick."
She frowned. "And that mission report was meant to

have been destroyed."

"Do we spooks ever do anything we're supposed to?" His eyes twinkled, like that of a toddler about to cause some major mischief. "Never mind, I thought they'd found out when they transferred me to Team Seven."

"Yeah, I heard about that, congratulations," he joked. They all got in the car with Jamie in the back. "So what are your orders, Nick?"

"To return you to the Pentagon for re-assignment Buchanan. Seems an Admiral Clark wants a favor from the one person that can help him."

XXX    XXX

Team Seven was just settling in to the first dance of the afternoon at the reception when the Teams' phones all began to vibrate or chirp at once, breaking through the band music with their own song.

Absolutely perfectly timed, and so typical; the men had almost waged bets on when it would happen.

Husbands kissed wives, leaving them to party alone, boyfriends slipped away with promises to call, and all those unattached just left, all of them making their way over to the base as fast as they could. Mathew had a feeling the moment they got texted, that it had something to do with Jamie and whatever was going on with Mel's team. So, when all of them were in their ready-room on base, waiting for the newly married Lieutenant Commander MacCafferty to brief them on the situation, Mathew was not at all surprised to hear what he said.

"Seems our new team member has a situation that needs our back-up, men," he said. His dress whites were replaced by the standard issue camouflage garb they were all now wearing. "Let's get our shit together and get going. I want us on that transport in no more than ten minutes' men."

"Where are we headed?" Petty officer Richards asked. Folding his dress pants in to a creased ball and putting them in the bag at his feet. "We are to rendezvous with Jamie on a carrier somewhere off the coast of Pakistan in the Indian Ocean. I'm waiting on a final brief to come down from Navy Intelligence. I'll let you all know more when I know more." The silence they had given their commanding officer was replaced with talking as MacCafferty left the room.

"Did Jamie call you yet?" Steven asked Mathew as all the men made their way out to their cars to deposit all items they wouldn't be needing before getting in one big truck to take them to the transport fueling up on the tarmac. "Not yet." Matt answered. "I'm guessing she hasn't had a chance since I last saw her."

"And what exactly happened after you two left the party last night?" Kevin asked with a grin.

"He knows too?" Steve asked as he laughed.

"Kevin heard some rumors."

"Which, after last night, leave no doubt in my head Taylor, that you are banging the doc."

"I don't like the term banging." Matt laughed as he reached the truck.

"You aren't seriously gonna use the L word are you?"

Steve got in first looking back. "Because I might just have to gag if you do."

XXX     XXX

Having been aboard carriers most of her adult life, she knew how things worked. A simple thing as ascending to another deck did not mean using one single staircase, but using multiple, and in different locations about each deck. She maneuvered with ease, and was just grateful her sea legs were still with her. Jamie had just hoped she would be on land longer than a few weeks before being sent back.

The man and the woman at the Air Force base had known little about why she had been flown in, and the connection it had to a mission she would rather forget, and thankfully their conversation was about everyday things. Unfortunately, she had barely endured Nick back six years ago when they had been forced to work together. He was a hulk of a man who had very little common sense. His idea of a successful mission meant any way he could use a MacGyver move from the eighties TV show, and when that worked you would hear about it over and over.

So okay, in hindsight the memory actually made her smile.

After two hours in the Pentagon, waiting for someone named Admiral Clark, they had told her she was to go back to the airfield to get a transport to the fifth fleet out in the Indian Ocean. There she would finally get briefed on what was going on. On the way back, Nick had informed her that he and Dumont were going with her; inside she groaned. She knew if they were sending them too it wasn't a very good sign.

Once aboard the USS Abraham Lincoln, she had been taken straight to the command center that had been activated to high alert since the Marine team had gone missing. Already there was a White House representative, a man who looked too young to shave, by the name of Simon Townsend. He was constantly in contact with POTUS (President of the United States) and the embassy inside Afghanistan in the capital Kabul. He looked green, not only because of seasickness, but at his job too. The fleet Admiral, an Admiral Cavannah was talking to some of his high-ranking officers, and there in the corner was her old boss Robert Wakefield, a top man inside of the CIA. The rumor was one day Robert would become the youngest man ever to be appointed director of the CIA. Robert was looking at the wall where the large screened TV displayed the satellite map of the border between Afghanistan and Uzbekistan.

Jamie walked over nervously to the man she had not spoken to, or seen in over five years. There was a large amount of unresolved issues, and a deep history between them that she knew he wouldn't mention right there; wrong place, wrong time, and that was probably a very good thing.

Robert was his job one hundred and fifty percent. He was tall and built sleekly like a panther; with dark brown hair always in perfect condition and styled professionally, and the suit pants and shirt she always saw him wear. He was the same handsome man she had once loved uncontrollably.

"Robert." Jamie said standing next to him, looking at the image of dry dusty land that stretched for miles on the screen. "Jamie." He turned to look at her, his eyes holding something she couldn't decipher. "I'm sorry we had to bring you out here." He apologized.
"Don't apologize Robert. Just tell me what the hell is going on. Why bring me here? What has happened to my sister?"

He turned back to the screen, obviously unable to look at her when he spoke. "Intel tells us that Mel's twelve-person team was ambushed at a small, relatively unknown Marine camp, just outside Konduz. They were taken by surprise as soon as the sun went down."
"Casualties?"
"Four of the twelve are confirmed dead. A team of Marines, who were to rendezvous with their team, arrived to find the bunker burned out with very little left except a few bones and debris, some pieces of uniforms and four dog tags."
"Was my sister one of them?"
"I'm sorry Jamie, they identified her tags with the others."

Jamie could feel her legs weakening beneath her, and Robert caught a hold of her arm, shouting for one of the officers to bring a chair over. Once sitting, she felt him putting her head low between her legs of jelly stop the room from spinning. "How is she?" She could hear a voice from behind her, one she didn't know. "She'll be fine, I just told her about her sister." Robert's voice was low and barely audible.

"We'll give you a minute, then but the clock is ticking." The same voice told him.

She felt the gentle hand that had ensured she keep her head low let go and as her head rose slightly, she came eye to eye with Robert, who was now kneeling before her, Nick and Dumont stood just behind him. "Jamie." He said as if he wasn't sure she was mentally there.

"I'm fine Robert." She sat up some more, but his brown eyes followed her movements. "Just tell me why we are here. This isn't a normal ambush is it, and what does our last mission have to do with this?"

"The cell that did this left a clue in the way they murdered the Marines in the bunker."

"The Muslim group Black Death Rebels." Jamie answered her own question, before she even asked it.

"That's right. Now do you see why you and I are here Jamie?"

"But we terminated Abdel Karim Atwa five years ago; did they get a new leader?"

"It seems Atwa is still alive." Robert said looking away.

"I saw him in that car with my own eyes, Rob. Don't tell me I fucked up something like that."

Robert stood up, offering a hand to pull her up from her chair. "You didn't fuck this up Jay, we all saw what you saw; hell, I saw Nick's bullet hit his neck. I saw the autopsy reports from the wreckage. He is out there Jay, and eight Marines might still be alive."

"Has Atwa contacted anyone yet?"

"He sent a video to the US embassy in Kabul. FBI agrees with us, it's him."

"What does he want?"

"He wants you, Jamie."

# CHAPTER NINETEEN

"What does he want from me?" Jamie rested back in the chair.

"Revenge pure and simple Jay. He wants you to pay with your life for what happened to his son, and the shame his family name now carries. He said on the tape that if we dropped you within a certain location in the next twelve hours then the Marines will go free."

"What is the plan?"

"You know Jamie; this is a suicide mission. You can say 'no' whenever you want. We'll find another way to get them." Nick said coming from behind.

"It's my mistake and I'll make it right."

"Jamie." Robert put his hands on his hips and shook his head. "You aren't going in; I won't authorize it."

"It didn't stop you last time." She snapped. "I'm sorry." She muttered under her breath.

Jamie walked over to the screen again holding her arms around her, as a cold shiver ran throughout her body. "I have to go, it's the only way."

"Hold on. Navy Intelligence and the Pentagon are going through scenarios right now, to calculate every possible answer, to find a different approach that doesn't mean using you. Jay; Team Seven have already left California to back this operation." Robert moved closer to her again.

"Do we know where he's holding the Marines?" She asked.

"He has a safe house somewhere inside the Konduz perimeter. Intel is searching the tape for any clues."

Dumont joined the conversation.

"Use me as a diversion. Put me in the middle of the co-ordinates, and let the fucker find me. Get the Marines out, and then come for me. I can wear one of those biological undetectable trackers like the ones we used for training at Langley."

"I can't let you do this." Robert turned her to face him, both his hands holding her upper arms. "I have to Rob." She rolled her head to the side to relieve some stress. "No you don't Jamie."

"That bastard killed my sister, I should have made sure he was dead. I screwed up."

"Jamie I...." Rob was about to say something when she stopped him, by saying.

"I need to get ready to go, so why don't you, and the rest of the brass, figure this out, and when there's a plan let me know. Otherwise I am on a helo to those co-ordinates in six hours from now."

## XXX     XXX

"She agreed to do what?" Senior Chief Chris Polanski asked Robert, Dumont and Nick, after they had been introduced in the Command center upon Team Seven's arrival. The official briefing was due to take place in twenty minutes, when the final orders came down from POTUS and the advisors at the White House. But because Jamie and some old boss of hers had insisted that she would play in to the orders of the terrorist, none of them had even had a say.

"Jamie is going in to let the Marines go free." Robert

said again to the man second-in-charge of the team. Danny was engaged in a small briefing with the fleet admiral and his men. "What guarantee do we have that this Atwa will keep his word?"

"None, that's why we'll send your Team to his hideout, when she is being picked up."

"She's been in a SEAL team as a non-SEAL less than two weeks. What is she doing going in there? Explain to me how you know her, and why she is involved."

"That's classified." Nick answered for Robert; he knew his boss was so mentally distraught over the situation, he might just tell the Senior Chief the truth, the truth about Jamie.

"Classified my ass." Polanski bit out at the big man.

"She'll be tracked the whole time, and I am making sure nothing happens to her." Robert spoke.

"You can't guarantee that she'll be safe."

"If I could change places or even persuade her not to go, I would. All I can tell you right now is that Jamie isn't new to these situations. There's more to her than any of you know."

"Oh I know. I've been trying to figure out who trained a doc, to shoot, and be in shape to run our "O" course, as well as a mountain of other tests we've given her."

"Then I think you already know."

"She's a goddamn spook?"

"Was."

XXX     XXX

"Who is it?" Jamie shouted at the knocking on the temporary quarters that had been assigned her. "Lieutenant Taylor," a male voice she recognized, answered.

"Come in," she invited. Onboard, there would have to be formality and none of the things that would get them both in trouble, not that her mind was anywhere near thinking about that.

She sat at the small metal fold down desk that was clamped on to the wall that held two lockers that mirrored the two bunks on the opposite wall. Her unpacked bag on the bottom bunk, sitting next to her garment bag, was just as equally discarded there. Before her on the desk was some paper-work.

Mathew walked in and closed the door, his hand still on the door-knob, as he said. "Jamie." She was not only out of uniform, but wearing cargo pants and a tank top that accentuated all her perfect female curves. Her hair pulled back in a ponytail was so blonde, that he was momentarily daunted by the thought of her being in Afghanistan; she would stick out like a very American thumb.

"The JAG lawyer on board thought I should have all my affairs in order before I leave." She made it sound like a joke. "I heard upstairs that you volunteered to go in there."

"I have to go Matt."

"No you don't."

"Matt, there's something you don't know."

"You worked for the CIA once?" His arms crossed,

and she wasn't sure if he was pissed, or looking for her to explain the large hole in her life. Was there more like this that she was hiding from everyone?

"It's something I can't talk about, it's all classified, Matt."
"That's something I know a lot about, but this is you and me inside this room right now. No one can hear." He waited a moment. "Tell me Jamie."
"All I can say is, this is my mistake that I have to fix, before someone else gets killed."
"Let us help, let the Intel people do the job they're paid for, and maybe you won't have to go in."
"You can't change my mind," she said stubbornly.
"You aren't super woman."
"And you aren't super man." Jamie saw the tightness in his jaw, and it was safe to say the last one hit a nerve. "Atwa wants me. He'll get me, Matt, so that those Marines can go free, and then the plan is you and the Team will get me after."
"Someone upstairs mentioned your father is arriving shortly." Matt changed the subject.

"Great." she said, looking like all the air had just been knocked out of her. "What the hell has he got to do with all of this?" she asked.
"I heard the Admiral say it was because he wants to know what's going on with your sister."
"Typical. I'm sure he knows I'm going in there, and all he'll think is that I was the one that let this happen." She turned from him and picked up three sealed envelopes. "These are just a couple of letters and my last will. There's a letter for you, and one for

my father, in case you are right, and I'm getting myself killed doing this. Can you give these to the JAG later?"

"Sure. I don't want a letter though, Jamie."
"What do you want Mathew?" She asked looking tired.
"I want you here safe, as far away from this Atwa as possible. I want to be able to finish what we started last night, finish everything we started." He took her hand in his, looking for her to back down and stay, to say all she needed was him and let someone else play bait. "I'm going to be leaving straight after the briefing." She informed him, taking her hand back, and looking as far away from him as possible in the small room.

"I'll have a tracking device on me, so you'll all know where I am at all times."
"So, when the blip becomes too constant in one spot, I should just assume that they've killed you then." He didn't like the sound of his own words, he felt the muscle in his jaw tighten again, but it was a very possible outcome. "Matt." Jamie turned to face him with anger and tears on her face.
"It's true Jamie, if you leave the safety of this ship, and do what he wants he will kill you."
"I killed his son; he'll kill me to make it even."
"You are coming back."
"I'll be there twelve hours before they'll let you come in."
"But when we do, your whole Team, your family will not let you stay out there. We'll bring you back,

Jamie." He paused. "I promise you with everything I have that we will."

"I can just imagine what the senator will say in that briefing. He wants retribution for his daughter's death. Why the hell would they let me, the one that didn't stop him the first time, go in to do that for him. He'll call it a waste of time." She was changing the subject.
"Then he'll be wrong. You'll be the reason eight Marines will be coming home."
"Remember that for my eulogy."
"I'm going to ignore that, and I think you'll be surprised about how your father will see you in all this."
"That will never happen Mathew, even over my dead body." She turned away from him.

"Care to explain to me why?"
"Ask him yourself. Of course, he'll deny I'm related to him, until he's blue in the face. He'll embellish, maybe even spit, as he talks, but the core of it will be true. One good thing about the Senator, he has never lied."
"Really?"
"Yeah, but I was young, remember that will you. Don't blame him for taking everything at face value; he believes all that he knows is true."
"How about you tell me the truth about everything on the way home to Coronado?"
"Sure," Jamie said not really believing that day existed. She stood up on tip toes and kissed the side of his mouth, as she held on to the back of his head

for a moment, wishing with her entire being that she could turn back time to where he had been deep inside her.

XXX    XXX

Everyone involved on the mission was assembled in the command center at 1800 hours; the meeting was headed by the fleet admiral and Robert. They went over the plan, Jamie had four tracking devices on her person, and they would take her by helicopter, unarmed, to a location just inside the co-ordinates they had been given. She would proceed to the exact center of those on foot, and using a GPS device.

They knew many of the terrorist organizations had bunkers scattered all around the desert land of all the Middle East countries. It would no doubt take less than an hour for her to be picked up, and taken to where ever Atwa was hiding out. Once inside she was to try and get as much information from them with regards to any other plans against the Americans, but mainly to stay alive.

Team Seven were listening to Danny go through their side of extracting the Marines, and their destination point, when a petty seaman came in to collect Jamie. Mathew watched from across the room as she got up, passing final items to a man who had been introduced as Robert, her old boss. He stood up and hugged her briefly, and Mathew's mind went on alert at the very intimate way they seemed to be saying goodbye. In fact, after the embrace, as she walked towards the door, quite a few officers and personnel stood and shook hands with her. At the last point in the room she seemed to scan the darkness for a face and when her eyes came in to contact with his own, he swore he saw a lone tear trying to stay inside.

# CHAPTER TWENTY

For two hours, everyone in the command center knew that the blip on the screen was safe as their fellow officer was being transported to the drop-off point. They knew, because they felt it too, that game time was fast approaching. The spooks kept to themselves in one corner, the men of Team Seven in another; the men of the fleet and the White House rep. were spread out, but keeping things quiet as they stood around, waiting for game time to begin.

Team Seven was ready to leave at a moment's notice, all their gear checked and rechecked. Coop, Chris, Danny and Lee, the senior officers of the Team, were huddled together to the side of their men going over plans and ideas as they were either passed down, or came to mind. They, at the end of the day, would be the ones going out to collect everyone up, and they had no intention of having anyone come back in a body bag.

Steven had slipped out to find Matt, who had been inside for only a few minutes after the briefing had wrapped up. He had been sitting next to his friend when Jamie had left, and had noticed his change at seeing her leave.

The deck was pretty quiet, the sounds of the ship's engines hummed along with the crashing of the waves. The occasional jet taking off or landing was the only thing to disturb what normally would be a very tranquil sound. The air was cool, and the stars twinkled clear, and out in the safety of the safe zone on the flight deck was Mathew, sitting on the edge, legs dangling, with his arms over the safety rope. Matt's feet almost touched the rope net that spanned the entire perimeter of the decking so that anyone who might fall overboard would be caught in it.

"Hey man." Steve said within a few feet.
"Hey." Mathew didn't turn around.
"I thought you'd like to know that Jamie landed safely."
"Yeah, thanks. Like I'm not already thinking about her out there unarmed right now."
"Sorry man."
"She's all alone in one of the hottest terrorist spots in the world Steve."
"You gotta stop thinking about that, and concentrate on us getting them all out."
"She wrote me this letter earlier and told me to read it when she left." He waved the opened envelope in the air with little enthusiasm.

"Letter?" Steve waited for Mathew to continue.
"Jamie believes she's not going to be returning." He paused. "Alive."
"I hope she does, but Matt, she might not."
"I just wish there were more people wanting her to come home. Someone she knew who would have stopped her from going in the first place."
"You couldn't stop her?" It was a question not a statement.
"No, she was adamant."
"What about her pops, the senator?"

"Him? Seems they haven't spoken since she was a teen, and the dad even told her twin sister to never talk to her or about her."

"Fuck, why?"

"I don't know the details, but it makes me wonder about everything, you know."

"She loves ya Matt."

"You think so?" Mathew managed a weak smile and kept his focus on the ocean. "You know we were getting pretty heavy when she got the call."

"You mean aside from the entire last week which you hid from me, your best friend?"

"Yep; after I dropped her off after dinner, she went out to her pool and called me to see if I wanted to come over, because she was wired and wanted company. We talked a bit until she went in to the pool and told me to come in. One thing led to another and she was gloriously naked, and we were, you know, again."

"And?"

"And what? You want me to tell you how good it felt? It did. I realized right then, when she was so close to me, that I've been falling hard for days."

"I haven't spoken to her much, but she seems really cool. You need someone like her."

"I do? Why?"

"Look, for six months you've been moping around because of that bitch Anna you were dating. She couldn't deal, and she broke your heart. You used to be such a mellow guy, overly polite in that old movie star way and so happy. Now you're as gruff and bitter as me and O'Rielly."

"I know."

"But hey, I noticed this past week how relaxed and like your old self you were. I hate to say it, but you had a real sparkle in your eye."

"Really?"

"Hell, yeah. I partly blame that dress Jamie was wearing, of course."

"Of course, but what a dress huh?"

"Fuckin' hell, yeah."

They both sat there for a moment contemplating life. Steve wasn't sure, but he could swear Matt was also picturing the dress a little like he was, but the lucky son of a gun had images going deeper and more naked than him, and he sure would sell his soul to see the commander naked.

The landing lights behind them on the deck came on, illuminating everything around them. "Incoming." Mathew said.

"Must be the senator." Steve stood up. "I'm betting this should be very interesting."

XXX    XXX

Sitting on the flat surface of a small rock, she looked out at the horizon; the stars were bright, and the land eerily dark. To the north about a few clicks were the mountains that bordered between Uzbekistan and Afghanistan. Afghanistan itself looked very much the same as the neighboring country, except Jamie was aware to her toes, of where she was sitting. Since her drop-off an hour earlier, this had been her third stop. Walking in squares getting further and further in each time.

The cities of Konduz and Faizabad were either side of her in the far distance, and glowed on either horizon like beacons. Other than the moon, that was her only real source of light. Of course if you didn't count the lighter and pack of cigarettes she had bought aboard the USS Abraham Lincoln. Robert had told her she couldn't take anything and especially something from a habit she had kicked years ago. "Watch me." She had told him.

Now, sitting there, watching as the embers burnt away at the tip, she wondered what the Team was doing, especially Matt. She'd tried hard not to think about him, but he kept crossing her mind since she left the carrier. Now, with the night facing her, she wondered what Mel's last thoughts had been, being ambushed at night, and having God knows what happen. Feeling a rush of tears, she choked them back and drew a large lungful of nicotine into her blood stream. She had quit smoking when she had seen her first emphysema riddled lung, the urge never popping up until she had been faced with this mission.

Throwing down the butt of her smoke on to the dry ground, she felt a strange sense of calm and serenity. A light shone from behind her, casting her own shadow and that of the rock, to the ground. 'This is it', Jamie thought to herself, as she slowly turned to see a small flashlight aimed directly in her eyes.

"Well, shit." The voice with the light said. "What the fuck are you doing here?"

# CHAPTER TWENTY-ONE

"Who the hell came up with that idea?" The well-dressed man had a vein popping out on his forehead. "Who gave the authorization for that?" The senator had gone directly to the command center, where everyone was watching the screens for any indication that Jamie had been found. The fleet admiral and Robert were joined by Danny to calm this man down, and everyone else in the room looked on as if his head might just blow off.

"Sir." Robert said calmly. "If there was any other way to do this, then we would have done it but we have no real Intel to tell us where the Marines are being held." "So you send in a weak, poor excuse for a commander and a somehow Navy doctor?" His anger was still at boiling point. "Jamie is no weak doctor sir, if you would just let me...." The senator cut Robert off, going on to, "That woman isn't trained to infiltrate a terrorist organization. You really expect her to succeed? I hope you have figured out how you're going to explain to those eight Marines families why their loved ones are returning in caskets."

Chris walked over and positioned himself between the three calm men and the pissed-off senator, who by all looks was about to try and take out each of these three, much younger and much stronger men. "Sir." Chris broke in. "I'm Senior Chief Chris Polanski of Team Seven anti-terrorist SEAL squad."
"Senior Chief." Senator Richard Buchanan never

gave up the staring contest with Robert. "Your daughter is a part of our Team. She agreed to this mission, sir."

"Mel's a SEAL?" The senator broke eye contact for a moment, but he did frown, a different facial expression from the one of pure anger which he had been wearing since he arrived. "No, Jamie sir."

Richard let out a short blood curdling laugh. "She is no daughter of mine, and I suppose I'm to believe she earned a spot on the SEAL team with her MD? Tell me the truth; who did she have to sleep with to get that position?" The senator looked over to see the SEAL team holding one of their own back. A man who, compared to himself, was younger and much more in shape, and could probably do some serious damage to his body which already felt the signs of arthritis. Years ago he had been quite good-looking, but gravity and the effects of hair depletion had caused him to age like everyone else.

"Looks like I'm right." He smiled at the young SEAL. He hadn't noticed Robert's own hands clenched at his sides, holding back an impulse to deck the senator. "With all due respect." Danny stepped in front of Chris, his words filled with contempt. "I know Jamie has proven herself to be able to perform in this Team, to the point that if needed I would have her back me up one-hundred percent. I'm not sure where she learnt all she knows." He looked at Robert who met his gaze for a moment before breaking it off, and walking a few steps back. "But I believe that she can do this, that she will show you what she is made of."

"Interesting." Richard tilted his head to the side. "Obviously, you don't know Jamie so well; mentally she is weak and only good at screwing up everything and everyone around her. This mission will end in disaster, and I can't wait to see you all explain this."

The room remained so quiet you could hear the faint hum of the engines, and the sounds from the landing pad a few floors up. Team Seven, one by one, stood up and walked towards the door. "Sir, I hope you never run for senate in San Diego." Chris said, and with that he joined his Team outside.

XXX    XXX

"What the fuck are you doing here? And who the hell let you out dressed like that?" Mel asked Jamie, as they both sat on the rock Jamie had been occupying alone earlier. "I came to get myself captured."
"Why the fuck would you do a stupid ass thing like that?"
"It's a long story."
"It always is with you Jay." Mel jumped down on to her feet. "Why don't you explain it to your little sister?"
"Explain what?"
"I dunno, the reason the Navy and the government would go for the idea of having you out here. If I'm not mistaken its usually your team that get sent in to rescue people not you, a doctor."

Jamie got down from her perch too, standing in front

of her sister, coming half an inch taller than her.

"You're not the only one who can be tough." Jamie sneered. She knew what her sister's problem was; she could see the twitch, the vessels in her dilated eyes. She knew everything in one moment of looking at her about what had really happened to her team. "What did you think I was doing the year you were at rehab?"

"Oh, are you trying to tell me you learnt how to be Rambo?"

"No. I was out there, earning my way in this world, something you've never had to do huh Mel?"

"Meaning?"

"Oh, c'mon little sis, who was it that didn't want to lose their trust-fund huh?"

"We're back to that are we?"

"Why not?" Jamie turned away from Mel. "Where were you when your team was taken down?"

"I was using the head about half a click away. I heard the gunshots and the screams of Sanchez, Adams and Silver. It was awful Jay; their pain was so...." Mel turned away as the recounting of what had transpired brought the sounds and visuals flooding back. It was going to take hours of therapy to erase those, Jamie thought thinking of the six months intense debriefing the CIA had forced her to endure.

"The fuckers stood outside the bunk and shot them in the knees so they couldn't escape the fire they were running from." Mel continued. "The other eight were being blindfolded and bound, and loaded into trucks after the men got in some serious beatings to my team."

"Did you get a good look at any of the men? Who was in charge?"

"No, it was too dark, and most of them had hoods." She watched her sister's face, a face that although looked like her own, was a total stranger to her sometimes.

"Why? What do you know?"

"All I can tell you right now is that the year you went to rehab, I was working outside the Navy and ended up here, undercover. The man who ambushed you and your team is after me for what I did to him and his family." Mel's eyes were wide open as if Jamie was telling an outlandish fairy tale. "What government organization?"

"Does it matter? You need to know as little as possible, because he wants me and he will try and use you. He's promised to release your team when he has me, but we don't believe him so Team Seven is on standby to collect them, and you now, if he doesn't comply."

"What did you do to his family?"

"I killed his son."

"You?"

"Yes me. I can't say anymore."

"Fine. So what are you carrying?" Mel reached for her own guns.

"Nothing, I'm here to get captured, not fight."

"Those assholes let you come here with nothing?"

"That's what I said."

"Well it's a good thing I was thinking straight." Mel removed the two M16's she had been wearing over her shoulder. "I can't take that." Jamie stated flatly lighting a new cigarette. "Fine, but do you mind if I use them?"

"If you wanna get your ass shot, sure."

"By the way." Mel asked, taking a cigarette from the pack Jamie was holding out and lighting it. "How is everything with you and Matt?"

# CHAPTER TWENTY-TWO

Hanging up his cell phone from a call back to the states, giving his wife an update on the situation, Richard Buchanan looked up and down the hall outside the command center. After an hour of meetings, going over the plan and worst/best case scenarios, and what could be done if the complete thing was a total clusterfuck, his head was beginning to pound.

His daughter and his last child had died, and they were sending in a screw up to avenge and clean it up. He wanted a strong drink, but knew alcohol was considered contraband after being aboard carriers like this most of his adult life. He was going to have to settle for coffee.

Knowing his basic way around; after all, these ships were pretty much identical or close enough, he found his way to the mess hall at the stern of the ship a few floors down. Inside were a few officers and over in the far corner were the group of SEALs he had seen upstairs earlier. Inside he groaned, wanting just peace right now to grieve for his precious daughter, but he knew sitting in here he would be approached by one of them.

Pouring a large black mug of coffee that burned on the way down and tasted like yesterday's brew, just hot instead of cold, he took a seat at a small table as far away from the SEALs as he possibly could. He had noticed the looks and the drop in the conversation level from the group of men, as he had entered. They no doubt wondered why he was so cruel about James. How he could be so callus about his own flesh and blood. It stung him deep in his soul. Not the whole Jamie thing, but the fact that those men should be his brothers, talking it up and taking his back. Once a SEAL always a SEAL as they said; instead, he had their bitter hatred. Having them follow on in his and others footsteps made them family, all of them. His would be fellow brothers.

It was that feeling that perplexed him the most; he looked up at them to see an angry face glaring back at him. It was the young face of the Lieutenant that they had held back upstairs; the one he accused of sleeping with James so she could get in to the illustrious SEAL team. The young man got up from his seat and made his way over towards him. Richard watched and waited as the young man pulled out a chair opposite him at the table, and looked him straight in the eye.

"Yes, Lieutenant Taylor," he said setting down his mug. He had asked the man's name earlier; he had planned on apologizing, but he would hold off on that until he knew what Taylor was about to say. "Can I ask you something Sir?"
"Go ahead."
"Sir, I was wondering if you could explain to me why you can have one daughter in your life and not the other? I mean, I know both of your daughters; Jamie lives next door to me. I don't understand how a father could do that."
"James's neighbor huh?"

Richard studied the young man a second, wondering if there was more to the neighbor's line. "Take a piece of advice, son." Richard said condescendingly. "Whatever your relationship is with James, keep it professional."

"Why?" Matt asked.

"She's like cancer Lieutenant, once she gets inside you she slowly eats away until there's nothing left."

"What did she ever do to make her father abandon her and say such things?"

"Abandon her? Huh, I like that Mathew. Can I call you Mathew?" Mathew nodded his answer. "I didn't abandon her, hell I paid for her to go to school, and to get as far away from me as possible."

"You sent Mel to the same school."

"Only because she couldn't live without her sister by her side. They were so close once, even had their own little language as toddlers." He may have sounded like he was recollecting a happy memory, but the look on his face was steel and ice.

"What did Jamie do that was so bad, Sir?"

"Why do you want to know? You are taking being neighborly a little further than you should?"

"I'd like to understand why she keeps herself locked away emotionally from the world; why talking about her past, herself, is so bad."

"I'd say simply it's because she is ashamed of her past, Mathew."

"Why would she be ashamed?"

"If you're sleeping with her, and I don't care if you are, it's your problem. I would just make sure there's no one else doing her too."

"Jamie hasn't been sleeping with anyone." Matt was finding it hard to control his respect for elder's rule, as he tried to forget Richard's last comment. "You are so sure because she is your neighbor, and you know everything about her?"
"We have hung out a few times, and I've never seen her be anywhere except home alone, or on base."
"Right, you are with her twenty-four hours a day." Mathew didn't respond, making Richard ask a question. "Did James ever tell you about her Mother?" He stood up and walked over to refill his cup with the sludge his headache was responding well to. He gestured to Matt with the coffee pot, asking without words if he wanted some, to which Matt shook his head. "She said she died." Matt answered. "She didn't say why, or how?"
"Like I said, she doesn't talk about anything."

"My late wife had quite the reputation on the base we were stationed at when James and Mel were, I think, eleven. Yes, because Ricky was twelve."
"Ricky?" Mathew asked.
"My son." Richard shook his head. "Jamie has never mentioned him? I'm very surprised about that." He looked truly shocked to hear that.
"No, she never mentioned him."
"Well, she probably wouldn't. He died of leukemia when she was twelve; anyway, that's a completely separate story. As I was saying, my wife was sleeping with a few of the officers on base."
"Why are you telling me this?"

"You wanted to know about James's past, and why I don't call her my daughter. I'm trying to explain it for you."

"Sorry, go on." Matt got the sinking feeling he wasn't going to like what Jamie's dad was going to tell him, but he remembered her strange words of 'he believes everything he knows is true'. Maybe her dad would give him a clue to understand that statement.

"When the girls were eleven, their mother was killed in a car accident. She and her lover were drunk and beyond any safe alcohol limit. They had been driving down an expressway when they crashed in to a set of concrete beams that support a bridge. It was a very horrific time, and it was especially bad for the girls, who were in school and teased about the rumors around their mother." Richard paused a second, taking a drink of his coffee that was getting cold. "Mel was devastated, so was Ricky, but James never even shed a tear that I ever knew about, not even at the funeral. To begin with I thought she was just in shock, you know, losing her mother like that, what with all the humiliation on top of it too."

"Can I ask, were you and Jamie close before this?"

"She was Daddy's little girl and Mel was her Mother's."

"Maybe she blamed you, your career?"

"I thought about it, but that never made sense. I had been home with them that night, and we'd had a great time at the base carnival. James and Ricky had dragged Mel on to the tilt-a-whirl, and the poor thing looked so green when she came off. Ricky and James were always a lot closer when they got older; Mel was the outsider in some ways."

"Jamie and Ricky? I thought Mel and Jamie were close, and stuff," Matt interrupted.

"They were as sisters are, but there was a stronger bond between the other two. I'd find them picking on Mel, or leaving her out, because she was too chicken to do whatever they were doing." Mathew watched the sudden pain of talking about his children pass across Richard's face. "Jamie became uncontrollable, would disobey orders and curfews, and a couple of times she ran away."

"Where did she go?"

"I never found out, and if Ricky had known he didn't let on. She wouldn't talk to me, would just walk around as if I didn't even exist."

"You never once found out? That seems hard to believe."

"There were a few times I found out, but they were later on."

# CHAPTER TWENTY-THREE

"About six months later, we moved to a base in Georgia." Richard continued his story. "James decided she was going to up and leave for a few days. This time she left a note for us." He seemed to chuckle at the thought of the memory. "The note said something along the lines of 'doing a paper on the Salem witch trials, gone to Massachusetts'. I hit the roof. I wasn't even sure she had been honest, and was really somewhere close to home, just pulling our leg to see how we would react. God, she was twelve, and I didn't even know where she would get the money to go all that way, or how."

"Did she go?" Mathew asked.
"Yes, she did. She hitched rides from different truck drivers along the way. I had put in a call to a friend up at Hanscom Air Force base, who contacted the local state troopers. Together, they found her doing what she said, looking around Salem and doing research for her class."
"She was lucky nothing bad happened on the way there."
"She was. They put her on a plane back to me."
"What did you say to her when she got home?"
"I tried to talk to her, but she went straight to her room and slammed the door in my face."

"She was twelve; you are her father, you should have done more. Maybe she needed to see that you cared." Matt knew he had said something the older man didn't like hearing, when he bit out.

"Trust me I tried everything from yelling to bribery, even family counseling. The shrink told me it was just a phase, and it would pass eventually. She was pushing me away as part of a defense mechanism, to protect herself from getting hurt if I died too." At the end of the sentence, as the last verbal note died out, Richard seemed off-kilter, and loosened his tie a little as he sat back in his chair, a little less ramrod straight. "You believe that?"
"Not at the time, but I have to admit, that was when we found out Ricky was sick."

"I had to take a leave of duty, and focus everything on him. The girls stayed with neighbors, wives of other Navy officers. Then; when Ricky died four months after we found out." Richard looked away and up to the overhead lights, obviously trying to push away any tears that might be surfacing. "What happened after Ricky died?"
"James became even worse. I had time to make up, and was gone just as much, but when I was around, it was just a constant battle, forever pushing the limits and my buttons. She even got in to fights with her sister who was just a wreck. It went from her ignoring me to her screaming at me, whenever I tried to talk to her, calling me whatever crude name she had heard on base, and from friends."

"She ran away more, usually in the middle of the night, to where I can only guess. She was pissed at me and the world, and even more when I was then transferred to San Diego, only a short time after everything had happened in Georgia. She retaliated by not going to school, and taking my car for joy rides at night."

"She was a kid with no license."

"She may have been thirteen, but she looked older, and acted like a mature eighteen-year-old. I noticed how the young men new on base would look at her, thinking she was older." He paused a moment. "There was the drinking, where she would come home at four am, if at all, sleep until late afternoon, and then do it over again."

"And you saw this but couldn't stop it?" Matt thought it was incredible: he couldn't control his daughter. "I was a single father in the Navy, running a SEAL team very similar to yours."

"She was your daughter. That means more than a job, a rank." Richard seemed to ignore his words and continued.

"By the time we had been in San Diego for a month, she had gotten into drinking, and drugs, she stole from the Navy Exchange, went for rides in my car, and would be gone for days at a time. It was around then that I met Margaret my current wife, who I was too ashamed to bring home because of James's behavior."

"What does she think of all this?"

"I don't know, and I've never asked. It's an unwritten rule in my house that no one mentions James, or Ricky."

"What happened next?" Mathew knew there had to be more.

"I got a call from one of the Master-at-arms on base,

telling me they had just arrested James and a seaman recruit, out by the edge of the base near the water, on their patrol. It was the final straw in all of this. They had been arrested because James and this nineteen-year-old had been fucking in his car, and they knew exactly how old she was; she was two months from her fourteenth birthday." Mathew's eyes were wide with shock. It sounded nothing like the Jamie he knew; yet a small part of him wondered if it was correct. "Are you sure?"

"Oh, it was consensual, I found out she was charging him too, my daughter the prostitute."

"I can't believe he agreed to it."

"As I said, she didn't act or look fourteen; he said he had no idea of her age and was dishonorably discharged. I persuaded the MAA to release her to my care and we went home."

"Good."

"Not really. I sent her to rehab the next day."

"Did you talk to her about the seaman? Did rehab help?"

"She wouldn't talk to me again. She was in rehab for a month and she made up wild stories while she was there. The shrinks told me it was her way of testing me, to see if I really loved her, and would rescue her. But I kept her there, she needed the help." Richard moved slightly, and rested his right ankle on his left knee. "After a week of her being home, I came home to find a bunch of the base kids in my living room, smoking weed and making out with each other; even her sister was high. That was it I put my foot down harder, and screamed back at her as loud as she had been doing to me. It was four days before Christmas and by Christmas Eve she had left again. It would have been our first Christmas with Margaret"

"Every day for four months I expected to get a call from the police to say they found her dead body. I was so scared for her, I really was. I called the hospitals every day, and filed reports in as many states that would listen to my ravings. Mel was always in her room crying, and I thank God for Margaret, she helped me through that. It was then I knew she was the woman I had always been looking for. But that is an entirely different and much happier story." Richard moved to leave.

"That was it? She left and neither one of you ever spoke again, and you never knew where she was?" Mathew stood up to block Richards's path to the door, as he rambled off the questions he wanted answered. "No, there was more. I got a call from a cop in New York City, letting me know they may have found my daughter from the missing person's report and her picture."
"She ran away to New York from California?"
"Seems she had stashed money she had stolen from my wallet, and bought herself a plane ticket. But don't worry; she was perfectly fine. They had spotted her in mid-town, and when they brought her in for questioning it turns out that she had met a young college boy at Columbia Law school, and had told him some sob story. She had been living with him, working as a waitress in a diner in Times Square, and going to high school too. By all accounts she was

supporting herself and that made me proud."

"That made you proud?" Mathew's eyebrows were raised in disbelief.

"She was always a smart child; I was expecting a lot worse Mathew. She had lied, sure, but not to this young man who she seemed to genuinely care for, and he seemed to care for her. Of course, I only saw him once when I picked her up to bring her home."

"You took her away? If she was doing so well, why not let her stay?"

"She was fourteen." His voice was raised, and a few men looked over at them.

"Deep down I just wanted her to come home with me, and find that happiness in my house. Of course, I thought a lot of things, but I thought having Margaret around would soften her just a little. But it didn't, and she told me either to send her to some boarding school in Chicago, or she would run away again, and that this time I would never find her."

"That's when you sent her to St. Theresa's?"

"I sent both the girls. Mel was always brighter when her sister was around, but because James had been studying while in New York, she was bumped several grades higher than Mel, and left the school a year and a half later to go to college."

"When was the last time you spoke to her?"

"I called her for her graduation. She didn't want her stepmother or me there, but I had to call and tell her how proud I was of her. She said nothing, but I always thought she was crying. That was the last time I ever spoke to her, and the last time I knew for sure where she was. I sent her a check for college, but it was sent back."

"Didn't she live with an aunt in college?"
"Aunt? No. Mel told me she moved in with the boy from New York, although I found that out years later."
"Did she marry him?" Matt didn't know where that question had come from but he went with it. "I think she probably wanted to, I think she has problems emotionally that keep her from getting that close to anybody though. She hurt me and her sister when she left, and I'm surprised Mel has anything to do with her now."
"She loves her and can see past all of that probably."
"Maybe, but she put me through so much, and made it very clear she wanted nothing to do with me."

"Do you know whatever happened to the boy from New York?"
"Why do you want to know?"
"I'm just interested."
"Well then, you should probably know he's upstairs and from the look he gave me earlier he still loves her. I'd say if you want anything to do with James you'll have some competition on your hands."
"Who upstairs?"
"The CIA agent, Robert Wakefield."

Matt had not seen THAT coming.

# CHAPTER TWENTY-FOUR

"This is fucking crazy." Mel fell to the ground in a complete temper tantrum. "How many times do I have to apologize for not having a weapon?" Jamie asked, stopping next to her sister.

"No dipshit, I'm talking about this." She said waving her arms around at the surrounding nothingness. "It's night time." Jamie answered.

"Do you think fucking terrorists sleep, Jay? Especially when they are supposed to be coming to get you?"

"They're playing a fucking mind game Mel."

"Fuck them."

"No fuck you." Jamie pointed her cigarette at her sister.

"We are right here and we could be dancing the fucking Macarena and they'd still not find us."

"In a rush to go with them, are you?" Jamie sat down next to her sister as she was obviously going nowhere soon. She knew why her sister was antsy, and she wondered if and when that snap would happen. "No, but I wish they'd get their asses out of the sand."

"You didn't need to come; this is my mess to clean up."

"Clean up? Sounds like that guy from that Bridget Fonda movie."

"The assassin?"

"No, the point of no return. Do I need to point out how stupid this is if they don't show up?"

"You don't need to." Jamie replied softly and Mel turned to look at her.

"You fell in love with your fucking neighbor."

"Matt?" Jamie looked wide-eyed. "You think I was? Oh, no I wasn't"

"Can't fool me babe." Mel laughed.

"Don't be so sure."

"Okay Jay, whatever you say. I don't have the energy to argue. By the way, I don't suppose anyone on board thought to give you any MRE's?"

"Chicken or meatball?" Jamie simply asked throwing the finished smoke to the desert floor. "Holding out on your sister, huh, Buchanan?"

### XXX    XXX

"Where have you been?" Lee asked over the commotion going on in the command center as Mathew walked in. "Talking to Jamie's father."

"Lucky you." Steven came from behind Lee.

"What's going on in here?" Mathew looked at his two friends who looked at each other. "Jamie's signal just split up." Steven told him

"Maybe she dropped one of them?"

"No Matt. You don't understand." Lee put a strong hand on his friend's shoulder. "Both trackers are moving in two separate directions."

"When?" Matt looked over at the clock display. It was 0110 hours; Jamie had been gone a little over five and a half hours. "About two minutes ago." Lee finished. "One is moving towards Konduz, the other east of there." Steve said pointing behind himself to the large screen on the wall.

"Intel is trying to get a satellite feed of the two trackers to see if we can figure this out." Lee continued to explain.

"They don't think?" Mathew asked worried about the answer.

"No, I don't think so. I think they are probably believing that Jamie got a tracker on one of the men to help us locate the Marines." Lee tried to ease his friends mind. "Remember, Jamie is smart. I definitely think it's something that she would do."

"Me too." Steve agreed.

The three of them looked over to their commanding officer, Danny, who was head bent with Robert and the fleet admiral. Mathew felt a stab of bitterness towards the CIA agent, knowing now that he and Jamie had been a couple and shared a history he wasn't privy to. It made him wonder how any man could let the woman he loved, shared so much history with, could let her go out there and get herself killed. "I think we're finally going out there." Lee whooped up as Danny and Chris now walked towards them. Chris let out a load whistle to get the Team's attention.

"Hey, hey." The Senior Chief got everyone's attention. "Team Seven; we are getting in the helos in ten minutes. We have satellite pictures that inform us that a team of men are travelling from the rendezvous point ,to go to the house we know Atwa uses for his operations, just inside the town perimeter of Konduz. We'll go in on the usual extraction routine, using the setup we all know works. Lieutenant Commander

MacCafferty will remain in one helo with Mathew in another."

"Why do I have to stay behind?" Mathew asked his commanding officer.

"Nothing personal Matt, just we need you in the game, and you know as well as we all do, that Jamie could have been compromised."

"I can handle it, Sir."

"I don't doubt you son, but this has been recommended by the spook over there and I promise you it won't go down on your record this way."

Mathew backed down. Obviously, the men knew more about his feelings for Jamie than he did, and deep down he had to agree. If they had even hurt her just a little, then he wasn't sure if he could handle it. It was one of the arguments about why females didn't belong in the teams. A bad one but at that moment he had to agree. He looked over at Robert who was watching him, his arms crossed over his chest, his fresh shirt sleeves rolled up on the sleeves.

"Also, we'll have two extra bodies," the Senior Chief continued. "Nick and Dumont from the CIA are coming for the ride. Nick, it seems, has previous experience at the house."

"Which tracker are we following? Did Intel figure which one it is?" Steven asked. "We're following the tracker that went to the Konduz house. The other tracker went northeast towards Faizabad, and to everyone's knowledge, Atwa wouldn't be there. They reckon Jamie tagged a tango, and they've moved to an outpost," Chris finished.

"Gear up men," Danny added at the end, as the Team started to pick up all their gear.

Mathew, with his bag, walked over to Robert who was still watching him. "I'm Lieutenant Taylor," he introduced himself, holding out his hand. The other man took it and shook it firmly. "I know who you are Mathew. Jamie told me who you were before she left."
"What did she say?" He was stunned and saddened that she had talked about him to Robert. "The question is; did you believe everything her father told you?"
"How did you...?"
"Know? Nick saw the two of you in the mess hall earlier." Robert returned his focus to the screen before him. "I don't know what to believe, except the Jamie I've gotten to know now, is nothing like the one he talked about."
"She's not." Robert turned back. "Only half of what he told you was true, and then there's a half he doesn't even know about. Jamie is a great woman who has only wanted to be loved Mathew. Can you love her?"
"What? I thought you two...?"
"We have history. I loved her, well I still do, truth be told. But she couldn't love me. When I realized it, by then she was focused on getting her life started without her father's loathing."

"I don't understand." Mathew honestly was puzzled why he was being told this.
"I got Jamie in to this six years ago. I was the one

who requested her transfer. I thought it would bring us closer, but it just put a bigger wall up between us. She asked me to make sure you weren't in the team that went out, but I'm sure I couldn't do anything to stop you, even if I wanted to. I have no authority here. But I did ask your commander not to let you in there as Jamie wished. She doesn't want you to see her if Atwa followed through, and avenged his son's death by killing her."

"Do you think he would?"

"He's a twisted fuck, Mathew. That's all I know."

"Just tell me why he wanted her." Mathew asked, heaving his flak-jacket over his shoulders. "Jamie killed his son on my orders. I'm sorry, that's all I can tell you. But Mathew, tell me, do you think you could love her?"

"I already do." He said firmly and with conviction.

"Then go get her, and tell her that. God knows, she deserves to be happy because she seems to like you a lot too."

XXX    XXX

Two small trucks had driven towards them with no lights on. The sand billowing out from the tires in the back looked eerie in the night, with just the moon to light up the desert. They had known, from the moment they'd heard the sound of the engines, that it was game time.

A dark bearded man who had sat in the passenger's seat of the front truck, had gotten out and walked over to them, studying Mel's face as he walked closer to her. "I get an American soldier, too," he said in his broken English. "This is a very good day I think. And look, they are twins." He moved over to face Jamie; a smile widened his dark features, and a sparkle lit his eyes, eyes Jamie would never forget. His teeth were so white they seemed to pop out of his face. "I did not know Jamie to have a twin. Maybe the American President will give me more now?"

"The deal was you take me and let the others go. She's with them." Jamie said.

A blow to the back of her head caused Jamie to fall to the ground. She was sure it had been the butt of a machine gun, and thankfully it had been only slightly swung, to send her off balance, not to hurt her badly. "You say nothing," the man informed her. "I will send your look alike to my house with the others, and you and I will go for a little drive. My men will treat her like a princess." He let out a crude laugh. "And you will be my guest until I decide exactly how you will be used."

A second blow; this time a foot connected to her stomach, and she fell face first in the dry dirt. She tried to blink out the harsh grit that stung her eyes, knowing her hands would be covered in the same; it would just cloud her eyes more. She barely saw Mel being knocked to the ground too, and being hog-tied both her hands and feet. The other men carried Mel like a dead deer to the back of one of the trucks, and then the truck was in motion.

She felt her hands being forced behind her back, but

only her hands were tied. She was dragged to her feet by two men she couldn't make out as more than blurs, through the sand in her eyes. "Ready to have fun?" Atwa asked in his native tongue of Pashtu, grinning at her as they covered her face with a cloth bag which smelt almost bad enough to make you suffocate.

## CHAPTER TWENTY-FIVE

The SEALs were all loaded along with the two CIA agents into two separate helos, one being manned by Chris, the other by Danny. They sped along just above the surface to avoid radar, and the propellers whipped up the sand and loose rocks, as they traveled to the drop-off site. They were going to land a quarter of a click from the perimeter of Konduz in a dark, isolated area. Few locals would hear them arriving, about half a click from the safe house.

Chris watched his men check and recheck their vests and guns, a way they passed the time, keeping their minds focused on the job ahead of them. He watched Mathew, knowing the fact the guy wasn't allowed to leave the helo was sticking in his side like a thorn. He could understand why, because if it were actually entered in to his service record, why he was left out, it would hinder his career. Luckily Robert Wakefield of the CIA had made the call so Danny could keep the real reason between them.

With another ten minutes until the insertion point, he caught a glimpse of Mathew looking out to the distant city. Mathew turned and Chris saw something that spooked him. It was a look that made him believe that he knew what they would find inside.

Team Seven's coordinates set them down just outside the far north-east corner of Konduz. The morning sun had only an hour before it would break over the horizon, shedding light onto their operation. The first of the five Muslim daily praying sessions were about to start soon, so time was certainly an issue.

Everyone aboard the two helos, with the exception of the pilots, Mathew and Danny, hit the ground running towards the city, and what would await them. The team had been ordered to split and remain in their two teams to retrieve the packages. They would insert themselves into the building as one, with Nick leading, and then they would separate.

The Team's XO 'Coop' would be with Nick, along with Steven, Lee and O'Rielly. Their task was to find Jamie and get her out. Expecting to find Atwa, or a group of his men, guarding her, they had the most skilled weapons men, and the most senior of the men in the first team. Team two, headed by Chris with the two Richards's, Vasquez, Vincent and King, joined by the very butch-looking Dumont, the silent CIA agent; their task, to find the eight Marines and get them out to the helos.

They had lucked out, and had found a newly crumbled section of the town wall, and had entered without being noticed, and without having to climb or repel down the wall. Proceeding together as one, they moved without any sound, even their breathing could barely be made out.

Locating the safe house, they took their positions, team one in front and team two around the back. The way the house was built, they would enter either side but would see each other down the long, wide corridor, leaving no room for any tangos to escape. They were hoping that if there were any bad guys they'd all be asleep. If there were any on the main floor, they could use the syringes of a sleeping drug, to ensure they wouldn't wake up. They had silencers on their guns in case they weren't so lucky. Of course, if they were really lucky, there would be no tangos at all, but that was just plain wishful thinking.

Coop's team made it in, and with the flashlights on their guns, found no hostiles near their door. Holding their weapons ready to use they watched as fifty feet away, team two, headed by Chris, broke through their door. Walking towards the staircase to the basement with symmetry, Nick had explained that the tangos did not use the upstairs two floors except for look out. Keeping prisoners, especially American Military, was far too dangerous for them to do when people could look in. Now that the American soldiers occupied most of the towns in Afghanistan, local people were more likely to tell them where the prisoners were, to get the reward money.

Nick opened the door, spilling out so much light for a second, it was like looking at the sun. Inside the door was a flight of stairs that looked like they had been carved out of the raw ground. The only noise around them was the slow drip of water. Nick turned back to all the men and waved for them to follow him down.

XXX    XXX

"Repeat that, team one." Robert said into his headset;

he had been waiting for them to find something, and get the ball rolling. He needed to be focused and ready, he just wanted to get this all over with, now with Coop's words telling him something that at first didn't make sense, he needed the officer to say it again to make sure he hadn't heard wrong.

"Base, we have made contact and have found eight packages so far. Over." Coop's voice was clear, and the moment it was gone the static of the air waves came across. "Is there any sign of the new package? Over." Robert asked, referring to Jamie.
"Negative, sir. Over." The radio was silent a few minutes, and Robert looked at the men next to him. The fleet admiral and his two-right-hand man, the White House rep and the senator, a man whose presence he could do without.

"Sir, you are never going to believe this. Over" Coop's voice broke through the static. "Go ahead. Over." Robert replied.
"We have another new package. Over."
"Explain. Over."
"We have a female in a USMC uniform, the new package's doppelganger. Over." Coop explained as covertly as he could. The senator grabbed Robert's arm. "My daughter?" He asked with hope in his eyes. "Sounds like he's referring to Mel, yes." He turned away. "What is her status, over?"
"Seems fine except for a minor beating. Over."
"Is there any sign of the other new package? Over?" Robert repeated.
"Hold on. Over." Coop informed him.

Everyone in the command room waited patiently, checking watches, as the only sound they could hear was that of the static. It was just mental torture, as everything seemed to slow down, seconds took hours, beads of sweat took forever to roll down the center of his back as Robert feared for the worst. "Boss. Over." Nick's New York accent grated over the airwaves. "Go ahead. Over." Robert didn't dare look at any of the other men around him, and instead focused on the live feed from the helo now waiting at the rendezvous point. "We have a problem. Over." Nick said. "Explain. Over."

"Our new package is not here but a video camera is. Our tango has a new message for us. Over."

"What is the Goddamn message? Over."

"We won't be seeing the package again unless we follow his orders. Over."

# CHAPTER TWENTY-SIX

The door creaked with age and rot. There had been two guards sitting at the bottom of the stairs to the basement. O'Rielly and Steven had administered a dose of sleeping med's to each, with only the look of shock from the men's dark eyes, before they fell back in their seats with the two of them making sure they didn't fall and make a noise. They placed their used syringes in the little bright orange bio-hazard box they carried as part of their pack. With the two tangos' down Nick waved on the team leaders. Indicating Chris's team should go to the door on the right and Coop the door on the left.

Chris's team walked into a dark room with the smell of stale air and human excrement, their flashlights picking out the forms of eight humans scattered all over the room. Some were conscious, others, like the Marine with a fractured leg, with the bone sticking through the flesh, were out cold. Each SEAL took to working on a Marine to get them ready to move to the Helos where they would perform the more advanced medical assistance, such as IV's and cleaning out wounds.

The kind of job Jamie was supposed to be there for.

Standing in the doorway, Chris watched his men working away and turned his attention to the other team in the opposite room. He couldn't see very much, but what he saw made his blood run cold.

## XXX    XXX

With the other team already getting to work, Cooper, Nick, Steven, O'Rielly and Lee took the next room in one very swift move with Coop going in first. The room had one bare light bulb hanging from the ceiling; sitting directly underneath was a Marine who looked like hell. The face was so bloodied and cut and bruised in places, it was hard to tell whether it was a male or female. The buzz cut didn't help.

Steven moved over and began to untie the Marine from the coarse rope at the back of the chair. Lee was the one to see what damage the tangos had inflicted on the Marine. As he lifted the head to see the face clearly, his breath drew in so fiercely, the other men stopped dead in their tracks.

"What?" Coop asked, coming over to get a better look.
"I thought Jamie's sister was in that burnt out building." Lee said.
"Maybe they put Jamie in a uniform." Steven suggested.
"No, that's her sister Mel." Nick the man of few words said.
"How do you know?" O'Rielly asked.
"Because of this." He held up a video camera. Pressing the play button, he saw Atwa in a room very similar to the one they were in. Jamie was in the background, tied to the roof above her and gagged from being able to say anything while they were filming.

"We need to get this back to the specialists to have them analyze this." Nick said, as Coop came over from Mel to see for himself. "I just radioed in and informed them of the new package."

"This is so not good. We need to get out of here now." Nick told him and something in his voice made Coop tell Lee and Steve to hurry up getting Mel out of the chair and up to the surface.

Mel came to as they exited the building, the final run to the last helo, the other one already rushing back to the carrier. Steven was carrying her like a rag doll over his shoulder. Lee being right behind saw her head come up as the look of realization also joined her face. "Mel, you're being rescued by Team Seven of the United States SEAL division. Don't panic my name is Lee and we're getting to our helo and we'll take care of you there."

"Jamie." She said through what sounded like a mouth full of blood and spit. "Don't worry." Lee said comfortingly.

"Save her. You have to save her." She said before coughing up some vile liquid that landed on the floor at his feet, which he dodged as they ran.

"Mel, calm down, we will." He tried to reassure her again.

"I found her out there." She said her voice getting a slight quiver to it

"Out in the desert?"

"Yes. It's funny, she hates the dark." Mel passed out as they reached the helo. Danny was there waiting for them. "Are you sure Jamie is not in there?" He asked his men, as they hoisted Mel in and buckled her down on a stretcher. Lee began cleaning the facial wounds as O'Rielly checked her for body wounds. "Atwa will have taken her somewhere else." Nick said over the roar of the blades spinning faster so they could get off the ground. "How do you know?" Danny asked.

"He is a shit head and gets off on games, that's how I know."

"What do you think the possibility of us getting to Jamie before he kills her is?"

"With Atwa, it could be a matter of minutes or days."

XXX     XXX

Mathew hated being out of the loop, and as he was helping the Marines on the flight back to the carrier, he knew there had been a reason they had insisted on not letting the two teams hear each other's radio messages, but it was killing him. He had absolutely no idea what the other team had found or where Jamie was, and the thought his heart would beat right out of his chest, he felt so angry and useless.

Chris pulled him aside as the last wound was being tended to, all they could do had been done for now. "Matt, I just heard from Danny over on the other helo." The older man's face was pinched and looked its forty years. "What?"

"They found Mel. Looks like she'll be fine, she's unconscious right now, but was awake for a few minutes."

"What about Jamie?"

"She wasn't there."

"But the tracker?"

"Nick thinks she planted one on her sister. Seems Mel found Jamie when she was waiting to be picked up. Maybe the other blip on that screen back at the carrier was Jamie."

"Was there any clue to where she is?"

"Atwa left a video for us. We'll see it when we get back aboard."

Mathew looked out of the helo door as the wave of nausea floated into his stomach.

# CHAPTER TWENTY-SEVEN

The flight on the helo back to the carrier took an hour, and the whole time Mathew just wanted to get off and go find this video tape Chris had mentioned, and to talk to Mel. They landed a full twenty minutes ahead of the other team carrying the wrong sister, and after helping a few of the injured down below deck, Chris had pulled Mathew aside, told him that Danny had requested his presence for their arrival, because of Mel and the state she was in.

Up on deck, the water was shining and the air humid and windy. Mathew had to hold on to the railing to steady himself from an opposing breeze. He wished he had kept his flak jacket on, the breeze was burying itself in the thin t-shirt he was wearing, and the blazing sun and humidity seemed like an afterthought. Standing and waiting for the helo was Robert. He had his back to him, and the perfect unwrinkled shirt he had been wearing earlier, was now hanging out of his pants, and blowing in the breeze.

"Hey." Matt said walking closer. "Can you tell me any more than I already know?"
"What do you want to know?" Robert asked, not turning around.
"For now; how about why I was requested to be here for the other team's arrival?"
"Mel is pretty upset; your Team have had a hard time keeping her calm."
"Yeah, I heard that already."
"We found out why Mel wasn't in the vicinity when

the others in her team were attacked."

"Why?"

"You don't need to know that Lieutenant. The NCIS agents and I will take care of her."

Mathew watched as the cool CIA agent turned around and looked at him through the thick darkness of his aviator glasses. "NCIS agents?" Matt crossed his arms. "What did Mel do?" For them to bring in the Navy investigators, it was a pretty good bet it was bad. "Did the senator tell you anything about his star daughter?"

"Mel? Nothing more than how Jamie made her miserable, and that she was the emotional daughter."

"Typical. Well, Jamie has been covering for her hopeless sister for years; she has the scars to prove it."

"Want to explain that?"

"I can't."

"Can't or won't?"

Robert moved closer, leaving a very small gap between them. "I promised Jamie that no matter what, I would keep her secrets. I've helped cover for some of them too. I'm just afraid I can't do it this time, and that I will be letting her down. Mel will be court marshaled at the end of all this, and all the dirty laundry in their lives will come to the surface. The good senator will realize his blindness, and the one person who doesn't need to be hurt further, will be."

"Jamie?"

"Yeah." Matt was beyond frustrated. He wanted to know what these cryptic clues and hidden secrets were. He also had a feeling that Jamie's oldest 'male' friend wasn't about to spill her secrets to anyone, especially him.

"If you won't explain any of that, will you at least tell me what you think the chances are of getting to Jay before Atwa kills her?" Robert turned back to the view; in the far distance he could make out the helo coming in to the fleet's safety zone. Behind them the stairwell door opened with a metallic creaking of age and seawater. Joining them on deck, were two MAA's and the onboard NCIS agent with a team of three medics. "I won't lie to you Matt. You seem like a nice guy. I wouldn't doubt that he's already killed Jamie, and he's going to suck this for everything he can."

XXX     XXX

Mel was in pain. All of her body, and everything mentally, just ached like she had been head on with a semi-trailer and lost. The men of the SEAL team and the big hulk of a man she thought she remembered someone calling Nick, had said very little to her after she had come too on the helo.

She was strapped in to one of the floor restraints, and every time she moved her arm to scratch something, or touch the swollen parts of her face, she was reminded of that. The men didn't look at her, and seemed to be huddled together. She couldn't make anything out because of the loud roaring of the helo's engines. She looked at all the men trying to remember the nice one who had talked to her on their way to the helo. Over the pain from her body, she couldn't really think of anything except not wanting to breathe, for fear of moving and making the pain come back.

The man she recognized from the ground came over, and his face was pulled in a strange way, as if he were trying hard to hide something. Lee, his name came to her in a flash. "Lee, what's going on?" Her voice sounded funny, thanks to her split lip. "Mel, how are you feeling?" His eyes were so caring, she thought to herself. "Like total shit. What's going on with the rescue? Did you get my sister?"
"She wasn't there Mel. Look, I know you're in pain from your...." He paused like he was unable to say the words.

"Beatings?" She helped him out.
"Yeah, anyway; I have to inform you that an NCIS agent is waiting for you back on the ship, and we know why you weren't with your team when everything hit the fan." Mel's eyes watered; even the one swollen shut seemed to find a vent to escape some salty liquid. "What?" Her voice squeaked out, and her body started to shiver and shake, as though the air had suddenly turned icy cold. "Your team leader Major Evans told the NCIS agent on the carrier when he came too. He was pretty badly injured, but he made a statement."
"He told them what?"
"That you were out getting high, when you were meant to be guarding your platoon."
"I...." Mel couldn't stand to hear the words, as

everything started to spin around her. "I was." Still she couldn't seem to connect the relevant words together to deny what she couldn't admit, even to herself.

"Mel." She heard Lee's voice but couldn't pin point exactly place where he was. "Mel." She felt his hands holding her upper arms. "Ah, shit. Hey, some help over here," Was the last thing she remembered before blacking out.

XXX    XXX

The helo had landed and the men had all exited. Nick came out after a few moments carrying Mel in his arms. She looked small and still, like a sleeping child. "Some help over here," the large man shouted. The medic team from behind Matt and Robert seemed to appear out of nowhere, yet Matt knew they had been there since their arrival six minutes ago. One of them was carrying a folded seat that the team sometimes took on missions, if they knew beforehand that the package was injured and needed to be more stable than thrown over one of their shoulders.

They buckled her in, and as the three men moved away, Matt could see that Mel had one eye wide open and was thrashing around in her seat. Danny pulled Matt aside and spoke closely to him. "She's been like this on and off since Lee told her we knew what she has been up to."
"How can I help?" Matt seemed confused.
"She asked for you a few times."

"Me? I met her one time, two weeks ago."
"I don't know what to say, but she was asking for Jamie and the seven dwarfs too, so...." The man shrugged. "I'll be damned if I know what that means." Danny patted his shoulder and continued on his way.

Walking away towards the rest of the Team, Mathew watched his commanding officer, before looking back at Mel. Her face was bruised and cut, the short hairstyle nothing like the sister he had been thinking about for the last twenty-four hours. In the moment that their eyes locked, he got a severe cramping feeling in his stomach. The men had been right, if and when the time came to go in to get Jamie, he wasn't sure he could handle the situation. Visually he knew the differences between the twins, but deep down they looked enough alike for the knowledge to hit home, and hard.

Her voice seemed small and childlike; Matt crouched down in front of her and noticed that her hands had been carefully tied in restraints to the arms of the wheelchair. The welts from the rope or metal that had bound her hands earlier in Konduz, peeked through the soft restraints and looked very sore, but she seemed to be free from the pain, even from the facial bruises and swelling.

"Mathew." She repeated again, looking through one hazel eye.
"Mel, I'm here." He reached for her left hand. She grabbed on to it, and held with a very unfeminine

strength. "Jamie. Get Jamie. I need Jamie."

"Jamie isn't here."

"But I don't know what to do." With her voice sounding so small and the small stream of tears flowing like a leaky faucet, she seemed haunted, and not completely with-it. "Tell me what I can do, Mel."

"Mathew is that you?"

"Mel. Do you know where you are?"

"I'm in trouble Ricky."

Mathew rocked back on his heels and let go of her hand. She had just called him by the name of her dead brother. "Do you want to see your dad?" He asked

"No." She shook her head fiercely, trying to wipe her nose but couldn't, using her shoulder instead. "If he finds out we'll all be in trouble."

"Why Mel. Tell me why." He moved closer again.

"Dad is going to be pissed. I don't know what to do." She looked long and hard at him. "I never know what to do. My sister, she can fix anything."

Matt pulled Mel in to an embrace as the flood of tears came cascading down. She sobbed so hard it was only a brief second before he felt the moisture soaking into the t-shirt on his shoulder. "Please bring her back to me. I can't do any of this without her." She spoke softly into his ear. "She's falling in love with you, you know."

"She is?" Matt couldn't keep his voice steady.

"She wanted you to know that. She made me promise to tell you when I saw you again."

"Well, she'll get a chance to tell me herself soon, okay."

# CHAPTER TWENTY-EIGHT

The feeling in her hands was coming and going; they were tied behind her back with some sort of thick rope. She had been unable to free them from the tightness, back when she had known there were still hands back there. The rope was making her skin burn, a feeling that she knew from the past; the moist burn on her skin that felt like it was seeping its way to her shoulders through her blood stream and nervous system.

Her knees were up near her face, bent so tight that the moment they were going to be straight was going to be a painful one, and one she was not looking forward to. It was a good possibility the people holding her captive wouldn't wait if she asked them to give her a moment to get the blood running again. They had put her in a crate or something similar, no doubt to transport her unnoticed. She had come too, not knowing for an instant what was going on; everything had come flooding back with a sharp realization that she was never going to get out of this nightmare.

Wherever they had put the box she was in, it was dark and smelled damp and musty, like when you opened that wet bag of soil from the garden center. There were no outside noises, and no sounds of life. For all she knew she had been left somewhere to rot, or had been buried alive.

Jamie had been conscious earlier, as she had been videoed by one of Atwa's men. He had been speaking a message for the American government in the background where she couldn't see him. They had hung her from a rusty beam in the basement of an old desert hut somewhere; they had let her hang like meat in a meat factory, while he talked about what he wanted from her and her government.

He had let them hurt her; her body ached to its core.

Atwa had ordered his men at the beginning not to speak unless they were outside the door, because he knew she spoke more than English. She had shown him most of her talents six years before, when she had been given the unfortunate pleasure of meeting him; but she still had a few tricks up her sleeve though that would shock him.

Hoping that by now the Marines would have been rescued, and that her sister was safe and in the arms of the loving senator, she relaxed a little inside; that part of the mission was complete. Thinking about Richard made her even angrier than she already was. When she had been with Mel she had figured out what was going on with her twin. She knew Mel hadn't been off, going for a piss. She knew her sister well enough to know that the last five years of sobriety was probably too good to be true. For the last year, she had been fearing the stress of being a Marine may be getting to her. Mel's normally sparkly façade had been crumbling, and maybe Jamie had chosen to ignore it rather than admit everything was going to come right back, to haunt them both.

She hoped Mel would be okay until she got back.

Then she realized that she had thought about the future.

The future; as she lay on her side, cramped and uncomfortable, she thought about it some more. What she would do when this nightmare was all over. She would tell her father all of the truths; the truth she had been holding on to for so long. She would take a vacation, maybe even resign her commission, and move somewhere tropical. At the top of her list, she would tell Matt how she had fallen for him, the first man to make her feel complete and totally loved, no games, just absolute love. She would go home and do everything in her power to make sure that he loved her as much as she knew she could love him.

XXX     XXX

With everyone from the two teams back on the carrier, Robert was getting the video ready for all of them to view. A copy had been emailed to Langley and the Pentagon, in hopes that either one of their own or NSA might be able to read anything in it, including Atwa's plan, and where he might be holding Jamie. The second tracking device that had obviously been on Jamie, had stopped working not long after the teams had left. He had Dumont going through files trying to see if there was any clue in the direction they were headed, to make an educated guess where they could have gone.

That tracker had been hidden very well on her, so if it stopped working, it would be because they had either found it, or from what they were doing to her. It was going to be hard to see this message.

Nick and Dumont were setting up things behind him. They had made up lists and info booklets for the SEALS who were now on a new mission, to assist in the recovery of Commander James Buchanan MD. The very thought, that she was already dead, was constantly going through his head a thousand miles a minute. In that stapled collection of pages was some of the old mission records from when Nick, Jamie and he, along with the now deceased Agent Bradley had undertaken, six years before; the root of all the problems they were now in. Bradley had been killed on that mission by Atwa, now he had Jay. God, he wished he could take something to relieve the sense of no control; the feeling was a new one to him.

These SEALs were going to see some of the classified information at such a high level that no one but he and the fleet admiral had clearance. He had forced his boss and the boss above him to let them see the information once it had been partially redacted, to show only what was necessary. They not only needed to see the reasons why this happened, but they might just be able to figure out a solution, being fresh eyes to the file and everything.

He rested his palms down on the desk in front of him, trying to crack the tight muscles in his neck. The noises of all the men and those from the Marines able to leave sick bay, were almost done taking their seats, and he knew in just a moment he would be watching a tape that just might make him loose the little food he had in his stomach.

Turning around, he tried not to focus on anyone, but he caught site of Mathew, looking right at him at the same moment, and he knew the younger man was looking forward to the viewing of this tape, as he was. He managed a tired smile at Matt, and took a deep breath before beginning. "In a moment I am going to be showing the tape that was recovered in Konduz by team one. I need for the Marines if they recognize anything or anyone, to let me or their XO know after this. SEALs, I have placed on your seats a copy of the mission report from five years ago, along with a bio on our package." He caught a few SEALs in his peripheral vision shifting in their seats as he used the word package.

"Langley and the Pentagon have received a copy of this video, and are standing by to patch any new communications straight to us." Robert continued. "I must warn you, I have no idea what is on this tape. Something or all of it may be disturbing, but please remember we need to watch this to figure out what he wants and where our package is."
Someone in the middle of the room coughed out the name "Jamie."
"Right now, we want to stay focused on this mission. I'm sorry if my impersonal approach bothers you, but keeping it non-personal might just keep Jamie alive."

Turning away from the room, he took in a deeper breath and steadied himself for what was to come on the large screen in front of them. The lights in the room dimmed, and the screen suddenly came ablaze with a picture of snow, followed closely by a grainy image on the screen.

There for everyone to see was Jamie hanging by the ceiling in the middle of a dimly lit, dank, dirty looking basement. Robert couldn't keep his eyes from the face that he loved, that was void of emotion and bruised and covered with dry blood.

She was gagged, her arms looking strained against the ropes binding her above her head. Her once clean cargo pants and tank top were soiled and grubby-looking. Robert wondered if the marks he saw were boot prints or just his imagination.

The camera zoomed in closer to her face, showing the purpling bruises and a small cut above her right eyebrow. She seemed less beaten than her sister had been, but he knew there would be more to come. Her eyes shone, the usual deep blue was sparkling, not from tears or a sad emotion, but from defiance. He had seen that look twice before, when she had been a young teenager and during their time together years ago.

A hand came in to view and removed the gag. In the split second, the foreign body part was recognized from its dark tattoo on the inside of the wrist. It was one of Atwa's men, the symbol of their organization.

"Speak," a foreign voice ordered Jamie. Jamie just licked the lips that must have been dry and sore, keeping her gaze directly at the camera. A few minutes passed, and she had blinked exactly once, but never moving or showing signs of following their orders.

"I didn't remember you to be such a strong\-willed female." The broken English that said it, was the voice of Atwa himself. "I wonder for how long?" he taunted. A dark, dangerous man came in to view of the camera close enough to see Jamie in the background, his face unchanged from the years or life's hardships. "Maybe we can do something about that." He waved his hand, and as the camera panned out another man, this time wearing a hood to cover his face, came into view. With the AK47 he was holding, he raised the gun high and struck Jamie right above the knees. She let out a noise that was neither a sob nor a sound of protest, just a deep breath. Her eyes stayed clear and focused on the camera.

"Maybe something more?" Atwa said, his voice not changing, just neutral. He waved again to the hooded man who this time, used the gun like a baseball bat. He hit Jamie at the base of the neck. Her body lurched forward and her head drooped for a moment before returning to its vigil of watching the camera. Moments later, the hooded man hit again, this time in Jamie's stomach. With her hanging there like that, she was now putting a great deal of weight on her arms, the cords of her muscles were showing signs of strain.

Robert turned away, unable to watch as the hooded man at Atwa's whim used the butt of the gun to hit Jamie square in the face. The sound of bone cracking rang out through the room, the speaker system picking it out like a firecracker exploding. Robert turned back and saw Jamie, hanging there, completely out of it, her head hanging down so they were all unable to see what injuries they had caused.

The hooded man said something, it sounded muffled. Robert used the remote control he had been almost crushing in his hand, and paused the tape. "Did anyone get that?" he asked the room of very quiet military personnel. "I did." Lee spoke up, he was sitting next to Matt and Steven. Matt's face was ashen. Robert felt for the poor guy, he felt just as bad. "You sure?" He asked Lee.
"He was speaking in Pashtu." Lee looked at his friend and then back at Robert with the rest of the people in the room looking at him, waiting for his response. "I made her bleed good."

# CHAPTER TWENTY-NINE

The video was still playing. Atwa was walking around Jamie, his gaze one that made the hair on Matt's neck stand straight up. Her head was lolling from side to side as she was obviously coming too. Jamie's face came back up, and she seemed to be pulling harder on the restraints above her; the lower part of her face was covered in blood. It was hard to tell if they had broken her nose or split her lip, but from the sound of bones crunching, it was most likely the nose.

"Maybe I under estimate you James," he said, moving his face so close. "My son of course, knew nothing of your real person. I think if he had known he would not have shamed me." Jamie just glared at him with her eyes holding a ton of fury, which was getting deeper and deeper. The eruption inside her she was obviously holding back, looked ready to blow. He waited again for Jamie to talk; and when she didn't, he sighed. "No matter. I will have plenty of time to make you talk. Maybe I should tell your American country what I will do to one of their military."

Jamie cracked the muscles in her neck, Atwa saw her lack of respect and his rage flew out along with his hand gun from the back of his pants. It was cocked and loaded, ready to kill, Jamie did nothing but hang there, void of showing him anything.

The gun was pressing in to her temple, and everyone in the command center seemed to be holding their breath to see what he was going to do. "Talk." He ordered again.

"I'm glad I killed your son, and I wish you had died too, when we shot you inside your car." She finally spoke. The gun was still pushing in to the side of her head, but he withdrew it, satisfied that she had spoken, if only to say something like that.

Atwa ordered something in his native tongue again, and Robert paused the tape, without looking at Lee; the SEAL translated the words. "She is willful like a mule. See that she remembers who's in charge." Lee looked at the floor, sitting forward in his chair and rubbing his forehead. "What does he mean by that?" Simon Townsend asked. "They are going to, err." Robert coughed and looked at The White House Rep. "He just ordered his men to beat her."

Turning back, unable to see the shock and outrage on Townsend's face, Robert pressed the play button. "James." Atwa said eerily. "You will soon beg me to let you talk." He turned towards the camera as four hooded men came in behind and began hitting and kicking Jamie. There was a second of shock in her face before it turned off and all that she was, seeped out, and left the shell behind. It was like someone had turned a light off and no one was there. The men using their bodies and guns did not let up on their attack. Most of the people in the C.C. couldn't keep their eyes on the screen.

"You will give me what I want." Atwa said to the camera. "And I will return your Navy doctor, when I am done with her." He finished with a jeer; a small laugh that was simply blood curdling and sent shivers down more backs than men who would admit to it sitting in the room. Then the camera moved away from him, and the last view before the film ended was of Jamie, spitting out blood on to the floor, giving the camera man one last defiant look.

XXX     XXX

The room stayed quiet long after the tape had been turned off, and the lights were back on at their blaring fluorescent strength. Robert and the Fleet Commander were joined by Danny, Chris and Nick talking in their little group about what they had just witnessed; Lee, Steven and Matt remained seated, as the other men and some Marines began getting up and walking around.

Mathew had his head close to being between his knees. The room was off-kilter, and the image from the screen was bound to haunt him for a long time. Uneasiness and nausea were ruling his emotions, and once the adrenaline kicked into gear, his anger and hatred would come out. Lee was reading the file next to him, and Steven was sitting nervously, no doubt unsure what to say or do, looking and watching all the people around them. If any of the team would lash out in a maddened way from the video, it was Steven; there would be a hole in something and not long from now.

"Well, shit." Steven drawled. "Looks like someone's

father caught some of the show." Matt and Lee turned to see an ashen-faced senator standing in the back, right next to the door. "I wonder how much he saw?" Lee asked to no one in particular. "Hopefully all of it." Mathew muttered under his breath.

Their commanding officer came over to them. All the SEALs behind them moved forward to hear what he was about to say. "Richards." Danny said to one of the SEALs behind Mathew. "We need you to see if you can find any holes in the security barrier around the personnel files," he asked the Team's computer wiz. "Yes sir. I'll get my lap-top from the lock up." The petty officer left without questioning his orders. "What is David looking for?" Coop asked.
"In the video Atwa referred to Jamie as a military person twice. The second time he called her a Navy doctor. Wakefield swears he doesn't know how he found out, so we need to find out how he knows."

Danny took a breath. "You guys should have some down-time. We'll be going out the minute we know where they are holding her. I think after that we all need to get some air. Stay close by though, okay." He dismissed his officers. He pulled Steven aside as the rest of the men left. "I need you to keep me informed on Matt. If it looks like he can't do this you have to tell me"
"Sir, I don't think we could keep him out of it, but I think he would step down himself, if he thought he had to."
"I know he's the one man you can count on in everything." Danny braced his hands on his hips.

"I'm going to call Kirsten; I suddenly need to talk to her. Keep an eye on Matt okay."

"Aye, aye sir." Steven stood at attention, feet together, before leaving the C.C. in search of his friend.

XXX     XXX

"How can this have happened?" Robert was flying off at a tangent, paper and other light items that had been on the table were being sent airborne. "Sir." Dumont came over from where she had been on the phone next to David Richards. He was eagerly waiting to see what holes if any he could find on the net. "Yes?" Robert stopped for a second, Nick, just a few feet away, had stood and watched as his boss had gone off on a wild rage mission.

"I spoke to the boys at Langley, seems Atwa had a few places between Konduz and Faizabad, that he liked to use."

"How many?"

"Around twelve."

"And here I was hoping they'd say one." Robert's face was full of anger, mainly at himself.

"Don't be so quick to dismiss this, sir." Dumont continued. "Eight of those places are now gone, thanks to the coalition forces out here, since nine-eleven."

"Where are the four still remaining ones?"

"One is in Herat, one in Kunar, and just two between Konduz and Faizabad."

"Well, that's good news then." Nick spoke up. "I mean; we know that one of the trackers was heading north-east from the rendezvous point before it vanished."

"David." Robert turned to the Navy SEAL. "Have you or anyone else found anything yet?"

"I'm on with Peters at the pentagon. Seems there was a black-out at the facility about a year ago. When they got all the terminals back up, they found no anomalies. He's checking the main frames."

"Why the main frames?" Dumont asked.

"Because they have four separate generators working them in case there's a blackout."

"What was the cause of the blackout?" Robert asked David. David covered the mouthpiece with his hand. "There was a total blackout for half of Washington; everything south of the Potomac River, about eighty blocks, was out."

"But what caused it?"

"Peters said something about a faulty circuit at the main power source."

"Get him to find out more." Robert ordered. "I want to know how that information was leaked, and I want it one year ago."

# CHAPTER THIRTY

Danny and Chris were talking with Coop in the corner of the CC, waiting for anything any of them could do. Both Danny and Chris had called their wives and felt just a little more comfort, knowing they were safe from harm, and far from the kind of torture Jamie was in. Danny's new wife had not been happy about the shortened wedding reception, but had understood when he had explained briefly what he could, without getting in to trouble on the phone.

Chris was holding on to the file Wakefield had given to the SEALs in the meeting. It had been cleaned up, and gave just the basic outline of the mission; who had been involved, and what the outcome had been. The job Jamie had done had been a tough one.

She had masqueraded as a college student, pretending she was a second year med student at Yale. She had become instant friends with Hassan because Robert had been one of their teachers, and had assigned them as partners. A quick relationship had blossomed and at spring vacation he had asked her to come with him, to visit his family. She had gone, and had been welcomed by hostile father; Atwa had been outraged that his son would think to bring a female like Jamie into their house. He blamed the fact that he had sent his son to America to study.

The report read that after a few days, Hassan had followed in his father's footsteps, and thought he had the right to strike Jamie. She had hit back and by the end of the paragraph he had been shot dead with her 9mm Sig Sauer, one single, fatal shot to the head. This had all gone down not far from the men meant to guard the boy, and soon they were pursuing Jamie and an agent that had been close by, an agent Jeff Bradley, who had been shielding Jamie as they ran, when he was gunned down.

"Excuse me." A male voice said. It broke Chris out of his summarizing. He looked up with the other two officers, to see an awfully pale looking Senator standing before them. "Yes senator?" Danny made no point of hiding his tone of disdain. "I need to have someone let me see my daughter." He said pleadingly.
"Which one?" Danny bit back.
"Melanie of course."
"I'm afraid we have nothing to do with that. You'll have to take it up with either the fleet commander or the senior MAA on shift." Danny walked away from the senator to speak to Robert for a moment.
"Maybe the NCIS agent could help you." Chris offered, getting down from the table he had been resting on.

"Can I ask you if you caught the video we were just watching?" Coop asked the senator.
"I saw a few minutes of it, yes."
"Did you feel anything?" Danny asked returning.
"Of course I did, seeing Melanie beaten like that."
The eyes of the three men standing there popped out of their sockets. "That wasn't Mel." Chris informed him.

"What?" Richard seemed genuinely confused.
"That was the video the rescue team found with Mel.
That was your other daughter, Jamie." Danny picked
up his file and some other papers. "If you'll excuse us
senator." He walked away followed by his two
officers.

XXX    XXX

Mathew had forced himself to watch that tape, and
now as he lay in a bunk trying to get some shuteye,
all he could see was the last defiant image of Jamie,
her face bloodied and no doubt suffering from other
injuries too. He thought he had known the nervous
Navy doctor, had begun to understand the depth of
her character and some of her life and past. Now,
after what he had viewed, and the contents of the file
Steven and Lee had highlighted on their return to
their quarters, he doubted he knew her at all.

But then, she had told him there was a past, a
darkness she was terrified for him to know. In the last
twenty-four hours he was beginning to learn, and his
feelings for her weren't wavering. He just wished he
knew everything, could understand what it was the
twins were involved in.

He was just totally scared he'd never see her again.

"I can't get any sleep." Matt sat up in bed; his two
friends and O'Rielly were playing cards to pass the
time. O'Rielly was notorious at winning every hand,
and most of the Team wouldn't play him, but as he

watched for a while, he noticed that none of them were really playing, other things being on their minds.

A knock at the door made the four men jump slightly. Lee, who was closest to the door got up and opened it. On the other side was a Master at Arms, a scowl on his face. "The presence of Lieutenant Junior Grade Taylor is requested down in the brig's hospital," he said, like a robot.
"That's me." Matt said, jumping down from his bunk. "What's the deal?" He asked.
"Follow me." The MAA answered in the same monotone.

Doing as he was ordered, Mathew grabbed his jacket and followed the MAA. Down the corridors of steel and more steel, descending a few floors below until they came to the medical area of the brig. Behind a plexi glass wall he saw Mel, lying strapped to a bed by restraints. "Are those necessary?" He pointed to the restraints.
"Buchanan is on suicide watch." The robot answered.
"Fair enough but tying her up. She was tortured and bound, isn't that going to send her even crazier."
"That is none of my concern." The MAA answered.

"I ordered it." A new voice said. Matt turned around to see a female doctor behind them. "You must be Mathew Taylor," she said. She was only five feet tall with a mountain of auburn hair. With fair features, her peanut butter Navy uniform and her white lab coat totally washed her out. "Yes, Ma'am, I am." Matt stood straighter, realizing the doctor was a

Lieutenant commander. "I'm Doctor Catherine Johnson. I should have guessed you'd be cute," She said, turning back to retrieve something from behind her.

"Excuse me Ma'am." Matt almost choked; the MAA seemed to smirk before re-taking his post at the door to Mel's room. "Sorry, I have a way of speaking my thoughts out loud." She smiled. She was holding a metal tray with a syringe and a small vile of medicine. "I know Jamie. I saw her to give her a quick physical before she left, and she mentioned you briefly. We served on the Comfort together for a few years. Actually it was her recommendation that got me this post."

"I see."

"Anyway, her sister, who I didn't know even existed till today, when they brought her in, has been asking to see you, and the NCIS agent afloat figured, if it kept her quiet until they take her back to the States, then you should talk to her."

"I spoke to her up on deck when she got here."

"I know she had to be sedated a while ago, because she was getting so upset."

"What was she upset about?"

"Well, she's coming down fast from a seriously wicked high." Her voice had a slight Bostonian twang to it. "Other than that, she kept saying she needed to speak to you?"

"Like I said, I spoke to her up on deck." Matt followed the doctor to the door to where Mel was. "We told her that her father was coming in because he was here. She began to go berserk, so we've had to keep him out of here."

"That's strange, she did mention she was scared of him finding out about everything though."

"Yes it is. Anyway, give me a minute to administer this." She nodded to the tray. "And then she'll be all yours."

"Is that going to knock her out?"

"No, it's just a mild sedative to keep her calm, help fight the effects of withdrawal."

Watching the doctor, he saw her as she tried to get Mel to stop moving. It was obvious that Mel didn't want whatever they were pumping into her system. She couldn't move much from the restraints but still was trying as much as she could. He couldn't hear what Catherine was saying from behind the door, or even see if she was speaking, because her back was to him, but she most definitely said something, something that had made Mel lift her head and look towards him, a smile spreading across her face, and a look of relief in her eyes.

Catherine came out with the used medicine on the tray. "She seems very happy you are here." She said. "When you are done in there come and find me." Catherine smiled and left Mathew standing there looking in at Mel. Bracing himself for another crazed visit with Mel, he slowly opened the door, and closed it quietly behind him. "Matt." Her small voice spoke from across the room. "Mel. I'm here," he said. He pulled the visitor's chair over from the corner, and set it down next to her. Sitting, he reached for her hand that she was offering, even though it was tied to the bed at the wrist. "Thanks for coming."

"What can I do?" He asked.

"I wanted to talk to you. You said you spoke to Richard."

"Your father? Yes."

"He tell you about Jamie? All the bad things she has done?"

"He did."

"Did you believe him?"

"I don't know, he told me a lot of tough stuff to manage right now."

"What is happening with Jamie? Is she back?"

Matt let out a loud sigh. "No, she's not back. They're trying to find her now."

"Did Richard tell you about Mom?" Mel changed the subject without blinking at the news of her sister.

"That she died?"

"Yeah, thanks to him."

"She was having an affair, Mel." He felt her hand tighten at his words.

"Only because he drove her away." Mel paused. "When Mom died, Jamie became numb. I became angry at Richard."

"You were the angry one? He thinks you were crying all the time."

"No, that was Jamie."

Mel stopped for a second. "Do you know she left me a letter? The doctor read it to me."

"What did it say?"

"She wanted me to tell the truth about everything."

"Have you."

"Not yet. That's why you're here."

"Why me?"

"Why not?" The question hung in the air a while.

# CHAPTER THIRTY-ONE

"Your father and I talked about everything your sister did, Mel, was it all a lie? Was it really you?" Matt sat there, his head spinning with everything. "Do you know what Jay and I used to play when we were kids?"

"I dunno, Mel."

"We would pretend to be each other."

"Is that what you did as teenagers?"

"It was easy; Richard was around less after Mom died." Mel looked closely at Matt, and he saw the deep differences in the twins. Far beyond that hazel pigment in her eyes and a trouble that rested there, where Jamie's held secrets and mysteries.

"Jamie was affected for a few days, then she changed, but then she and Ricky were always better at coping; they were used to doing everything for themselves, as our parents either fucked around with other men or their career."

"Who went to Boston?"

"Jay did. She needed the time to get herself together. But she felt really bad after, because the time she was gone was a little time left she had with Ricky, before he was in and out of hospital, and too sick to do anything but lie around and sleep."

"She felt bad?"

"She blamed herself for him getting sick."

"He had Leukemia. There's nothing she could have done to make that happen."

"Yeah. But man, it was like they were the twins not

me; they were closer. Then not long after he died, she came to me one night, Dad was already back at work, and she told me she would never let anything happen to me."

"Big promise for a twelve-year-old."

"Jamie was never twelve; we might be twins, but I swear to you when we were twelve she looked and acted eighteen, she was taller and had the body to match."

"Who took Richard's car and ignored him?" Matt asked.

"I took the car, and she ignored him, but he would never have known the difference; he never has."

"What about the seaman recruit?"

"That was Jamie, but it wasn't like anything he probably told you. His name was Cory, and he had caught me driving off-base in Richard's car. He told me I had to do him a favor, and meet him one night, or he would tell."

"It was you?" Matt asked; his eyes seemed to stay wide.

"Yeah, Jamie was the one who met with him to protect me. She was supposed to just tell him off, and say she would inform his superiors he had blackmailed a minor, but it all went wrong."

"Did he hurt her?" Matt couldn't say the actual words, but Mel knew what he was asking. It was an obvious question if you heard Richard's side of the tale. "Rape her? No, but he probably would have, if the MAA's hadn't gotten there when they did. I'd called them because I didn't trust Cory. Maybe it was because I'd seen how he looked at her, always leering. In his defense, I don't think he knew her age, but she was only thirteen."

"Why does Richard think she was prostituting herself?" Matt asked.
"Because that's the tale the seaman told, and she never denied it. She'd rather let him believe that his Jamie was making money, than walking into a stupid trap."
"And she was sent to rehab?"
"Yeah, but she never did drugs. She drank a few times because I goaded her, but that was a way to get back at Richard for ignoring her and me." Mel shook her head as if in a fit over a fly, and Matt loosened his hold on her hand. She grabbed on for dear life at his movement. It stopped her own flailing, and refocused her to their conversation.

"They left her there, but when she got back after a month, she was different. She was really pissed at Richard and vowed she would leave, and never look back. She promised she would go and come back for me later. I think something happened in detox, because I had never seen her be like that before."
"Did she ever tell you?" Mel looked away and the tears she was crying ran down her face untouched. Matt stood and leaned over her to turn her face back, wiping the tears away with his own hand.

"I don't know what happened, and I should," Mel sobbed. "I only know what I heard Jamie say on the phone before she left again; then what I heard my

Dad say to Margaret. I don't know Matt, but I think she was hurt in there."

"What?" Matt didn't think he wanted to hear this; he already wanted to kill Atwa; now he'd have this unknown person he'd want to kill too. "Hurt how, Melanie?"

"I'm not sure, but I think one of the orderlies raped her. I asked Richard, but he told me to let it go, forget about it. My sister was saying anything to get out of the rehab, and would stick to it after, to make him feel guilty."

"That's when she went to New York?"

"That Christmas Eve; she was gone for four months; she went to school and worked to pay for everything. She lived with a guy she'd met through someone on base who said she could stay with him. She called me once in that time, promised me she would be back soon for me."

"But she didn't?"

"No." Mel was getting angry now, and the tears were drying out. "She never came back for me. Even when we were sent to that horrible boarding-school, she never did anything but try to get out of there. I never saw her, and we never talked there. It was like old days when she had Ricky."

"Did that make you angry?"

"Only when Dad, who hated her so much, seemed to be proud of her even after everything she had done and put him through."

"And then she left you again after she graduated." Matt added he was hoping he didn't already know the ending to the story he was hearing. "Yeah, didn't bother to call me again till after she was in the damn Navy; she did that just to please Dad, you know. She was the smarter twin with her doctor position in the Navy and everything. She broke Robert's heart."

"She what." The jump in conversation topics had confused him for a second, as he digested until she mentioned the other man's name, the one who held a history to Jamie. "Did she?"

"He wanted her to marry him, but she wouldn't, said she wasn't worth the love he wanted to give her."

"So Jamie left him too?"

"She's good at leaving. But she covered for me every time I went to rehab and made promises that after, I could go with her away from Dad. She was the one who persuaded me to join the Marines, you know." Mel's voice softened. "I love her so much Matt. I was just so scared I would lose her too. When we were out in the desert together, she told me I didn't know her at all. I laughed at her, we're twins, right. But she was right Matt, wasn't she? Why did you all let her go in there?"

"She has history with the terrorist."

"What kind of history?"

"She killed his son five years ago."

"My sister?" She had disbelief in her eyes. "I don't understand."

"She was part of Robert's CIA team who went undercover to get this guy Atwa. He's the one who has her now."

"You have to be straight with me Matt. What's going

on with her? Has there been any news, a ransom? A communication from them?"

"There was a tape."

"Did you see it?" She gripped his hand tighter.

"Yeah." He almost choked out at the memory. "I won't lie to you, it's not looking good, and Jamie was trained not to give in."

"You know they told me, once I get back state side, I'll be dishonorably discharged from the corp's."

"I heard."

"I need to get my shit in gear. I've fucked everything up so far."

"Yes you do." Matt smiled. "I better go and see if they have any news."

"Matt, let me know when something's going on, okay"

"I will." He promised, letting go of her hand and walking away.

XXX    XXX

Being in the dark was starting to drive Jamie slowly crazy. She didn't know when, or how, but someone had moved her out of the cramped box and into a dark space she guessed was a basement.

There was a noise, very faint, but it was the only thing her mind could concentrate on. It was a slow drip, making her think she was in some sort of basement.

Her hands and feet were still tied, but not as tight as they had been when they were behind her in the cramped box. The feelings in her fingers along with her other pains running through her body, were the only thing that reminded her she was still alive.

If there was really a heaven, then there would be no way she would feel so bad, or at least, she hoped.

Jamie's stomach was growling deep inside, and her mouth was so dry. If someone tried to order her to speak she wouldn't be able to. She wanted so much for Atwa to call upon her again, and try to get her to talk. Since the recording of the video, she had not seen him; but then to her knowledge she didn't even know how long she had been out of it They were obviously giving her something to keep her knocked out.

It was probably only a matter of time before they did it to her again.

Part of her face felt numb, something felt dried to her skin and she knew it was probably a mix of dirt and blood. When she moved, even slightly, the raw skin at her wrists and ankles stung, as the tender skin met fresh air.

Something ran over her bare feet and she stifled a cry, she didn't want anyone who was outside listening, to know she had come too.

Moving further against the wall already pushing in to her back, she noticed for the first time that her skin could feel the cold dampness of the floor and walls. It took only a second for the realization to kick in that she was no longer wearing the cargo pants and tank top she had been in earlier, but just her underwear. A new anger pumped through her veins, and she pushed out all bad feelings about whatever had come in to contact with her, and screamed.

She screamed so loud that it was a mere fraction of a second before the door swung open, to reveal a bright white light and a shadowy figure, she couldn't make out. An eerie laugh came from the shadow as it came towards her and at that moment, bound and defenseless, Jamie knew she had to do something.

Self-preservation took over.

# CHAPTER THIRTY-TWO

Robert was scratching his head, waiting for answers. They were taking far too long, and the longer Jamie was out there, he knew the worse it would be for her. The clock was recording the time since her insertion, and although it had been only eighteen long hours, it felt like an eternity.

David was still on his little laptop, and waiting for someone on the other end of the phone to return. Nick was reading over files on Atwa, and the known movements of his team of terrorists. Dumont had gone to receive some satellite pictures they had requested from the pentagon an hour before.

He watched as the senator and the White House rep sat together on the other side of the room, talking away, not sure what it was about, but he would make a guess it would concern whatever the latest Capitol Hill buzz was. The older man had been ashen-faced since seeing the end of the tape earlier, and Robert had heard his other daughter had insisted she didn't want her father anywhere near her. It was likely going to make his grey hair white with all the stress.

"How's it going?" Robert asked Richards, who was looking thoroughly bored. "I'm on hold while Peters finishes the trace on the missing files." The SEAL looked at his watch. "That was forty minutes ago. You know, if they'd just give me the info I could have done it by now." He held a cocky grin on his young face. "Not to mention the elevator music, they have really sucks. I'm going to be humming some song I don't even know the name of, for the next week."

Robert actually felt his face lighten up in a smile; it felt good and strange compared to the scowl he had used for the last day. The team's commanding officer walked in, looking fierce and ready to go and get one of his own as if they knew where she was. "Robert," Danny said, coming to stand before him. "I just wanted to see if there were any updates."
"Nothing solid yet." Robert answered. He could see Danny wanted to break something, to relieve the stress level that was building.

"Look, all the men in the Team, except Richards have rested up, and are now down in the gym and mess hall. I think it might be useful if he could take a battle-nap for at least a half hour. If I get him to bring me up to speed, can we let that happen?"
"He's been waiting for a reply from a guy at the Pentagon, but I don't see why you can't hold the phone. He was complaining about their choice of music just a minute ago." Danny seemed to let the corner of his stern mouth turn up in a very small smile. "I'll go tell him." Danny walked over to his man and Robert watched their friendly comradery.

"Boss." Dumont thumped her way back in to the room, her girth and flat footedness making her sound like a running bison, and not a five-foot-six female. "There's been another communication. The pentagon is patching it through right now." Robert turned to

Danny who had heard all of that, and was already getting in to action; David was running over to the ship's comm. to get all the SEALs back to the command center.

The fleet admiral came in seconds later with his second in command, and stopped to speak to Danny. They were followed closely by many of the men in Team Seven, and another of the ship's own crew, a young seaman Robert had never seen before, but went straight over to Dumont as if they knew each other. A pile of large satellite pictures in his hands were handed over to the agent, and Robert hoped they had the answers.

He watched the bustle going on, as the room filled to the max with everyone who was needed. Dumont was looking at the pictures with Nick, and Nick turned to his boss, a slow smile creeping up his cheeks. "Rob," Nick said moving his head to signal for him to come over.
"These were taken earlier by one of our surveillance planes going over an area south west of Faizabad, about thirty kilometers," she said.
"These are trucks going to an area next to a ground bunker."
"Yeah, but look what the last of the three trucks are carrying." Nick pointed out to the clearest close-up picture. There on the back of the truck was a large wooden crate. "If I was Atwa and wanted to move a female without having her spotted, I'd put her in a gun crate. It's the right size for a female." Nick said.

"Get the exact co-ordinates of that bunker," Robert ordered Nick. "Good job Dumont." He patted her on the back. "I have to go and talk to the Admiral before we hear the new message." Robert moved over to the mass of men.

XXX     XXX

Shivering in the humid darkness of the small concrete cell seemed wrong. The fact that there were no windows or any source of fresh air was becoming bearable. What was completely inhuman to Jamie, was the fact that she was in this hole with only her underwear, and the after marks of the beatings they had given her.

After she had screamed out, a guard had come in and foiled her attempt at getting up, and knocking him out of her way. She was far too weak; just trying to get up had been a real effort that her body couldn't respond to. He had seen the need she had to lash out, in the light reflected in her eyes, and had knocked her back on herself so hard, that her head had hit the wall and she had blacked out.

The abuse was getting tougher. The entire lower half of her face and nose was sore, the back of her head throbbed. At least two of her fingers on her right hand had been broken, her ribs, although not cracked, felt like they were, her abdomen no doubt had quite a few bruises on it, from several large boots kicking her. The worst of her whole-body ache was the burning of the rope around her wrists and ankles; the skin there was as raw as it could be, and try as she might not to move, those restraints, still felt like they rubbed.

Right now she wished she hadn't been so quick to give Mel two of the four tracking devices that she had been given. No doubt the reason she was still in this hell, was because they had no idea where she was. She hoped the others were safe, and back on a US owned Navy fleet, or at least, on soil where they could be treated like humans.

The noise of footsteps on the gravel outside the door was getting louder. They stopped, and the noise of the metal bolt sliding open rang out. The door opened to reveal two hooded men with big guns strapped over their shoulders. Atwa's men walked in and picked her up by her arms, dragging her almost lifeless body out the door along the rough and dusty ground. Her feet were getting cut up, and the stinging sensation was nothing that really registered, against all the other pains. They pulled her about fifty feet along an almost darkened tunnel, before they turned into a room.

The room was sparse, except for a rusted tub in the middle. Filled to maximum with water. A hook was connected directly above it to the ceiling; they lifted her bound hands and effortlessly connected her with the hook to leave her hanging just mere millimeters above the water.

Atwa appeared and his two men moved back into the shadows. "James, I am so glad to see you are still with us," he mocked. "I see you have seen this tub, yes?" Jamie stayed still, looking away from his gaze. "And you are still defiant, of course. No matter, I know now what I will ask from your government and I am sure I will break you in the time it takes them to come to your rescue." Jamie turned to look at him, and Atwa knew she understood. "That is right James. I have no intention to return you, at least, not in one piece. After all, don't we need to ensure you repay for my son's stupidity?"

He watched her eyes for any hint she was weakening, which there wasn't. "You are telling yourself that they will find you, yes?" He laughed. "I will send them a little message to make sure they see you one last time." He waved for a man to come closer, the one she called the cameraman, the one from earlier with the scar on his darkened cheek. She could see the flashing red light on the side that told her he was indeed recording. He took his time to get the gritty image of her hanging there, in nothing but her underwear.

Waving to his two henchmen, Atwa remained out of the view of the camera as they lifted her hand bindings to detach her from the hook. They took her down in to a laid back position, and Jamie let out a loud. "Ahh." As they pushed her down into the tub, the water was warm, and she swore it had a bad, stale smell. "Let me see how long you can hold your tongue now." Atwa laughed, and his distorted laughter was the only sound she heard as her ears filled with the vile water.

XXX    XXX

Having been able to get a short combat nap and some chow, Mathew felt like a new person, minus the happy feelings of another new day. He had been in the gym with a few of the Team, when they had been called back immediately to the command center.

Everyone was gathered there; the lights were dim. As Mathew looked around, he saw Robert standing at the back of the room, blocking the person he was talking to. Matt was curious as to whom would be important enough to be speaking, when the room was in a buzz over the latest contact from an evil man holding one of their own.

The person came in to view, and it was Jamie's father. The senator was deep in conversation with the CIA agent. It looked like he was disagreeing with whatever Robert was saying to him, and after a few minutes the younger man seemed to give up; and walked away. He came to the front of the room, where he stopped and spoke quickly to Danny, then locked gazes with Mathew. What those dark blue eyes' told him was not what he had been looking to see. There was anger and sadness in them.

Mathew was not surprised when his CO came over and ordered Steve to go and sit two rows in front of them, in the seat he had just vacated. Danny sat down next to him and leaned close enough for him to hear. "Seems this tape is pretty bad Matt; if you want to leave, no one here will judge you."
"Sir, I can handle this." The look in his eyes must

have been enough to reassure his CO because Danny got back up and moved back to his seat, sending Steve back to Matt's side.

Unlike the last tape viewing, Robert said nothing before he pressed the play button. But like before, the tape started off fuzzy before coming into focus and showing everyone the real gritty image of a fellow officer in the most hideous of ways.

Matt knew he heard the heart of a father behind them breaking down.

They watched as a body was being held under the water for minutes at a time. Then they pulled the pale- skinned person up for a quick gasp of oxygen, before pushing them back to where their lungs would inevitably burn with the sensation of drowning. It was a widely used form of torture in the third world countries, one that a lot more than the American military would ever admit to being done. All the SEALs had gone through training against this being used to extract anything from them, such as valuable information. Matt hoped Jamie had been lucky to get that training too.

The torture stretched on, and it began to seem as if the person they could barely see was just a lifeless rag being held down there. Something was spoken in a foreign language that Matt heard Lee translate under his breath. "Hang her up." Lee rubbed his neck, looking down. Sure enough, there for everyone to see, Jamie's panting body was being hung by her bounded hands to something in the ceiling. The big shock was how little she was wearing, and the image of her skin bruised and cut around the tiny garment's fabric. Sure, he had seen her in a bikini, and her underwear was black like that too, but it was the purple bruises and cuts that made it all ugly.

A few gasps from the Team and the other men around them broke the silence in the room. They all seemed still around him as he sat in his seat fighting the urge to stand up and throw something from the anger building up inside of him.

# CHAPTER THIRTY-THREE

Senator Buchanan was standing at the back of the darkened room watching with everyone else as the video showed the grisly, grainy image of the daughter he had given up as a lost cause. She was showing her strong will and strength in defying others, as well as her lack of acknowledgement over her multiple injuries and bruises, while hanging like a slab of meat from the dank rooms ceiling.

His body was stuck in the room, even with his mind telling him to turn away and not look back. His eyes tearful, but unwilling to shut to let that one drop of salty liquid pass through. His heart went out to his little girl as she hung, trying to catch her breath, dressed only in her underwear, and shivering from the cool air around her. He wanted to shout to the young CIA agent to turn the damn tape off. He wanted to go to wherever she was, and be the one to rescue her. To hold her in his arms, wrapped in a big soft blanket, and smooth her hair out of her impossibly beautiful but beaten face, and tell her he would never let such ugliness happen to her, ever again.

Before him, the man responsible for his daughter's torture showed himself on camera for everyone to see; it was the face of a monster with the aged and dark skin of a man who had lived in a country where terrorism was a way of life and a way to make money. He had a smile that made Richard want to hit it so hard that his teeth ended up in the back of his head. There was a glimmer in the man's eyes that Richard had seen before when he himself had been a young SEAL and on a mission; the look that meant only one thing. If things did not happen fast, his daughter would never see the light of day again.

"I want for you to know that I would have killed her sooner, but I figure she may be worth something," he heard Atwa say in his broken English. "I will agree to letting her return to you if you give me what I want. I think it a fair trade. Just give me one hundred million US dollars and a black hawk helicopter filled with weapons and I will release her. I will let you decide what kind of weapons; but if I decide I don't like, then I keep my prize." Atwa walked over to Jamie and pulled her by her wet hair until her pale and dirty throat was fully exposed. "I will slit her throat from here to here," he told them. "And I will watch as her life drains from her body."

The screen went black and Richard watched as the whole room began talking and moving as the lights came back to their full capability. His mouth was dry, and he felt still stuck to the floor. A burning feeling ran up his left arm, and before he knew it, he was closing his eyes and falling sideways to the hard steel floor.

XXX    XXX

A piercingly load whistle silenced all the men and the few females in the room. With the silence restored, the sound of something falling was thunderous. Everyone turned to see Senator Buchanan out cold on the floor. A few of the men closest to him had come to his aid. "His pulse is thread," one of them said, looking up at all the eyes looking back at him. "Medics are on the way," the fleet admiral announced, holding the onboard com in his own powerful hand.

Robert brought the attention back to the front of the room, as the back door opened, and a few Navy medics came rushing in straight to the fallen man. "Now that we have seen this, I know that all of you are itching to get out there as much as I am," he said, for the first time hinting at any personal issues in the case. "We will not pay the ransom." The White House Rep spoke up for the first time, showing his backbone and aggressiveness in his position, the first time since Robert had first met the pale faced man on the transport over to the USS Abraham Lincoln. "Our country will not give in to the demands of these terrorists," he finished.

"I wasn't expecting we would," Robert told him. He motioned for all of them to sit back in their seats as he continued. "What Atwa just asked us for he knows we won't give him; he's playing with us. He's cocky and thinks we'll sit on our thumbs wondering what to do while he gets some more pleasure out of torturing Jamie, and us. It is very clear that he has no intention to ever let her go. He'll ultimately kill her, but when, is a wild guess. It could be too late yet, he may keep her for a few more rounds of 'let's torture my son's killer'.

He has wanted her from the moment he realized he could have her. His vengeance for what she did when she was working for me has driven him to this moment, and he will never give up the satisfaction of seeing it through. What none of you know is that I gave the order for Jamie to kill Hassan. He was becoming violent with her, and as I and the team watched her being abused on his father's ordering I knew it had to stop. Hassan found out who Jamie really was, and I knew he would tell Atwa, and then Jamie would never get out alive. So I had her take him out first.

I'm telling you all this now," he said, as he looked at all the faces in the room. The file they had received had been vague and had stated only that she had killed the target, not why, and with details. He felt now they needed to know everything. He was risking his own job here, so they would know, and because Jamie needed them. "Well, because, Jamie was trained for six months in undercover terrorist tactics at a Langley facility, she has a very strong and defiant will, and breezed through it. Nick and I put her through a series of test situations before we were ready to let her get in to the assignment. She had never met Nick before." Robert turned around and glanced at his large burly right-hand man who carried more secrets than he did.

"The simulation was one not too different from the one we just saw. Most of the operatives that go into this never pass this phase, especially if they are females, because of the extremely high level of intimate invasion to their bodies. Basically...." Robert coughed and looked down at the floor as his chest tightened at the sudden remembrance of that time. "Nick attacked her, and tortured her for hours, for so long we actually thought she would never break."

"She never broke," Nick interrupted. "I broke down and I couldn't continue. She and I went through that for over ninety hours, and not once did she even break a sweat."

"So you see. If Atwa doesn't see a change in her strength soon, he will become even more hostile and dangerous. We need to get her out of there and we need to do it now."

"That's fine." Danny said standing up from his front row seat. "But how do you suggest we do that? Go in to Afghanistan and just comb it for the next year till we get lucky?"

"Just before we got the video, Dumont found some satellite pictures of a bunker he once used. Its thirty k's from Faizabad, and yesterday a plane took these." He held up the large pictures. "At least a dozen trucks entered the compound. One carrying gun boxes, boxes big enough to store a female in without getting caught."

"I'm making the call on a hunch. I'm sending in Team Seven as soon as they can get there, to get Jamie. Lieutenant Commander MacCafferty. When can your men be ready?"

"We are ready now, Sir." Danny stood up squarely, his Team following suit. "We will need a layout guide of that installation, and we can organize our plan on the way there."

"I'll have Intel send you a full map. Seems the bunker was emptied and mapped a year ago by our own men."

"We'll be standing by for it then." Danny turned round and left with his entire Team close on his heels.

XXX     XXX

"What's going on?" Richard asked as he came too in the ship's hospital. It was a very sterile looking room and he didn't remember being there before he blacked out, unless of course he had been downstairs with Melanie; but he didn't think he had been. His daughter had made it clear that she didn't want to see him. "Senator," a Navy doctor said to him, a pencil light flashing in his eyes and his arm getting squeezed by what he guessed was a blood pressure cuff. "What?" he asked again, his head was hurting like hell.

"Senator," the doctor said again, and he managed to focus his eyes on the small man looking down on him. "You're on the USS Abraham Lincoln. What is the last thing you remember?" he was asked. Richard searched his memory, and as the vision of Jamie and how she had looked came in to his mind, he heard the loud beeping of some electronic machine. "Steady Senator. Your blood pressure is way too high."

"I was in the Command center," he finally answered. The doctor shared a look with what could have been a nurse on the other side of him. From the looks, they already knew what he had witnessed.

"That must have been pretty graphic, because I believe it gave you a mild heart attack, sir" he was told.

"A heart attack?"

"Yes, we have arranged for a medical transport to take you to Germany immediately. I want to make sure you get the best care, in case you have another one waiting to come out," the doctor explained.

"I don't want to. What's going on with my daughters?"

"A SEAL team just left to go and get Commander Buchanan," the doctor told him. "And your other daughter is still downstairs. Although I hear she has been asking for you. If you want, I can get someone to go and get her? I'd rather you didn't get up right now."

"Yes, I would like that." Richard thought, at that moment all he wanted to do was hold both his daughters close to him.

# CHAPTER THIRTY-FOUR

Sitting in the loudness of the helicopter, Mathew went over the events of the last few weeks. He had fallen for a female who had changed in so many ways before his eyes. It was hard to believe that the same timid and shy girl was the trained and defiant body he had now witnessed along with everyone else on the video tape. She had been through God knows what, and still found the strength to defy her captor. He, along with everyone else aboard the helo, only hoped they arrived soon enough to get her out before it got worse.

A map of the bunker had been faxed through to them, and each of the team members was given a few minutes to study it, and remember all the different areas inside. Their training had allowed them to absorb such information at short notice, and for once Matt thanked the Lord that he had a natural sense of memory.

Each of them was ready to go, the moment the small bird landed a few clicks from the bunker; the plan that the Lt. Commander and the Senior Chief had figured out, would have them splitting up. Four men would take out and secure the perimeter of the bunker entrance, and allow for the others to go inside where they would take out the men, one by one, as they cleared the bunker to find Jamie. The goal was to bring home their fellow officer, not to take any prisoners.

Each of them had been given a direct order and location for securing the bunker. The map showed there were three floors leading in to the ground, and they were going in blind, not knowing where she was being held. It wouldn't be the first time that they had done a rescue mission with such little Intel, but the possibilities for a clusterfuck were just as great.

The Senior Chief along with petty officer David Richards, Officer Vasquez and Lt. Kevin King would be securing the outside perimeter. On the first floor would be Lt. Ryan O'Rielly and the XO Cooper Lee. The second floor would be taken by Chief Petty Officer Peter Richards and Lt. Max Vincent. That left Lt. Commander Danny MacCafferty, Lt. Steven Schlome, Lt Lee Kelly and himself to get to the third floor and clear it to find Jamie. Danny had been sure, when looking at the map of the installation, that if they were there, they would be keeping her on the lowest level.

He had been surprised that they would let him go in that far. He had been sure they would stick him outside, but Lee had told him it was likely that they meant it incase Jamie was hysterical or broke down; he would be the only one she might respond to. He was grateful that his senior officers had the respect to let him continue the mission; it seemed somehow they all knew about his growing feelings for Jamie. Now all he hoped was that he could actually do what they hoped he could, his gut was tied in knots, and the urge to spew was so strong that he felt light headed.

The sun was setting in the horizon as the helo flew low to the ground towards their insertion point. Everyone was getting their night vision goggles ready, because they all knew from experience that night in this barren country was darker than hell.

Looking at his fellow officers, he knew they were all getting mentally prepared for what was to come, there was never an easy feeling having to terminate a tango, and the ones that did would go through a very serious set of psych reviews after, to make sure they had not been emotionally affected by it. SEALs were not killing machines; they were covert operation specialists, but each one of them had taken out a tango before, in the line of duty. Kill or be killed was a constant mental reminder.

XXX    XXX

Atwa sat in the comfortable seat in his office inside his hideout. Anyone looking at the scene would never guess where he really was, as his surroundings conveyed the idea he was actually in a high rise American office. He was two floors below the ground in an old bunker he had recently reclaimed after the coalition forces had emptied it, and made no attempt to destroy it, like the others around the country.

He looked at his laptop computer in front of him; the latest Apple had to offer the world. It had been a payment from the last people he had held for money; a gift he was very pleased to possess. On the screen he had set a twenty-four-hour countdown. He had no intentions on letting the bitch downstairs go free. He wanted her blood to spill like his dearest son had bled. In his world a son is treasured, especially if that son is the first-born. It is expected that the son will follow in the family line.

Deep down he had known Hassan was weak, maybe because of the school and American ideals he had picked up while studying over there. He wished he had never sent him there, kept him close, maybe sent him to a school in Saudi Arabia. But that was all in the past, and regrets would not bring Hassan back, but spilling her blood would quench his thirst.

The only problem was that he was becoming torn by the American woman downstairs. She was so strong and defiant. A complete contrast to the women of his own kind who were mere shadows of the men who controlled their every move, their bodies covered from head to toe, only their husbands seeing the sacred skin underneath. Having her hung up in her flimsy American made underwear was getting to his men, they were beasts, and he too was finding the attraction hard to resist. If a female from their country dared to be like that, they would be taken out and stoned or worse, for the lack of respect.

With the intense satisfaction building on being the one to take her life, he felt an urge to ponder one last idea. Maybe he would offer her something sacred to her; her life, if she would stay with him for the rest of her natural life, and be his secret mistress. He knew a life of solitude and demeaning status would never appeal to that female. But the thought of her soft silky white skin under his fingers, brought more lewd thoughts to mind of what he could do to her.

Earlier as she had lain on the dirt floor, trying to get her breath back under control, he had knelt beside her and run a hand from her shoulder all the way down her side to her thigh. She had shivered, but had looked at him with the eyes of death.

With only twenty-two hours left for the female, before he would have his two men kill her, he thought about whether he would give her the offer of her life, for the chance to be his for the rest of her time on earth. He picked up the file on the female, that was on his desk before him, and smiled to the picture of the Navy woman she once had been. It had been a stroke of luck that his informant had been able to get their hands on the file, but he knew now all he needed to know about her, and where she came from. He was sure her people would bow down to his requests, but they did not know he really had no interest in what they would be able to give.

Sitting back and closing his eyes he let himself think once more about the skin he so craved to touch. He wondered if there was a man in her country who had the pleasure of knowing how it felt, like he did. He was sure there was, she was a very attractive woman. He pictured her like a movie in his head, obeying him, and letting him know how grateful she was to have him. He let his mind drift off with this playing out, and sleep came on, lulling him to smile while he dreamed.

XXX    XXX

"Your daughter is here," the friendly nurse told
Richard as he lay back on the uncomfortable bed, still
connected to monitors and IV's. They were waiting
for a transport to come and take him to the American
military hospital in Germany, then on to the States,
where he would finally be home with his Margaret.
He would make sure that he got word about Jamie
when there was news, before the media back home
got wind of it. If the worst happened, he wanted to
tell his wife before she heard it on the news. He had
spoken to her before the video when he passed out
and she sounded worried.

His other twin daughter entered the room alone, with
no restraints or guards. A frown played across his still
handsome face. He thought Mel was under MAA
guard, but from the look of things it seemed what
they had told him earlier must have been the mistake
he had hoped it was. "Daddy," Mel said closing the
door behind her, and coming over to stand next to
him. "What's going on?" he asked her, as he reached
for her hand. She pulled it away, and held it behind
her, her eyes were full of tears.

"I'm going back to the states in twenty minutes. The
Marines are giving me a BCD." She looked down to
the floor like a bad child.
"Will there be a formal hearing?" Richard asked.
"No, but I won't be getting any job references from

them."

"What did you do? Is what they told me true Melanie?"

"I have a problem Dad. I seem to be fucking everything up. They were going to send me to the brig for a few years, but Robert spoke to someone, and if I promise to take the BCD and get help the minute I get back, then they'll dismiss all charges."

"It was drugs?"

"Yes." She said softly. "I've had a problem for years; Jamie's been covering for me."

"Jamie?"

"Yeah, Dad."

"Why did Robert help you?"

"He promised Jamie he would."

Richard lay there and contemplated it all for a second. "Tell me Mel. Was I wrong for all those years? About who was doing what? Did I make the biggest mistake of my life by pushing your sister away?"

"She only wanted you to love her, like you did before Mom died. She was trying to get your attention. We both were."

"I gave you both everything."

"No." Mel almost screamed out. "You didn't. You couldn't even tell us apart, and your job not only moved us around a lot, you were always away. We might as well have lost both our parents." A tear fell down her cheek; she wiped it away, trying to hide the fact she was being emotional.

"I don't know when I'll be able to talk to you, or where I'm going for treatment; but I wanted you to know something and I wanted you to tell me something truthfully."

"Anything."

"What happened to Jamie in rehab the month you sent her away?"

"What?" The question shocked him. "Why is that important?"

"Because Jamie never prostituted herself to that seaman," Mel explained. "That seaman caught me driving off-base in your car, Dad. He told me if I didn't meet him that night, he would tell you, and I would also get into trouble with the base commander. Jamie went only to tell him she was going to inform everyone he had blackmailed me, she thought it was going to be a harmless few minutes talking to him, but it wasn't, because I had seen him looking at her when we were around the base." Mel paused and could see her father letting what she was telling him sink in and sink hard.

"I called the MAA's because I didn't know what else to do, I was worried about Jamie. I would have come to you, except you were out on a training exercise and I couldn't reach you. The seaman told the MAA's what he did, to try and save his own neck; and Jamie let them believe it, because she didn't want you to think she was stupid enough to fall for such a dumb thing. The last thing she thought you would do is send her to rehab for the drinking problem she never had."

"But she was always drunk and doing God knows what drugs."

"Dad." Mel blushed. "That was me."

"You?"

"Yes me. So what happened to Jay?"

He sat there looking at the other daughter he had thought he had known, but just like Jamie, he realized he really didn't know either of them. After all, until now he had no idea Mel had a drug problem. Now he was faced by the upsetting thought that he had indeed wronged his beloved Jamie. All along he thought she just hated him for their mother and brother dying, and his absence. Now he would have to live with the fact she may have been telling the truth all those years ago.

Mel could see it in his eyes. The answer she was searching for had been given to her in one pained look. "You bastard." Mel began to cry freely, moving slowly backwards towards the door. "She was thirteen, and she wanted you to protect her and save her, and you did nothing."
"You don't understand. They told me she was telling lies to get out of there. A lot of the girls did that."
"And instead of believing her, you left her there. That was supposed to be me."
"I didn't know, I honestly didn't, Mel." He held out his hand for her to come to him but she had backed up all the way to the door, her hand on the knob behind her. "Please, don't leave like this," he said, his chest tightening, seeing her look at him like that. The same look as Jamie had given him as he had walked away from her, after she had begged him to let her come home from the rehab. She wanted to come home and would be good.

"I don't know how to deal with this." Mel turned and headed out the door, hearing her father call out one last time to her. She turned her back to his door and bumped in to the hard chest of a man coming in her direction. "I'm sorry," Mel said, not looking up but trying to wipe away the flood of tears that were coming out on their own. "Mel." A voice said. She felt warm fingers raise her chin to look up in to the most powerful blue eyes she had ever seen. "Robert." She said, slightly shocked at his soft touch, his thumb flicked out and wiped away a lone tear.

"I'm sorry." She said, pulling back, the heat she had felt from him left her, and a coldness returned. "I was just going in to see your father," he told her, shoving his hands in his pockets.
"Is there an update?"
"The team left twenty minutes ago."
"You know where she is?"
"I'm hoping we do."
"The senator will be happy to hear that."
"My, don't we sound like your twin."
"She suffered because of me, Robert, he did nothing."
"This is about the rehab center, right?"

Stunned Mel frowned. "You know about all that?"
"There's nothing I don't know about; remember I was there not long after. Jamie was hurt badly from all of it; emotionally and physically."
"I can't even imagine. It's all my fault."
"Jamie has never blamed you; she has only ever been trying to keep you safe."
"Why? If it wasn't for me...." Robert grabbed her

upper arms, silencing her.

"Stop it now. Jay wouldn't want you to go through this. What happened, it happened, and she has worked for years to get past it. Let it go, get yourself cleaned up, and do something positive. If you really want to make Jay proud, do that."

"I should thank you for getting me off the hook again."

"No need. I was paying Jamie back a debt from long ago."

"Do you still love her?"

"I." Robert rubbed his brow. "She loves someone else."

"I'm sorry." Mel paused. "Look, I should get up on deck to leave." She moved past him.

He grabbed her hand as she brushed by. "Take care of yourself," he said, a slight smile coming to his face. He put his free hand in his back pocket and pulled out a slightly stuffed wallet that he opened, and produced a small white business card. "I arranged for a rehab just outside Falls Church, Virginia. If there's anything you need, this is where you can reach me." He passed her the card, and she looked at it for a moment. "Anytime," he added.

"Thank you," Mel said, turning away again and leaving.

# CHAPTER THIRTY-FIVE

In the dead of the night, the stars shone above them and the temperature dropped only twenty degrees cooler than that of the daylight hours.

Team Seven had successfully inserted into the thick darkness of night, and were now just a click from the bunker they believed their fellow team member was being hidden by the tango Abdel Karim Atwa.

During the flight they had been told that an order from the White House had come down the chain of command, and they were to use all force necessary to get Jamie out. All they could hope for now was that she was still alive.

Moving with stealth like silence to their destination, they all came to a stop when the bunker was finally in sight. There were four tangos outside the bunker entrance; three of them sat around a small but bright fire pit, laughing and smoking. The fourth was walking around them, looking out for anything moving in the night.

Danny waved for Max and Jason to come up alongside the bunch of large rocks they were hiding behind. "We need to take them out before they can get any warning sign out," he told his two best sharp shooters. Max nodded and looked to Jason. "I'll take the moving asshole and the one nearest the trucks," he told Jason. "Okay." Jason said getting his gun settled on the ground, his and Max's bodies lying flat out, their eyes trained on the gun sight. "Now," Danny ordered as the two men motioned with their heads that they had their targets in view.

The four tangos fell to the ground. Not one of them knowing what was happening until their lifeless bodies hit the floor. All four shots had been fatal head wounds; there would be no possibility that they'd be getting back up. Danny once again signaled, using hand movements that they all knew. To an outsider it would look like some kind of baseball gesture. He told them without words that team one was to go up to the entrance of the bunker, so that the rest of them could get in without worrying about any surprises.

Watching the four men led by the Senior Chief make their way up to the entrance, the rest of them geared up for what would be a quick in and out, without getting any of them killed. It had been talked through on the helo, over, and now was the time to act out a rescue they had all spent their careers in the SEAL teams preparing for.

Chris used his pocket flashlight to signal that all was clear, and the rest of the Team picked up their gear and moved swiftly over to the other side of the clearing. As the men moved past Danny he pulled Matt aside. "Don't let anything in there get personal until after we get out," he told the younger man, not in a harsh way, but as a reminder that his sudden personal actions could cost any of them their lives.

Standing outside the entrance, the Team to secure the

first floor were ready, and at Chris's signal they entered the dimly lit bunker. Inside was a wide-open space with only one door that was closed, and no signs of human life. With their guns drawn, Coop and O'Rielly swept around the area, making sure there were no hidden corners. Then they motioned for team two to come in and take the lead to the second floor, followed closely by the team going in to get Jamie.

With Chief Petty Officer Richards and Lt. Max Vincent before them, they watched as the only door was opened, and a spill of human voices came flowing up the staircase. Danny halted the two men, and signaled to Lee to join them. He spoke their language, and hopefully, if any of the tangos called out as they descended, Lee would be able to tell them something to avoid any suspicion that they were coming down.

Mathew was getting a rush of adrenaline as he waited with the other two members of the team he would be going down with in a few moments. He watched as the light coming up the stairs began to move as if it was just a bulb hanging from a wire swinging back and forth. His heart quickened its pace as he knew what was going on down there. Trying to hold his breath, he heard his thunderous heart beating in his ears. It was so loud that he almost missed the voice of his best friend over the small earpiece, saying "All clear." Gripping his gun with his sweaty hands, he said a small prayer and followed Danny and Steven down in to the bowels of hell.

## XXX    XXX

Atwa had ordered one of his men to go and get Jamie
and bring her to the room where she would be killed
later. A video camera was on a ledge in the corner, he
wanted to have this private meeting recorded so he
could view it later on.

To his sick amusement he found the sight of the once
headstrong female being unconscious and dragged in,
as a big turn on; his men sat her limp form in a chair
that had been put in the middle of the room. Her head
lolled to the side as she slumped down, even in this
state she looked beautiful, bruised and cut, yes, but he
knew what was underneath. Even the flimsy under
garments she wore, hid nothing and his loins stirred
with the thought of her.

"Get me water and scented oil," he told one of his
men, as they both walked out of the room, closing the
door behind them. He took the moment alone to look
closely at her body, to run a gentle hand across the
skin from shoulder to shoulder along her elegant
collarbone; he realized he was enthralled with her. He
let his hand move down to brush against the inside of
her arm and then felt a new warmth as his knuckles
brushed her soft round breast. The sounds of his man
returning made him back away from her. He tried to
decrease the flow of blood to his male organ before
he was disturbed; there was no way he would let any
of the men know his true feelings and weaknesses.

"Put the oil under her nose," he ordered. His man

came forward and waved the smelly liquid under Jamie's nose. The fragrance drifted up her nostrils and seeped in to her mind, causing her to stir slightly. Atwa snatched the water-cup from the man, and waved him away. He waited until they were alone again, before he took the cup and placed it to her delectable lips, and raised it to let the fluid run to her slightly open mouth. He watched as she freely swallowed the liquid and as her eyes opened, the shock of who was doing it startled her, and the water going down too fast made her choke and splutter. With a look of surprise on her face, she moved up in her seat, as she tried to regain her composure of hatred for him, and stop her body from convulsing in loud coughing spasms.

"You worried me Jamie," he said, as he moved back to her, pulling another chair from the corner with him, to sit opposite her, their knees slightly touching. He leaned forward and she backed away as far as the chair would allow her. "Be still," he told her, and her eyes betrayed her fighting spirit, as she searched his face for a clue as to why he was being so gentle. "I was going to untie your hands," he said, reaching for them, pulling them away from her lap, causing her to move her body closer to his.

"They look very sore. Do they hurt you?" he asked in a softer voice. Jamie just watched him. "Still quiet I see. Here." He took her hands and gently caressed the raw skin around her wrists. "I have been thinking about you," he told her, looking at her for a response to his touch. "How nice it is to have such a female like you around." Atwa watched her as she looked over his shoulder away, from his gaze. "What would you do if I offered you your life if you gave me the rest of it as my mistress? I see now what Hassan saw, he was not so wrong in all his choices."

He watched as Jamie listened to his offer, and without hesitation spat in to his face. With the wetness running down his cheek, he lashed out, and using the back of his hand hit her across the face, making her fall hard to the floor from the chair. He got up and pushed both the chairs to the wall. He wiped his face with his shirt sleeve, and then began to roll the sleeves up, walking around her body that was recovering from the backhanded force. She touched her cheek to feel the warmth of her own blood flowing from the new cut his ring had made. "Shame, such a beautiful intelligent woman. What a waste. Tell me, is there someone back in your country that knows the pleasure of your touch?" He asked crouching before her, her face looking up at him; she was using her newly freed hands to push her body back up to a sitting position.

"Your son was ten times the man you are." She said spitting out the blood from her cut lip. "Ahh, he knew you intimately yes?" He leered at her, licking his dry lips. "But is there some American man that will curse my name for taking you from him? Someone that might come looking for vengeance? Tell me; tell me his name so that when I send a video to your government with your dead body, I may relay a message to him."

"Fuck you." She said through gritted teeth.

"That is what I had hoped for, yes." He let out a belly jarring laugh that sent a slight shiver through Jamie's body.

At that moment she knew she was going to die, and soon. She would never again see the light of the sun as it came over the horizon at dawn. She would never again see her country she served, or the men who had become her family in such a short time. As she closed her eyes and lay back on the bumpy floor, she pictured her sister, Robert even Richard in her mind. The image of Mathew brought a wetness to her eyes and Atwa did not miss this. "I see there is someone that you love," he mocked. He planted a kick in her abdomen as he walked away, and sat in one of the chairs, lighting a cigarette, and making the room smell of cheap nicotine. She opened an eye slightly to see him rubbing his small pistol on the material that covered his legs.

"If you are going to kill me, then do it now." She said, her eyes closed tightly.

"I will not kill you; one of my men will." He said putting the gun back into the top of his right boot.

"Why not you?" she asked, sitting up, facing him head-on. He saw that any emotion she had been showing a few seconds ago had vanished. "Why should I dirty my hands? I will be satisfied as long as I see you dead."

"We killed you. I saw it with my own two eyes five years ago."

"No, you killed the man I paid to look like me, there

is a reason most of my men have hoods, It's because some of them have been made to look like me."
"That's sick, you coward."
"Coward am I? Why? Because I will not dirty my hands with your life?"
"If you are going to kill me I want you to do it."
"Maybe I will, maybe I will show you what a real man could give you before I slit your throat."

XXX    XXX

After securing the second floor, Lee told them using his lip mic that they had cleared the area and that by using their infer-red detector, they were able to see that the floor below had five heat sources. Danny, Matt and Steven made their way down to see for themselves. Sure enough, there were five, three along what could have been a hall, and two close together in a space not far away.

Watching the heat sources move was like watching a movie made of colored negatives. The picture was the gross distortion of what was actually happening. Pointing to the body that looked like it was lying on the floor, Danny looked up at his men. "I think we can take a guess that is Jamie." Matt felt a wave of relief flood through his body, as he let the image sink in. As he did, he saw the other image move closer to it, and pull it up fiercely. "Sir, I think we need to make a move, and fast," Steven said beating Matt to it.

# CHAPTER THIRTY-SIX

"Is there any news?" Richard asked Robert, as he was being wheeled on a stretcher in to the butt of a Marine helicopter that would fly him and a medic to Germany. "The team has gone in, and the last report was that they had found the bunker. You know that until they get to safety, there will be no radio contact," he said to the older man. He wished he could give the man good news. After he had run in to Mel a short while ago, he had gone in to tell the senator that the mission was a go, and he had let Richard get all he could off his chest.

"I know. And thank you," Richard said. "Look it's probably a little too late, but I thought I should say thank you as well, for what you did for Jamie, back when she was young."
"Sir, it was nothing."
"I can't imagine what would have happened if she hadn't met you in New York."
"She didn't meet me by accident, sir." Robert smiled. "We didn't meet by accident." He began to shout over the roar of the engine kicking the blades in to gear, the medic and crew, getting ready to leave. "What do you mean?" he asked.
"My father was on one of your teams, sir."
"He was?" Shock and then comprehension came to his face.

"Captain Mike Wakefield." Richard let out a long laugh.
"Yes sir. He asked me to look after Jamie; she and my

Dad had quite a friendship."

"How is the old guy?" Robert asked.

"He died six years ago of colon cancer, Sir."

"Ah, damn, I'm sorry. He was a damn fine man."

"Yeah he was. He thought Jamie was one great girl too. He was responsible for helping her join the Navy. She would listen to him telling her stories about the two of you on your adventures, for hours. She went to him after the rehab incident, and he gave her the money to come to me, but he made her promise she would join the Navy and make you proud."

"She does." Richard choked.

"I'll let the crew know when I hear anything." Robert extended his hand to the man he once despised but had grown to accept by watching him learn and grieve about his mistakes at being a father. Richard put his hand in the other man's and then used his other to clasp his hand in between his own. "Thank you."

XXX    XXX

There was no way that they would be able to get down the small set of stairs that led to the last floor and take out the three men in the hall without alerting everyone down there, that someone had come into the bunker to rescue Jamie. Danny just hoped that by all going down quick and swiftly with their weapons ready that they would get two of the three men out and the third before any of their own blood was shed.

Steven and Lee would take the lead and he and Matt

would follow close behind. With their silencers in place and the power to go off and then on again in ten seconds, they would have exactly less than a minute, to get down there and surprise the hell out of whoever was there. Two of the three tangos were very still. If they were lucky they would be able to get a break, and they would be sleeping, giving them a clear shot of all of them.

Looking at their watches, they counted down the seconds, and on cue the power went out. Pulling down their night vision goggles with one hand, and taking the stairs down, they held their collective breaths as the moment of truth played out. As suspected, two of the tangos were asleep but the third was awake and alert, shouting at the top of his voice as he saw the green goggled men appear at the base of the stairs. He got off a lucky shot that hit Steven square in the shoulder, as he got off a shot back that caught the tango in the eye, propelling his body back with a thud against the door he had been heading towards.

"Man Down." Danny spoke into his lip microphone; he felt the stairs move as he made the way with Lee and Matt around Steven. It would be either Richards or Vincent coming to see to Steven. Even with a man down the mission had to go on.

Shouting came through the darkness, cutting the silence of the underground hall like a knife. One of the voices was definitely female, and definitely American. A single shot rang out and the deathly hush returned. The noise propelled them faster, hoping to hell they hadn't just killed Jamie with their rescue attempt.

XXX     XXX

Atwa had come towards her like a lion after its prey, stalking it with eyes of heat and death. He had circled her a few times, before coming to stop in front of her. She had backed up, her feet still bound, and so sore, that with every move, pain had ricochet through her body. The hair on the back of her neck was standing up, waiting for him to attack, to keep his promise to show her what a real man was like.

He had lunged, and her feet had lifted involuntarily to save herself. He had caught them midair and held on to them for a second before he pulled on the knot, loosening it, and letting her feet fall free to the ground, sending more pain through her. "I can't show you with your feet tied." He laughed his evil laugh. With all her effort she tried to back away but he lunged for her again, this time grabbing her elbows and falling on top of her, careful to avoid her knee she had brought up.

She squeezed her eyes shut as she felt his rough bearded cheek rub against her own. His breath smelt of cheap whiskey and nicotine, his body of someone in need of a shower. Bile rose in her throat as he pinned her arms above her head, her eyes not daring to open to capture an image she might take to her death with her. "No." She said over and over as he moved above her. She could feel his growing erection pushing against her body. She began to black it out, knowing she had survived it once, she could again; if only to get a few minutes more of life pumping through her veins. She could feel her body tense and a surge of adrenaline coursed its way into her blood stream.

"No." She shouted louder, as she tried without luck to free herself. She felt him move from her, and only then did she dare to open her eyes, the room was in total darkness. Without thinking she moved towards where she thought he would be and grabbed for his leg. She found it on the second wave of her arms, and her hand came in to contact with the coldness of the metal at his ankle she had hoped to find. "Bitch!" he shouted, as she pulled out the fire arm in the dark and pulled back on the safety, Atwa had heard it, and she knew he would come for it.

A loud thud made his footsteps stop for a moment, and she called out his name to make sure he was where she thought he was. "I'll get you, bitch. You'll be dead before they get in here." She heard the sound of a metal blade as it exited its sheath. She squeezed the trigger, and as the bullet fired everything moved in slow motion. The spark from the gun showed his body as he moved; blade raised above his head, towards her. She scrambled away as she heard the sound of a bullet hit flesh. He let out a grunt, and then there was the sound of metal hitting the ground.

The lights came back on with a squinting brightness.

She blinked a few times, and saw that her shot had hit him low in the abdomen. "You are going to die," he said getting off his knees and grabbing for his fallen knife. Jamie made the fight fair by getting to her weak legs, pain distracting her for a second, before the adrenaline took over and blocked everything out. He swung at her and the knife caught her upper arm. She winced at the pain as he lunged again, this time getting her across her abdomen; not deep enough to cause serious damage, but enough to stun.

One more lunge, but this time, she moved out of his way, and ducked towards the door. "Screw you," she said, as the door flew open behind her. For all she knew it was his men, and she expected to hear the bullets as they entered her own body. When they didn't, she took in Atwa's face, it was pure surprise and anger. Without wasting a second, she pulled back on the trigger again, and sent a bullet aimed to kill. It hit Atwa dead center of his forehead. His body and pieces of grey matter and skull, along with blood, flew back with him, hitting the whitened walls around him in a garish pattern.

Feeling the sudden urge to vomit, she fell to her knees, having forgotten that the door behind her had even opened. What little had been in her stomach lurched up, and the sudden chill ran through her, which comes with shock, and she could feel the room sway. Whatever energy she had felt in those seconds or minutes had just done her in. She could hear heavy footsteps around her, and feel the softness of a blanket wrapped over her. Her body broke down, and she slid to the floor from her knees. She could hear someone talking to her, but couldn't recognize it; her eyes filled with tears that ran like a hot spring down her face.

She closed her eyes and succumbed to the urge to shut down.

"Jamie. It's Matt, stay with me, okay." A voice called to her in the darkness. "Come on, you can do it." She heard him again. She imagined she could feel him too. Carefully she opened an eye, and there before her was the most beautiful sight she had seen in a long time. "Matt?" she questioned, as he stroked her hair from her face. They were still in the basement, and she saw the faces of two of the other men in the team, Danny and Lee. "We're here to take you home, Jamie," Danny reassured her. As she fell back in to the abyss from which she was being called, she felt the warmth of Matt's strong arms, as he carried her wrapped in the blanket.

XXX     XXX

"Sir, she's out again." Matt said, lifting Jamie into his arms. She felt small, and lighter than the last time he had held her, and he was just glad they had made it in time. "Let's get out of here," Danny said.

The three of them left the room and climbed the stairs to the entrance to the bunker. There they came upon Richards and Vincent helping the injured Steven make it out. They had wrapped a makeshift gauze around his shoulder, his arm tucked around his waist like a broken wing. "He'll be okay, sir." Kevin said. "Let's get to the helo," Danny ordered his men. They started running as fast as their legs could carry them, and under ten minutes they had the bird in sight. The remainder of the Team either stood inside it or kept guard on the ground, in case of possible tango retaliation.

Mathew reached the bird; Jamie was still out of it. He reluctantly passed her off to the Senior Chief so he could get in. Once inside he was pushed aside as Kevin came to check on her wounds, being the Team's most skilled corpsman. He watched as they removed the blanket from her body and displayed her injuries in the garish light of the helo. Kevin skillfully connected a couple of IV's to her arm and checked her over quickly; Matt could see the Lt. looked uncomfortable tending to her. When he was done he took the blanket and re-covered her. Turning to Matt and the three senior officers, he told them that she had no serious external injuries, and that all he could do was give her the IV's and pain medication.

With the helo on its way back to the USS Abraham Lincoln, Matt sat next to Jamie, holding a hand that he had pulled out from under the blanket. He didn't want her to wake up, feeling alone and scared again. He watched Steven trying to sit still as Kevin looked at his arm and also give him an IV in his other arm. Lee had come over a few minutes ago, and told him that the bullet had gone straight through the meaty part of his shoulder, and it looked like nothing was broken or ripped. Lee patted him on the shoulder, and returned to Steven, who was complaining like a girl.

"She's coming too," Mathew yelled over the helos roar, to his teammates. He sat forward and gripped harder on her hand. Her breathing had changed, and her head had moved slightly back and forth. As he sat over her, he noticed her eyes moving below their lids. "Jamie. It's okay, you're safe," he said near her ear. The rest of the Team, minus Steven who was ordered to stay put, came over to stand and watch as Jamie came too.

Rubbing his thumb along her forehead, he showed no hesitation at the personal touch that the men would have, under normal circumstances, teased him relentlessly about. "Jamie," he said again in his soft voice. Slowly her eyes came to and he could see her trying to focus on what was around her. "Matt," her voice rasped.
"That's right," he said. "We are taking you home, sweetheart." He gave her a reassuring smile.

Her eyes closed again, and he studied the face, that had been beaten. The eye that had been swollen shut in the video, now held only an ugly yellow and black bruise, the only sign that it had ever been hurt. "I'm so tired," she said, opening her eyes again, but only slightly. "Then sleep. You're safe now."
"Thank you." She said before her body succumbed to the weariness inside her. Kevin touched his shoulder. "Let her sleep." He told Matt, and with his face away from the men he quickly wiped a tear that had

escaped his eye.

XXX     XXX

The Command center had been so quiet. Everyone, even the Rear Admiral, sitting impatiently on the edge of their seats waiting for news, the team had landed thirty minutes before and they should have gotten out of there by now.

Robert was the only one standing. He was pacing his way around the room. Nick and Dumont had gone outside for air and it seemed all the people in the room were holding their breaths, or praying to whatever god they prayed too.

"Command center; this is Team Seven. Come in, over." Danny's voice broke out through the room with static around it. Robert had to run across the room to pick up the radio. "This is command, over."
"We are on our way home with our package, over." A roar of cheering broke out around him.
"How is our package, over?"
"Needs medical attention but nothing major; package is unconscious but vitals good, over."
"Anyone else injured, over?"
"One shoulder wound, over."
"We'll see you when you land, over."
"That's a roger." The connection cut and the Rear Admiral came up behind him and patted him on the back, taking Robert's hand in a firm handshake.

"Excuse me Admiral," Robert said, walking over to the table and getting his cell phone. He made it all the way to the deck before he let his emotions show, and with a face full of tears, he dialed the number of the hospital the senator would just have arrived at, leaving a message that his daughter had been found, and that he would call when he had seen her.

## CHAPTER THIRTY-SEVEN

The minute the helo had landed a team of medics had rushed over and whisked both Jamie and Steven straight down to the sick-bay. The rest of the team would have to go straight to the command center, where they would be slowly debriefed by the governing parties, about the mission, and then they would be able to clean up and get ready to go back home to San Diego.

After what seemed to him like an eternity, Mathew had finished the official breakdown of the mission and changed into clean camies, and gone down to see how Steven and Jamie were doing in the ship's hospital. From outside he could see the two of his teammates. Steven was getting stitches in his shoulder, and Jamie was wrapped in a blanket, sleeping on the other side of a curtain. Other than her head, the only other body parts exposed from her cocoon were her arms, because they were connected to various IV's and monitors.

Sitting in a seat next to her was Robert; he was holding her hand, his elbows resting on the bed rails; his head slumped as if he was asleep. Matt's stomach turned with the sight of the two of them, and he had to look away, supporting his body against a wall to the side of the window. He slowed his heart-beat down as it raced with the jealousy raging within. Uncertainty nagged at him, the two of them had a past he could never deny, and the love for Jamie was bright in Robert's eyes. He knew that look because he had seen it in his own eyes a lot lately.

Since the debriefing, he had been re-playing the last few weeks in his head, over and over. The videos were there constantly replaying in his vision; he was sure that the Lieutenant Commander would insist he go in for counseling when they returned to base, to explore every emotion he was feeling about everything that had happened.

For once he was looking forward to it.

He hadn't heard the door open, but he felt the presence of someone standing before him and he looked up. Robert, a sad expression etched on his face looked at him, Matt knew he didn't hate the guy, he was just plain jealous. "She's going to be fine Matt," he said pulling his hands on his hips and looking away for a minute. "I hear that it was close out there." "Yes sir, it was."
"Is it true she killed him?"
"We saw it with our own eyes." Robert shook his head, and let a breath slowly escape his mouth.

"I wanted to see her before I leave." Robert announced. "I have to get back to Washington, and answer to my ordering the mission before getting approval."
"If you hadn't we might have been late."
"Ifs aren't going to cover it, I'm afraid."
"They won't fire you, will they?" Matt asked with genuine interest.
"If we had done this right five years ago, I wouldn't

be held responsible for what happened to her today; and yeah, I ordered an unauthorized mission. If they don't fire me they will kick my ass." Robert made a small joke.

"I didn't want Jay to wake up alone. I thought I'd wait until you got here." What Robert said shocked Matt. "I didn't...." Matt started, and Robert stopped him.

"It's okay Matt, I know she doesn't love me, not the way I want her to. Her father knows everything. Mel and I filled him in earlier."

"How is Mel?" Matt asked.

"She'll be fine. She has to do two months of mandatory rehab, and then she'll be out. She got a BCD but that shouldn't stop her from being able to join the civilian workplace."

"How did Richard take the truth?"

"Like a man. He really feels bad about everything. And he should. Jamie has suffered so much heart ache in the past. Before she met you, she has never let herself love or be loved."

Matt blushed. "I do love her." He admitted for the first time. "But we haven't really had time to; you know, let anything really develop."

"You will. But you know she's going to DC too, until she heals, and then there will be a lot of healing for her to do, before she can return to her old life."

"How long?"

"I honestly don't know."

"Can I call her?"

"She'll be able to call you after a few tests. She can tell you herself when she thinks she'll be home."

"Good."

"Just do me a favor," Robert said. "Don't play with her heart. Help her to forget the past, there's nothing there for her now. She's been connected to it for so long, and I think everything has changed for the better. Show her that, okay."

"I will." Matt offered his hand to the man he felt sorry for; it was obvious it was hard for him to tell someone else to love Jamie.

Robert accepted the handshake and turned around to leave, stopping at the door and turning back. "She loves Chinese food and watching sappy romance movies, the black and white ones. Not that she will ever admit it," he told Matt. "And she loves to watch the sun rise over the desert." With that said, Robert didn't wait for a reply, and carried on leaving.

Watching his figure disappear down the hall, Matt took a deep breath and walked to the door. Squaring his shoulders, he went over to Jamie's bedside and took the seat Robert had been sitting in. Her hand now felt warm inside his, and the color had picked up, even around the bruising and cuts. He kissed the back of her hand gently, rubbing his lips tenderly across her skin. He watched her intently as her chest rose and fell with each lungful of fresh air she was breathing.

Just sitting there with her felt wonderful, knowing she was alright, that no one was ever going to get the chance to hurt her again, because he was going to make sure she knew how much he loved her. He knew he had from the moment he had seen her shock at finding out he lived next door. He was going to give her everything he could; he was going to ask her out on another date the moment she was well and back in California.

## CHAPTER THIRTY-EIGHT

Aching all over was something she had expected after everything she had been through. After all, she was a doctor, but not being able to move without her whole body hurting, was completely unexpected. Sharp pains ran through her when she tried to move just a finger. She was going to heal, she knew, but sitting, or lying still for a long times was not something she was accustomed to.

The first time she had realized she had been saved, before blacking out her heart had soared at the sight of Matt looking down at her. She had thought it was her imagination replaying all the dreams she'd had during the whole episode. She remembered opening her eyes in the helo and seeing him again, along with all the other faces. She had fallen asleep after just a few seconds, but she fell asleep feeling loved. Not just by Matt, but by the whole Team. She wasn't the outcast to them anymore; she had proven herself to them, and she didn't even understand why.

When she had felt hands holding her hand in the ship's hospital she had known it was Matt. He was telling her some funny story about Lee and Steven from before Lee had been married. As she let her mind wake up, she had listened carefully to what he was saying, telling her about the boat they all used for going out on their days off to scuba-dive, and how he loved being in the water. His favorite missions being the ones when they had been inserting through water to places he couldn't talk about.

When she finally opened her eyes, she was so glad to see his face close to hers, his chin resting on the three hands in front of him. "I was hoping you'd be here," she said, giving him a smile.

"Where else would I be?" He laughed, kissing her cheek.

"Far from me," she replied. "I must look really bad."

"You're beautiful," He told her.

"Full of it today aren't you, Taylor," she joked back.

"Never when it comes to you Buchanan," he said, his eyes telling her everything she hoped.

"I have to tell you something." Jamie told him trying to move and obviously hurting from it. "I thought about you a lot while I was gone."

"What did you think?"

"That I wish I had said goodbye to you properly, and that I would never get to tell you I had fallen in love with you."

"You just did. And I love you too." He told her, smiling. "When this is all over I want to take you out, maybe away for a few days, so we can be alone for a few hours without any interruptions, to show you how you make me feel inside."

"That sounds so nice." Jamie held his hand tighter. "When are we leaving for San Diego?"

Matt paused, looking into the eyes that reminded him of the ocean he loved. "The Teams returning soon, and they have you on a flight to DC first. You need to heel and get debriefed and stuff."

"Why can't I do that on base?" She asked.

"I don't know. That's all Robert told me."

"Robert." She said his name, and it was more like a question, wanting to know if he knew, no doubt.

"I talked to your father." She grimaced at the name. "He told me things and Robert explained them. So did Mel."

"Is she okay?"

"She was arrested, but it seems that she had a BCD and was sent back to rehab."

"They know about her problems?" Jamie looked worried. "Richard too?"

"Her senior officer did and when he came to, he told them. Mel told your Dad the truth about everything."

"Everything?" Jamie looked away. Matt pulled a hand free, and turned her head back to look at him.

"I don't know what she said, but yeah, it seems he does. And I don't think any less of you, if that's what that look is for. I'm proud of you for becoming the woman you are."

"But you don't know everything."

"So tell me."

"Did they tell you about him sending me to rehab?"

"I know what happened there Jamie. Mel had guessed from things she had heard over the years. You don't need to tell me anything, just let me be there for you."

"I guess you really do know everything. And you still want me? I don't deserve you, Matt."

"Yes you do. If anything I want you more, knowing you are human and not some mystery. I want to protect you from everything for the rest of your life."

"Is that a promise?" Jamie asked.

"With all my heart." Matt leaned over and brushed
the lips he had been dying to kiss, since all the other
kisses they had shared. She tasted like home and love
all wrapped up. He deepened the kiss as she let her
defenses of the past day's slip away.

A noise behind him pulled him from her as he
recognized the voice of their Team leader. "Well, I
thought I'd find you here, Taylor." Danny stood in
the doorway, behind him the rest of the Team were
talking with Steven, who was now walking around,
his arm in a blue sling. "How are you feeling Jamie?"
Danny asked, coming over and placing a hand on
hers. Matt had taken a few steps back at being caught
kissing Jamie. "Like I was used as a punching bag."
She let Danny's face change from a smile to a deep
frown before adding. "Which I was, thank you, sir for
getting me out of there."
"Thank all the men; I can't be a good Team leader
without a good team. And that includes the medical
staff on my team."
"Thank you, sir."

"Well, Taylor, we have to get going." He walked past
the younger man. "I'll let you kiss her again, but then
you have to be on deck okay."
"Aye, aye, sir." Matt answered.
"I'll see you soon Buchanan." Danny winked before
he left, pulling the rest of the team with him. "I guess
you better get going then." Jamie said.
"I wish I could stay."
"I'll see you soon enough."
"Robert said you could call me when you get to

Washington. Call me as much as you can, okay."

"I will."

"I love you Jamie."

"I love you too." She said, before he leaned over for one last heart stopping kiss.

She had watched him leave and was surprised at how lonely she began to feel. Feeling tiredness covering her again, she let herself shed tears of happiness, as for the first time in what seemed like a lifetime, she felt alive.

XXX    XXX

With Jamie in the custody of Nick and Dumont as she was traveling back to the States, on a transport not long after their own. Mathew relaxed and savored the feeling he felt in his heart, every time he thought about Jamie and that she loved him.

It had been close there for a while; everything had almost turned into a complete goatfuck, but had turned out all right in the end. All the men around him were asleep; they had all been running on nothing for so long, that now they could relax, they let their bodies catch up.

He had talked with his team for a while as they had started their journey home; he knew all the married and attached men were really looking forward to getting home, and holding their loved ones close, for as long as their next time at home lasted, before they had to leave again. He knew Danny was anxious as hell to get back to Kirsten, and begin his honeymoon. Until the CO got back from his two weeks leave, they would have the Senior Chief's wicked sense of humor to deal with, and that always meant fun and outrageous training missions.

Not one of them in there would soon forget what they saw on the videos, and it would silently haunt them for a very long time. Each of them would do at least a couple of sessions with the Navy shrink on base. They had been told to do as much from Danny, as a wedding gift to him, he had told them jokingly. It was going to be back to the office Navy SEAL style until the next call for help came in.

After close to eighteen hours of traveling, having stopped to change planes twice at different bases, Matt finally pulled in to the driveway of his little house. The emptiness of the house next door pulled at his heart, as he thought yet again of Jamie. He had done that on and off at least every minute since he had spoken to her last.

As naturally as if he had never been away, he dropped his large duffel bag on the floor inside the door and leaned over to press the play button on his answering machine. "You have three new messages" the machine told him, as he walked through the living room to the kitchen, opening the refrigerator and taking out a nice cold beer. "First message." He was told by the toneless voice. It was a reminder from his dentist's secretary that he had an appointment that had come and gone. The second was a call from a man trying to get him to sign up for a satellite dish. "Like I'd get to use it," he joked, hoping that one of the calls would have been Jamie. "Message three," he was told by the Machine.

There was a pause of air before her voice filled his house, and wrapped around him. "Hi Matt." Her voice sounded tired. "I'm here in DC. I thought maybe I'd get to talk to you, well I was hoping I would. Anyway, I'm feeling better, maybe the medication's kicking in, I dunno. So, I am being taken in the morning to Langley to get de-briefed and get some shrinkage done to my brain," she joked. "They have told me I won't be able to talk to anyone till all the shrinking's been done, and I don't know how long that will take." He walked over to the machine, looking at it, thinking Jamie sounded like she was going to break down.

"I'll call you as soon as I can. I love you." The machine rang out a dial tone before shutting off, the message replaying. Matt put the cold and sweating bottle to his forehead, and over to one of his temples, wishing he had been here to talk to her.

# CHAPTER THIRTY-NINE

High altitude parachute jumping was a dangerous part of being a SEAL, and the practice and constant training was important. They had not done one of these exercises in a month, so at four am on a brisk Californian morning; the Senior Chief had them out doing it. It was his last official day as their Team leader and thought they should finish off with a bang.

It had been three weeks since they had returned from Afghanistan, and after only a few days, they had been sent over to learn some new weapons in North Carolina. Danny had been ordered to go, so his honeymoon had been postponed an extra week.

Matt had not spoken to Jamie at all in that time, but she had called once more, that time sounding less tired, and more like herself. She had said nothing about what she was doing, but of how she was feeling, and that her injuries were almost all healed, or gone. He missed her so badly that at moments he didn't know what to do with himself. He may not have known her for long, but that old saying of love at first sight had been true for him, and he liked to think that was the same for Jamie too.

They were all surprised to see Danny in the truck with Chris as it pulled in to pick them up and return them to base. It was five miles back to base, and they had half expected Chris to call and tell them to get their collective asses and gear back to base on foot. He was unpredictable and evil sometimes. They didn't wait to be told, they all walked over looking forward to the end of the day that had already started, because it was a holiday weekend and they were free until Tuesday morning. They had all been suffering from weekday blues, and the TGIF had picked them up a little this day.

"You coming over for the barbeque Monday?" Lee asked Matt, coming to wait behind those in front of them getting in to the back of the truck. "Probably," he said vaguely.

"Jamie?" His friend asked.

"I haven't been able to speak to her since she called right after we got back from North Carolina."

"You miss her don't you?"

"It's crazy man, every time I'm home all I can do is watch her house, even though I know she's not there."

"You've got it bad," Steven joined in; his shoulder had healed nicely and today had been his first actual exercise since the injury occurred. "Give him a break." Lee stuck up for Matt.

"Hey Taylor." Danny called out, looking in the trucks side mirror at him. Matt passed his gear to Lee and ran down to the window to face his CO. Standing at attention, he said. "Sir."

"Relax Matt," the older man said. "I haven't had a chance to ask you, how Jamie is doing."

"I haven't spoken to her in person, but on the message she left last week, she sounded good." He shrugged a single shoulder. "And how are the two of you? Did you tell her you loved her yet?" Danny had a grin on his face; he had asked as a friend, not as a higher-ranking officer. "Yeah, I did."

"Good." Danny smiled. "You know what my wife says that means?"

"Sir?"

"Let me know when the wedding date is set okay. By the way, a call came in for you yesterday. The switch board forgot to put it through." He handed the folded paper to Matt.

Caller's name: James Buchanan
Contact Number: (619) 555-7017
Message: None

"It's from Jamie." He looked puzzled as Danny got out of the truck and walked around to the back to speak to the whole team, Matt on his heels. "Tuesday morning at 0600 hours you are all to report to the medical building for your new monthly physicals. Commander Buchanan will be waiting for all of you there." Danny turned to look at Matt as the realization sank in.

"Jamie's back?" David asked from the back where he'd had a hard time hearing.

"The commander was ordered back to active duty yesterday, and although the Rear Admiral and Washington are disbanding the medical SEAL program effective immediately, Jamie will still be a member of Team Seven and all of your personal physician for the foreseeable future."

With Danny wrapping up, an uproar of. "Hooyahs."

filled the silence around them.

XXX     XXX

Returning to base, Matt decided it had been too early to call Jamie; it was just after five, and he didn't expect her to be up so early. He had waited until lunch to call and gotten her voice mail. Now on the drive from the base to their houses he couldn't wait to get there.

He drove on to their street and saw a red convertible parked outside her house with two people leaning close together in front of it. His heart stopped as he saw Robert's face and the back of a blonde female head. They were holding each other close and kissing every other moment. The possibility that Jamie had called to tell him she didn't want him anymore, never occurred to him; but as he saw this he felt a sinking feeling in his stomach.

He managed to pull his truck in to his driveway, and sat there for a second regaining his composure. He was determined to act like a man, not a fool who had been waiting three weeks to get Jamie alone. He closed the truck door and went to the back to get out his gear. "Hi Matt." He heard Robert shout over to him. "Hey." He cordially shouted back, thinking what an asshole the guy was to rub it in his face. But as he was thinking that, the sound of the screen door of Jamie's house made him stop, he heard her voice and it wasn't coming from the direction of the car and Robert.

Looking up he saw her running over the small yard between them, a big smile on her face. He dropped his bag and picked up the run from his side. He stopped just in front of her, as she jumped into the air and landed square on his chest, wrapping her arms and legs around him. Pressing her lips to his, his surprise was evident as she pulled away to look at his face. "You thought I was kissing Rob, didn't you," she said, calling him on it.

"Yes I did." Matt took the first opportunity to turn to look over at Robert and the other female, only to discover that it was Mel he had been smooching.

"When did that happen?" Matt whispered in her ear.
"Sometime in the last few weeks I'd guess."
"I thought Mel was supposed to be in rehab?"
"He's taking her to one out here so I can go to treatment with her. He let her drop by to see me; I haven't seen her since the night in Afghanistan. Doesn't she look so happy?"
"She does." He kissed her cheek, looking away from the other two; he wanted Jamie all to himself. "Bet she doesn't look as happy as me." Matt kissed her mouth, loving the feeling of her legs still wrapped around his waist.

"We better get going." Robert said standing now right next to them. Reluctantly Matt let go of Jamie as she wickedly slid down the front of his body to the ground. Mel stood next to Rob, and she came closer holding open arms for a hug for Matt. "Thank you for getting her out." Mel hugged him tight. "I told her you were more than a pretty face, but she doubted it there for a while." Mel joked like she had that first day he'd met her. "Sorry if we gave you a heart attack." Rob held out his hand to Matt as he let go of Mel. Matt shook it smiling. "I won't deny it, I did, I thought you'd won her over."

"Her heart belongs to you." Robert put his hand around Mel, resting it on her hip.

It was then Matt noticed the other man's lack of suit and formal attire; he instead was wearing board shorts and a t-shirt and sandals. "How did the hearing go? They didn't...?" Matt asked Rob.

"Fire me? I didn't give them a chance to. But then a senator from Georgia informed the board that if it wasn't for my quick rule-breaking, the outcome would have been worse; they had no choice but to re-hire me."

"Then what's with the clothes?"

"I'm taking a well-deserved holiday."

"That's great." He saw how happy Mel and Rob seemed, and noticed that both of the couples looked happier than anything.

"Well, I better get to this clinic." Mel broke from Robert and gave her sister a hug, and then Matt. Rob gave Jamie a sisterly hug, and then shook hands with Matt again. "We'll talk to you both soon," Robert said, as they watched him open the car door for her sister, then go around and get in his own side, starting the engine and waving back to them as they drove down the road.

"That was a little weird." Jamie said first, lacing her fingers through Matt's.

"I'm glad you said it," he joked pulling her closer again, so that their bodies connected.

"Let's go inside," she said, and he picked her up in one swift move, carrying her effortlessly inside the house, closing the screen behind him. He carried her to the big oversized white couch before putting her down on the soft material. Jamie lay back and took in the feeling of Matt kissing her like it was all he needed to survive. He came down next to her and they lay there, making out like a couple of over horny teenagers. He had been dying to kiss her like this since they had been here together last, and now he was doing it and in heaven.

# CHAPTER FORTY

Matt had left to get Chinese food, and returned to find the soft light of candles filling the pool area as the sun left the smallest slither of sunlight slowly fall behind the horizon. The two of them had spent hours making out on that overly comfortable couch, and when they noticed they had been there for two hours, they decided to get food.

The candles were not the only thing Jamie had done since he had left. She had also changed into her black bikini. She was leaning against the back of one of the chairs, (her hands on the back of it). He put the food on the table and looked at her, she was more beautiful to him than ever, but the image he saw only reminded him of what had happened to her.

He looked in her eyes and could tell she knew what he was thinking.

"When I was at Langley, one of the doctors there said I had to share this with you." She held out her hand and guided him to sit in the seat she had been leaning on. She stood before him and looked in to the depths of his soul for eternity. "You saw me in the video, in a way like I am now, and I don't want you to."
"That's going to be hard to change." He held both her hands.
"Not that hard," she told him. Coming closer she knelt on the wood deck and placed his hands on her shoulders, putting her hands on his knees. "This is me; this is my skin. It's healed in the last few weeks

and there really isn't any sign I was ever injured."
She felt him instinctively move his hands down her
shoulders, sending a shiver through her body.

"Atwa gets his power from the fact we remember
how he had me. He never hurt me in an intimate way,
Matt. What's here now, that's all yours, only yours. I
can't tell you that I'm over it all, I wake up thinking
I'm back there; but it's not as bad as it was the first
few days. I still see his face too, but it doesn't scare
me as much as the thought that I killed him with my
own hands. It's hard for me to know I can kill, Matt; I
am responsible for killing two people."
"You did what you had to, Jay, he would have done it
to you if you didn't. You wouldn't be here with me."
His eyes told her he cared and she knew she was safe.

"I've done the psych thing. There's nothing more
they can do for me there. I need to return to
everything here. I feel alive here; I love being part of
this tight-knit team. I like being near you." Her voice
trailed off towards the end. Matt looked at the woman
before him, and all he could think was how lucky he
was. She was strong, intelligent and beautiful. "I love
having you near me." He pulled her up and on to his
lap. Cursing the fact he still had on his camouflage
work pants and a t-shirt, he wanted to feel her soft
skin next to his again, really badly.

"I don't want you to worry about what I think when I
see you baby." The endearment meant so much to her
as she snuggled her head into the crook of his neck,
her heart leaping like a teen fool in love for the first

time. "I am just so glad that you are here now, and that they'll let you stay at the base in our Team." "You are, huh?" Her hand wandered under his shirt that smelt of him, his own personal mix of deodorant, dried sweat and the ocean. "Especially when you do that." His back arched a little as her fingers trailed soft touches up his abdomen. "I admit the videos freaked me out, all of us were close to losing it; even O'Rielly admitted as much last week. But you are right; you do have a family here, and a best friend in me if you want it."

Jamie looked up at him, he was looking back at her, his arms felt strong around her, and it felt so good and so right. Her hopes that the past wouldn't haunt her might actually come true. She leaned up and lightly licked his slightly parted lips, her hand moving down to the band of his pants, fingers sliding gently below the buttons. A feral growl exited his mouth as the warmth of his lips caught hers and lost her in the feeling of him kissing her as if the very act kept him alive. His hands roamed her body, pulling her so close they might have become one.

"What did you get for dinner?" Jamie asked pulling away and trailing light butterfly kisses up the side of his strong jaw line. "And here I was hoping you only thought of me."
"I have been eating food from the bowels of Langley, and before that nothing. I am so hungry." Her eyes twinkled. "I need to have energy for whatever might happen later."
"Later? Why Commander are you suggesting

inappropriate relations between ranks?"

"Would you have any arguments?"

"Certainly not Ma'am." He winked.

"So what did you get?" She repeated giving him a big smile.

"Why don't you see?" He told her with a grin, as she sat up straighter on his lap and leaned to the table, pressing her body closer to his. He took the opportunity to kiss around the area next to her mouth, and he felt her body respond with a gentle wiggle. He heard the brown bag that had been stapled shut, being opened, and then a small laugh. "Did someone tell you I love Chinese food?"

"Actually I love Chinese food too." He wasn't lying at all. "But Rob did tell me."

"What else did he tell you?" She turned back, a little worry on her face.

"That I was never to break your heart."

"Will you?"

"I don't ever want us to be apart again."

"Never?"

"Why, you want to run?"

"Not run Matt, but the fact you know more about me than anyone, kinda scares the shit out of me. I would expect to have you running from me."

"I would never run, maybe jog," he joked, and Jamie slightly slapped his shoulder; he loved seeing her laugh and enjoy herself.

"How about we get married tonight?" Matt threw out there.

"Aren't we supposed to get engaged first?"

"Why, don't you want to? Worried I might find out you really do have a bad sense of humor like your sister?"

"Ha, ha. No, not at all. How about you move in here?"

"What about my place?"

"You could rent it out, then if you do find out I'm like Mel you would be able to go back. But I can guarantee you won't. You'll fall more in love with me."

"I'm sure I will." He moved the hair that had fallen over her eye with the slight breeze that had picked up.

"Why do I have to move in here? Why not move in to my place?"

"Well I have two words that will give my choice the winning vote."

"What?" He was anxious to hear this one.

"Swimming pool."

"Yeah, you win," he said, taking her back on his lap so that her body was almost flat against his, from his chest to his legs. Gently turning her face he kissed the side of her lips. "If this is how winning with you feels, I'll let you win all the time," he said between kisses.

"And if this is how it feels to give you my heart, then I'll be at peace."

XXX    XXX

The Chinese food had hit a spot inside Jamie, but the spicy food had filled only her stomach. As they had sat next to each other on the deck, and chowed down, they had joked and talked about small stuff. She watched as he ate bowl after bowl of the food. She wondered how much physical strength he was building up and what for, and a sly smirk came to her face.

Mathew watched her as she sat there watching him eating all the food. She had just come back from fetching a couple of new beers, and was leaning back languidly in the wooden chair, the perspiring bottle resting on her tan and tight stomach. He saw her give him a look that made him interested in what she was thinking. "What?" he asked.
"I was just wondering how much energy you thought you needed, from all that food you are eating." She slowly slipped into her sweater as a breeze picked up. "Really?"
"Yep." She took a long swallow of the beer, and he was fascinated by the way her lips came in to contact with the bottle. "Maybe I'm just trying to make you wait." He looked back at her.
"Wait for what?"

Matt put down the chopsticks and pulled her back over to his lap. He had been so interested in just watching her, that he had forgotten what she felt like so close to him. She had put on her zipper front sweater to shield her from the cooling air around them, and as she put down her cold bottle, he found the little pull and lowered the zipper until it was completely open. He kissed a delicate trail of kisses down the center of her chest, loving the swell of her round breasts as he moved past them. Her hands came into contact with his male chest from under his shirt, and her cold fingers sent a feeling akin to electric through his system.

Lifting up his shirt, Jamie's breath caught at the sight of his very golden and muscular chest. Thinking about how much she had thought about it over the weeks; what it would be like to touch it again. Without a fight Matt let her remove his shirt, and she freely gave way to his hands as her own sweater fell with his help, slowly down her arms. "The last time we were alone out here, we were interrupted," he joked, and then wished he hadn't, because that had been the night she had found out her sister had gone missing, presumed dead. "That's not going to happen tonight," she whispered near his ear, and the feeling of her hands going down his body made him squirm. "Why?" He asked.
"I disconnected the phone, and left our cells inside."
"Well," he said grabbing her gently and positioning her on his lap so that there was a leg on either side of his waist, and her chest pressed against his own. "Then we should be okay."

Jamie kissed Matt with the urgency that never seemed to end. With each of her breaths, she couldn't get him out of her system. With her lips still kissing him, she removed her bikini top and pressed up to him. "I need all of you," she told him, beginning to unbutton the pants he was wearing between their bodies. He moved his hands from her back and slid them down the smooth expanse of skin to her backside which he cupped easily, the small round mounds of flesh fitting like a glove.

Standing up, he let her legs wrap around his body and felt his pants make the fall down his legs to land softly at his feet. He carried them over to the pool and with just their bottoms on he walked down the steps and in to the refreshing feeling of the pool's water. He stopped at the bottom of the steps and lowered them both in the shallow end, nuzzling at her neck, he heard her moan at the feeling of his lips and tongue. He let his mouth wander down her neck, past her collar bone to the area above her right breast, lifting her butt up slightly so that he could take one of her fully erect nipples in to his eager mouth. He suckled and licked and felt her move so he could get more of her before he moved to the other breast using his hand to feel what reaction her body was having. With his spare hand at her bottom he slowly peeled the fabric down, and as he came to the obstacle of his own legs in the way of removing them, she moved again and helped him in his task of getting her completely naked.

Jamie was fully enraptured with what Matt was doing and slightly came to as she helped him to get herself undressed. Now all that was between them were his own black jockey shorts. Resting her naked form on his lap, she kissed his returning mouth and with a copy of his own motions removed his underwear.

The awareness of their nakedness brought both of them back to the ground. Matt looked into those blue eyes he could drown, in and saw the lust she had, his arousal, the one he had been fighting all through dinner was brushing against her feminine body, and driving him slowly nuts.

Jamie, the shy woman from long ago gently reached for his manhood and teasingly rubbed it up and down her female fold. Jamie, looking into Matt's eyes, was amazed at her own boldness, but enjoyed the look he was giving her. She stroked him from base to tip a few times, even showed the organ the familiar feel of herself before she aligned it with herself and gently slid down him, hearing his indrawn breath at the same time as she felt her own. He was pure male and physically amazing, the feeling of him buried to the hilt in her for those long seconds drove her over the edge. Those feelings from weeks before came back, and all he wanted was to finish it this time.

"Open your eyes." He told her softly, and saw her look back at him, the feelings going through her as he moved slowly and delicately back and forth were mirrored before him. "You fit so well," she told him, blushing slightly, and the color made her skin look new and delicate. "I feel like I'm home, where I'm supposed to be," he told her, taking her lips with his.

## CHAPTER FORTY-ONE

At four fifty in the morning, after a night filled with
the most sex he had ever had in one night, Mathew sat
and watched Jamie. Lying on her stomach, just
covered slightly by her soft white cotton sheets she
was sheer beauty to him. He had tied a towel he had
found in the bathroom around his waist, he wanted to
let her sleep and watch her forever, but he had a plan
that he wanted to put into action.

"Jay," he whispered softly to her, his hand snaking up
and down her bare back. She stirred lightly, a smile
drawing out across her face; he waited a few seconds,
and then said her name again, so that she knew he
was trying to get her attention. "You can't possibly be
able to go again," she laughed sleepily.
"With you like this?" He lifted up the sheet to reveal
all of her naked glory, a few fingers gliding across the
smoothness of one of her butt cheeks. "I'm always
ready to go."
"Then why are you not over here?" She sleepily
tapped the empty side of the bed, her eyes still closed.
"I want you to get up and dressed," he told her. Her
eyes shot open and looked at him. Leaning up on her
elbows, she looked at the clock on the bedside table
on the other side from her.

"Matt, it's almost five, and you've kept me up all
night."
"Please," Matt urged gently. "There's something I
want us to do."
"Is it that important?" She asked rolling over on to

her back and stretching like a lazy cat in the sun. The sight of her breasts and the place she had given to him more than once, stirred him to life again. He had to start counting back from a thousand to curb the rush of blood down there. "It is." He reached out and touched her cheek. "I'm going over to my place to get some clothes to bring back. I'll meet you outside in five minutes, okay?"

Sitting back up on her elbows, now fully awake, Jamie looked at Matt in the soft darkness, with the only light from the nightlight in the adjoining bathroom. "I'll be right down," she said watching him smile, and returned the quick kiss he gave her before she watched him, in her towel leave the room. Listening to his footsteps, she dropped her feet to the wooden floor and walked over to get her sweat shirt and pants from the chair she had thrown them on, less than four weeks before.

A sudden image came to her head of Atwa, his eerie grin and laugh. She stumbled for a minute, and caught herself on the side of the dresser. Breathing hard, she felt sick, her head spun and before she knew it the image was gone. She had been suffering from these since she had come to on the USS Abraham Lincoln, especially when it was dark. They were becoming less frequent, and smaller in length, but they still made her break out in a sweat.

Recovering slightly, she slipped into her clothes, and grabbed her flip-flops from near the closet. Taking a look back at the bed that Matt had made the most amazing feelings run through her body, she smiled.

She smiled because she knew she was safe, and that there would be a day when the dark and that man's face would never haunt her again.

XXX     XXX

Sitting on the cool dry ground, the breeze whipping around them as they sat huddled on the top of a dry rock, Matt sitting with his legs on either side of Jamie, holding the blanket from his truck, around her and himself.

All the way to the desert, Jamie had sat with her head resting on his shoulder. It was comforting and warm. She had said nothing until they had driven into the parking lot off interstate 8, a clear view to the east before them. "Sunrise." Jamie had said.
"I heard it's another of your favorites."
"Yes it is." She had seemed tearful. "How much did you and Rob tell each other?"
"Not much. I told him I loved you and he told me that you liked Chinese, and the sunrise over the mountains." She looked at him for a minute, and then changed the frown she had been wearing into a smile.
"You told him you loved me?"
"Yeah, I did." Matt sounded cocky.

"I'm glad you woke me up for this," she said, snuggling up to him.
"Well, it was touch and go there. Watching you asleep, and wanting to wake you up for other reasons,

but I wanted to do this."

"Well I like it." She turned her head to kiss his cheek.
"Good." He got up and draped the large blanket over
her shoulders. Coming to face her and kneeling
before her. He had both of her hands in his, and the
sun rising over his shoulder. "What are you doing?"
she asked.

"When we were on the mission, I realized a few
things and, well...." Matt sounded nervous and
Jamie's mind jumped at what was coming, and she
held her breath. "I know we've only known each
other a little more than a month, but Jay, I love you so
much that when you aren't around I miss you; it feels
like half of me is missing. I want to spend the rest of
my life with you and to grow old and care for you and
keep you safe, for the rest of time."
"Matt...." Jamie began, but she became distracted
when he reached into his pocket and took out a small
square velvet box, a box that could hold only one
thing.

"Jamie, would you make me the happiest man, and
marry me? It could be a long engagement if you want,
I...." Jamie touched her finger to his lips to stop the
words he was saying.
"I'm guessing you've been thinking about this," she
said.
"Every day since I got back. I dragged Steven in to
help pick it out. It was really a sight."
"I can imagine." She looked away a second. "I just
can't believe you want me."
"Baby, I never want to lose you and I've never felt

this way before about anyone."

Jamie stood up and pulled Matt up to her level; he looked green from nerves. "Matt, I would be honored to be your wife for the rest of our lives together, I too have never felt like this for anyone. When I was out there, all I could think about was you, and not seeing you again." She stood up a little to touch her lips against his, his morning stubble rubbing her chin. "Yes I'll marry you," she said, and Matt smiled, pulling her in for a bone crunching kiss.


EPILOGUE

It had been three and a half months since she had returned to her home in Coronado after the worst nightmare in her adult life. Everything had changed for the better. The ghosts of her childhood had been eased by the love of a good man, and the time in Afghanistan and Atwa had stopped haunting her and Matt. Life as Jamie Buchanan knew it was getting better and stronger every day.

Her relationship with her father had changed. He had called and apologized, and asked her to forgive him, and said that he wanted to get to know her. What finally broke down her defenses was his words of how proud he was of her, and apologies for not believing her when it was most important.

Mel had finished her rehab and moved back to Virginia where she was working as an assistant photographer. She had always liked the arts, and at St. Teresa's she had been very good with a camera. She was seeing Robert, but never made any comments about the future; she was doing what she had been taught by her councilors, taking it one day at a time.

Matt had moved into her house two days after she had agreed to marry him, and when all the Team and their significant others had found out about the engagement, they had all been very happy and supportive; they really had become a large family. Patti and Mary were even helping her arrange all the details, because the Navy was keeping her very busy. Mary had even been with her the day before when she had found out the best news of her life. Of course, swearing Mary to keep quiet about it had been hard. By later that night tonight every one of Team Seven would know.

Jamie had found out she was three months pregnant.

She had been feeling off in the mornings, and run down by the end of her days, and after a home kit she had a fellow physician take a blood sample. Sure enough, when she was out shopping with Mary the day before the same doctor had called her on her cell, and told her the good news. Telling Matt was going to be easy; she had snuck in to his combat vest a fax copy of the results. He should be finding them any time now as he wore the vest on all his training exercises.

Matt had been sitting around with the fellow men of

the Team when he realized that his vest was unusually bulky on his right side. Opening up the pocket, he pulled out the piece of paper and read it a few times. It had a lot of medical terms on it and he wondered what it was doing in there; obviously Jay had something to do with it. He had felt like he had been hit square in the chest when he figured out it was the results to a pregnancy test. He was going to be a Dad! He asked Danny for a few minutes, and had called Jamie at home, their home.

"Is this for real?" He asked before anything else.
"Yes it is." He heard the humor and joy in her voice.
"This is the best news ever, baby," he told her, and she could tell he was happy.
"God, I love you Matt."
"I love you too sweetheart. I think we should move the wedding date up now."
"Me too."
"How about we go out this weekend, maybe invite the team to celebrate?"
"I would love that," she told him.
"But you have to do me one favor." He laughed.
"Anything."
"Wear that dress for me, the black one."
"I think that can be arranged." She laughed down the phone line.
"I'll see you tonight." Jamie said.
"I'll be home as soon as I can."
"I'll be waiting."
"And Jamie."
"Yes Matt?"
"Thank you for giving me this."

"No, thank you." He heard her quiet tears that pulled at his heart.

Disconnecting the call, he turned to see all the men looking at him, wondering why he had such a silly grin on his face. "I'm gonna be a Dad," he said. "Congratulations." Lee said coming over, followed by the rest of the men, each congratulating him. "Well," Danny said, clasping Matt's shoulder. "Looks like my wife was right about everything." The men all laughed and as they jumped on the back of the truck, a round of "Hooyahs." Started by Steven, rang out.

# *Released August 2016*

## <u>SEAL Team 7</u>
## <u>Elisabeth's Island Vacation</u>

Lightning flashed through the small hotel suite like a knife, illuminating the sparse space. The French doors to the patio were open, allowing the swift wind to billow the sheer drapes that had earlier been tied back by the maid. The only thing stopping the rain from coming inside was the large covered balcony area that, during the sun-soaked days, held a positively amazing view of the waterfront and the tourists coming and going on boats from other islands.

The room's occupant had spent most of the day down on those docks, gathering information while posing as another ignorant American tourist who couldn't see past their own being, to what this paradise in the middle of the Caribbean Sea could offer. Now with his room in total darkness, aside from the sporadic natural illumination from outside, he stood below the harsh spray of the shower, savoring the cool water as it washed away the salty air and sunscreen film that had been covering his lean body.

His thoughts were going over the data he had collected since his arrival a few weeks ago. He had been Island-hopping for a couple of months, in search of his target; the handful of people who could ever detail him in any kind of investigation, would remember him as an early thirties American business man, looking to open a restaurant on one of the islands. He had explained to them, he was looking for someplace sunny and relaxing to start over after his wife and two kids had been taken from him in a plane crash eighteen months before. It wasn't the truth, but if anyone suspected him as anything else and checked him out, they would find a lot in the Boston Herald about the restaurant owner who lost his high school sweetheart and two angel faced children.

Turning off the stream of water, he reached out a tanned arm and grabbed one of the fluffy, soft towels delivered that afternoon. He wrapped it around his narrow hips as he stepped out, and walked over to the mirror, wiping away the cloudy sheen from the fogged-up glass. Resting his hands on the edge of the white, cool porcelain sink, he stared at the face before him. A few days of beard growth covered his jaw, and his brown eyes glared back at him, mocking him for being such a coward in accepting the project two years ago. He should have stuck around to deal with the break-up he had seen coming like a freight train at full speed, with headlights brighter than the sun. They had wanted different things, their worlds were so completely polar opposite, and like always his absence due to his job had killed whatever trust they'd had, because he just couldn't confide in her what he did the weeks he had been gone.

Sighing aloud, he pushed himself off of the sink and walked into his room. The thunder had subsided to the distance, but the wind was still blowing fiercely, and the lightning made his still wet torso glisten every time when the flash would slice through the room and hit him lengthways. He picked up the loose cotton sweatpants from the edge of his bed, and threw the towel to the floor, before pulling his crisp white t-shirt over his head. Clicking the muscles in his neck, he was about to bend over to retrieve the towel as another flash came through all the glass windows, and for a split second he swore he had seen a figure standing out on his balcony.

Not wanting to break from his cover, he looked over to the wardrobe that held his gun in the lining of his suitcase, and figured that if there was someone out there, he'd have no chance to get his only weapon before whoever it was lurking, could strike. Instead he eased back towards the wall, and as the sky lit up again, he knew for certain that someone knew who he was, and was coming to take him out.

He remained standing, back to the wall as the dark figure boldly made its way into the room through the balcony doors. He held his breath, watching as the person's eyes scanned the room, not seeing its occupant to the side of the entertainment center. The figure came further into the room as the light from the bathroom spilled out and cast everything towards the room's main door in a brighter light. Thinking this was the chance to get out, the room's occupant made a slow walk towards the door, but halfway there, the unknown stranger turned from the bathroom, obviously sure it was empty, and the two of them came face to face just feet from each other.

Even with all the training he had, without the gun he had hidden he was defenseless against this hulk of a being standing before him, decked out in black from head to toe. It was like being inside a bad Hollywood movie, with nowhere to go. The two of them stood there surveying each other, and as the hulk went for something in the back of his pants, he knew it was time to strike out with his fists. It had been one hell of a long time since he had to take anyone on by bodily force, and he hoped his training as a rookie a decade before wasn't lost.

In the beginning he had the upper hand, and quick jabs to the hulk's stomach, and a right hook, had caused some disorientation, not to mention a slight crippling in his hand from the blunt force. The stranger regained control of the situation, before he could do anything but surrender under the steady hold of the gun pointed right at his head. Within moments he was roughly shoved to the floor with his hands bound, and a crude strip of unknown material was shoved into his mouth to render him unable to call for help, before having the awful strip of duct tape slapped over his partially open mouth, to ensure he couldn't spit it out. The last thing he saw of his hotel room was the feet of the bed, and thinking if only he hadn't been so gutless back in the states, he wouldn't be doing this mission, that more than likely, had just written his ticket to hell.

Coming to on a boat he had the rain and the salt water from the spray of the waves in his face, and he was lying on the crafts back seat, near the roar of the propellers under him. He could see three men up near the controls, and couldn't make out anything but the occasional word, and that was in the island's French, and a mixture of their slang language which he had a hard time translating. He had a headache, to boot, that was going to take more than a bottle of aspirin to cure.

One of the men, not the one from his room, because this one was at least fifty pounds lighter came over and pulled him roughly so he was sitting. A quick scan from the corner of his eyes, and he knew he was off somewhere to the east of an island, the shore lit up on the horizon like a magical sea beacon.

"You asked the wrong question." The man's voice said; his voice had that sharp island twang to it. "I don't know what you mean." He answered, his tongue felt so dry and his lips dry and sore probably from when they'd ripped off the tape. "I know you do, and you aren't going to get a chance to tell anyone anything Mr. Walsh." The man laughed, and pulled him again, but this time to his feet. A harsh push and he was facing the ocean on his feet, the boat slowing slightly before he felt a hand on the middle of his back. "This is where we let you off," he was told, as he was severely hit over the head with what felt like a baseball bat, and blacking out seeing the crashing waves come closer as he fell, bound with his hands behind him, face first in to the chilling darkness of the moonlit ocean.